"You said we'd start over."

Annabelle was half-appalled at her own words.

Clint looked down at her and his expression softened. "Is that what you want, Annabelle?"

She nodded, not sure at all it was what she wanted. But she couldn't seem to help herself. *He is my husband.* Her mind kept tossing those words to the surface, forcing her to concede the fact. To accept him as her mate. Where did that thought come from? Her *mate!*

"God knows," he said, "it's what I want." He gripped her hand. "Come on. We have a day's work before us."

She marched along beside him, conscious only of the warmth of his hand around hers and the feeling of safety that surrounded her when he was near. *This man is my husband, and I am his wife.* She tried not to think what all those words really meant. . . .

Dear Reader,

This month, we are happy to bring you the next installment in Margaret Moore's Warrior series. *A Warrior's Quest* follows the path of the disillusioned Urien Fitzroy, a mercenary soldier who is no longer content to live his life by the sword.

Julie Keane has no use for an indentured servant more suited to be the lord of the manor than a common laborer, but Zachariah Hale soon proves his mettle in *Bound by Love,* from the writing team of Erin Yorke.

Web of Loving Lies by Barbara Leigh is a heartwarming tale of two sisters whose lives become inescapably intertwined with a man who falls in love with one sister, but is forced into marrying the other.

From author Beverlee Ross comes the story of a weary gunslinger, Clint Strand, who finds himself amazingly willing to be saddled with *Annabelle,* a feisty young woman who isn't afraid of anything.

Next month marks the release of our Western historical short story collection—UNTAMED. With authors Heather Graham Pozzessere, Joan Johnston and Patricia Potter contributing, this is one collection you won't want to miss!

Sincerely,

Tracy Farrell
Senior Editor

Annabelle

BEVERLEE ROSS

Harlequin Books

TORONTO • NEW YORK • LONDON
AMSTERDAM • PARIS • SYDNEY • HAMBURG
STOCKHOLM • ATHENS • TOKYO • MILAN
MADRID • WARSAW • BUDAPEST • AUCKLAND

Harlequin Historicals first edition June 1993

ISBN 0-373-28778-X

ANNABELLE

Printed in the U.S.A.

BEVERLEE ROSS

has been a nurse, dining room manager of the world's greatest Italian restaurant, a hospice administrator, a loan processor, an office manager, and she sang blues and jazz in her spare time. Now, living in Las Vegas, she is what she wanted to be: a writer. She credits her success to the support she received from Romance Writers of America—and a great imagination.

To the Group, who always believed and were
willing to share:
Paula Detmer Riggs
Ruth Jean Dale
Day Leclaire
Patricia Camden

Chapter One

Northern California, 1885

Clint Strand stood at the bar and with a shaking hand poured cheap whiskey down his parched throat. He shuddered as the liquid hit his empty gut. The raw taste of the liquor couldn't burn away the image of the dead man sprawled in the street outside in the hot September sun.

The acrid stink of black powder clung to his hard fingers, a grim reminder of the years he'd spent defending his miserable way of life.

The hated routine never changed. Shortly after his arrival in town some hothead seeking a "reputation" challenged Clint. He'd draw, shoot, then head for the nearest watering hole, hoping to blot the bloody scene from his mind with a prodigious amount of alcohol.

Only once had a shooting turned personal. The one time he should have killed a man, he hadn't. Somewhere that man still waited. Someday Bull Docker would ambush Clint or draw down on him in a dismal saloon just like this one. It was simply a matter of where and when; one of them would die.

Aching with weariness, he stretched his long, hard frame, trying to loosen his tense muscles. The bullet wound in his shoulder flared with a piercing pain and he winced. Damn, he thought. How long before some other first-timer did him in? A week? A month? A year from now?

He was quick enough that he didn't have to draw first on some kid who wasn't old enough to shave. Clint wondered, not for the first time, if he saw his own death at the hands of another gunman as his only way out of this life of killing and running. Beneath his sandy mustache, the corners of his mouth jerked in a mocking salute to his special code of honor, which gave the advantage to the challenger.

He closed his eyes and let his mind drift back to the beginning, when a few short days of being a hero had set the stage for years of deadly contests. Even after his father had offered a way out, Clint, drawn by excitement and fired by youth, had turned his back on all he loved and chosen this lonely, dangerous life. He'd given up on second chances years ago.

Numb with exhaustion, he longed for a steaming hot bath, a soft bed and an even softer woman—three things he was unlikely to get in this small mountain town. Nobody ever invited him to stay around after a shooting. For fifteen of his thirty-four years, his life had been made up of quick draws and short stays. God, he was tired. Sick and tired.

A dirty bar rag lay near his drink. He shoved it under his shirt and pressed it against the torn flesh of his gun arm, hoping to stem the blood seeping from his wound. A fierce look aimed at the hostile barkeep stopped the obvious protest forming on the man's lips.

"There a doctor around?" Clint knew he needed treatment and soon.

"Out of town."

Clint felt sure the man lied. He braced his injured arm on the rough surface of the bar and surveyed the dismal saloon. The room was spare on decoration and long on dirt, and the smell of stale smoke and unwashed bodies assailed his nostrils. He'd spent more hours than he wanted to count in places just like this.

Wary, unfriendly men watched him furtively, glancing in his direction only when they thought he wouldn't notice. No one ever looked him directly in the eyes. Other men's fears kept him isolated, lonely. One of life's pathetic jokes, he thought, that a rash, impetuous decision he'd made as a kid could shape his life and set him apart from everything he wanted.

Still painfully sober, he rapped on the bar for another drink. The movement increased the throbbing in his damaged shoulder. A fresh, bright stain blossomed on his shirtsleeve, leaving a smear of blood on the scarred wooden bar. A smug smile broke over the bartender's beefy face and he poured the drink with exaggerated slowness.

Clint removed the dirty rag and tore off a strip. He folded the remaining cloth into a thick pad and carefully replaced it over his wound, tying it securely.

He considered grabbing the smirking man around the neck and jamming his face into the bar, but this enticing temptation was replaced by a sudden terrible fatigue. When he raised the glass of whiskey to his lips, the sounds of a heated argument distracted him.

A very pregnant woman stood just inside the swinging doors of the saloon exchanging words with a stiff-collared preacher. Clint couldn't make out what they were saying, but even in the dimly lighted room, her angry gestures and rapid-fire words signaled her fury.

The preacher appeared to be pleading with her. Strange, Clint thought, a pregnant woman and a preacher in a saloon. His lips quirked in amusement before he downed the whiskey in one swallow.

An anxious silence settled over the room and her words carried to Clint. "That's all there is to it! He's responsible and I'm going to make sure he does it!" Clint looked around to see who she was after. Some poor bastard, he thought, who's having a drink and playing cards. Thank God no woman had ever tried to put a rope on him. He laughed to himself; what woman would want a gunfighter anyway?

As the furious little lady wove her way through the tables, several men tipped their hats and mumbled greetings, while others made snide, suggestive remarks. She ignored them all. Belly first, she came to stand in front of Clint.

Astonished, he took off his hat, ran a large hand through his sandy hair and quickly swept his gaze over her. Dressed in a large, pale gown, she looked like a freshly whitewashed barn.

He took in the bedraggled wreath of flowers dipping over her forehead and the wilted bouquet held tightly to her chest. Hard to tell her age with all that fiery red hair hanging about her face, but she seemed pretty young.

Her eyes, green as a spring pasture, were red-rimmed and swollen. Feathered with lush auburn lashes, they were the angriest eyes he'd ever seen. They betrayed something else, as well: a gut-wrenching vulnerability.

Something deep inside Clint responded to her so strongly he felt a sense of wonder. He recognized a kindred soul, one who was dealing with life in the extreme. This was a woman on the very brink of desperation.

The wild look in her eyes cautioned him and he turned wary. Best find out what she wants and move on, he thought.

"Ma'am?"

"Don't 'ma'am' me!" she snapped, and dropped the tired flowers to the floor. Fumbling in the folds of her voluminous white skirt, she pulled out a six-shooter and shoved it against Clint's ribs, poking him hard.

A quick shot of self-preservation jerked his body straight, prepared him for action; she represented immediate danger. "What the hell are you doing, lady?"

"Simple, you murdering..." She took a great, shuddering breath. "You're going to marry me." Her hand shook so badly she brought up the other to support the heavy weapon.

Clint's incredulous laughter broke the tense silence of the room and he relaxed a bit; he could handle this. "Lady, you are coot crazy." She nearly bored the gun through to his liver. He grunted. Through clenched teeth he said, "I'm not about to marry you."

Her eyes snapped wide with amazement. Clint decided the gun made her believe he'd do her bidding without hesitation.

"Your choice." She shrugged. "Marry me or I shoot you."

Clint moved his gaze over her child-swollen body and gauged his chances of taking the gun from her without hurting her. He could do it, but a strange new curiosity crept into his brain and stopped him. For some reason—one he didn't even try to understand—he needed to see how far she'd go. "Well, you'd better fire that thing, because I'm not marrying you or anybody, ever."

She cocked the gun. "Poor choice, mister, because I mean to shoot you right where you stand." She nudged him again with the gun, harder this time.

His eyes narrowed into hard slits with an expression that caused several men to back away from the bar—out of the line of fire.

Clint's mouth barely moved when he spoke. "You mind telling why I should marry you?" He tensed his body. Instantly he calculated the effect his wound would have on his reaction time as he prepared to take her gun. "If it's not too damn much trouble."

"The man you just shot...he was marrying me today."

"Damn!" Clint wiped his hand over his face. A hard knot of agony tied up his gut. Would it never end? he asked himself. His hopes had been so high when he rode into this beautiful, isolated valley. What could he say to her to ease her anguish?

Her skin looked as white as her dress and her eyes sparked furiously at him. She looked mad enough to kill. How the hell could he get out of this without knocking her cold?

"I'm sorry, ma'am, but he called me out when my back was turned. Hell, he called, I drew and shot." In his mind he saw again the body of the young man, crumpled at his feet.

She shook her head. "It doesn't matter how it happened. LaMar Tucker was the father of my child."

Never taking her eyes off Clint, she grabbed the preacher by the arm and pulled him forward. "Start the ceremony, Reverend Mills."

"Now, Annabelle..." the preacher began, his thin fingers pulling at his collar.

"Yeah, *Annabelle,*" Clint interrupted. "This makes no sense at all. I shot your... man. Why would you want to marry me?" He glanced at the throbbing pulse at the base of her throat. Her anger was his ally—he could take her. Still he hesitated. She wasn't much older than he'd been when he faced his first challenge. He needed to know what drove her to this desperate action, as if in understanding her, he would understand himself and the choices he'd made.

She sucked in a ragged breath. "You robbed my baby of its name. Now you're going to give it yours."

Clint admired the beauty of her logic. An eye for an eye. He took something from her, she wanted it back. He nearly smiled at her.

She drew in another deep breath. "My child will *not* be a bastard." The words seemed to infuse her with strength, and she jabbed him again with the gun. "I'm going to start counting. If we aren't married by the time I reach ten, you're food for the buzzards."

Logic be damned. He didn't want to be married—or dead. "Whoa! I can't make a decision with that...with a—"

"One."

"Gun slammed against—"

"Two."

"My gut. Give me—"

"Three." Her trembling finger began to squeeze the trigger.

"Sh—"

"Four."

The pain in Clint's shoulder edged him to a decision. She wanted his name; she wanted a fair trade. All right, he thought, but it'll cost her plenty. He needed a place to heal, and maybe to hide, if Docker had picked up his trail. Clint couldn't deny he owed her. "What the hell." He nodded his surrender to the minister. "Go ahead, Parson."

Sensing the danger had passed, the curious patrons of the saloon began to gather close as Reverend Mills pulled a small worn Bible from his pocket. With a nod, he acknowledged the witnesses and in a shaky voice began to read the marriage ceremony.

"Dearly beloved, we—"

"Five."

"My God," Clint said. "Skip the fancy part, just get it done before she shoots!"

"Do you, Annabelle MacDonald, take this man for your lawful wedded husband?"

"I do. Six."

"Hell, she's still counting!"

"Do you, uh ... ?"

"Seven."

"Strand! Clint Strand!

"Eight."

"Do you, Clint Strand, take this woman for your lawful wedded wife?"

"Nine."

"Yes!"

"I now pronounce you man and wife." The preacher drew a rumpled white handkerchief from his pocket and wiped his sweaty forehead.

Annabelle threw the gun onto the bar and looked Clint directly in the eyes. He could have sworn a kind of peace settled over her.

"Fine," she murmured, and weariness seemed to overtake her. Tears filled her eyes, and though she was still staring at him, he knew she really didn't see him at all.

She turned suddenly and left her new husband and the crowd of amazed men behind her. When she reached the door she brushed her wild red hair from her face and looked back over her shoulder. "Fine," she said again, a wan smile on her lips. The doors flapped back and forth in the wake of her leaving.

Clint grabbed the gun and whirled the chambers. Six bullets all right. That's one feisty lady, he thought. He picked up a bottle from the bar, poured himself a final drink and slammed it back in his throat.

A scared woman no taller than a sapling and with a voice whose harsh words were softened by the sound of the South had taken him on and gotten just what she wanted, without a shot.

Deep in thought, he stared at the still-swinging doors of the saloon. Once before, a woman in desperate circumstances had changed his life. Maybe, just maybe, he was being given that second chance. He made his decision and the guilty, painful knot in his gut relaxed and the grim lines around his mouth eased.

That little lady didn't know it, but she had just punched his ticket to a new life. He had a strong feeling it was going to be a rocky ride.

He eased his injured arm through the sleeve of his heavy woollen jacket and shoved the gun in his belt. He grabbed his hat and took off toward the door.

"Where are you going, son?" the preacher asked.

"Why, Parson, I'm going after my bride."

"Gonna have yer hands full, Strand," called a customer. "Nothing could be worse than being married to that one."

Clint pulled his hat low on his forehead and took a final look at the dreary saloon with its filthy, sawdust-covered floor and cracked, flyspecked mirror. The men gazed back at him, their eyes as empty as their lives. Nothing, he thought, can be as bad as this. He shouldered his way through the swinging doors and never looked back.

On a rickety wagon hitched behind a swaybacked mule, Annabelle, feeling foolish in her wedding dress, sat and blinked back the threatening tears. Crying was a luxury she couldn't afford, exposed as she was to the townsfolk—hardly her admirers even in the best of times. And this day certainly wasn't one of the best. Best days weren't much a part of her life.

She closed her eyes against the hot September sun and wondered if she had gone crazy. The images of herself running from the church at the sound of gunshots, LaMar lying in the road in front of the church, his blood pooling in the dust, burned themselves on her brain. The gunfighter walking away, through the doors of the saloon, unaware that he had taken everything from her and her child. Her sudden, explosive rage that once again life had dealt her a losing hand.

She had wanted to shake her fists at heaven, accuse God of abandoning her. But God wasn't the problem. It was a man, again. Instead of shaking her fists, she had taken LaMar's gun and forced the preacher into that saloon and the killer into marriage. Yes, she was crazy.

She fervently wished herself in another place and time, but she had nowhere else to go but home to her small ranch outside of Pleasant Valley.

This pretty town, set in a small valley watched over by the forbidding but beautiful Sierra Nevada, had been at the center of her dreams; it was clean, with well-kept homes and stores fronted with swept and sheltered wooden sidewalks. There was only one saloon, and the large, spired white church and freshly painted schoolhouse testified to the nature of the people of this town.

Tall timber kept the lumber mill going and employed those men who didn't farm or ranch. The sheriff presided over a one-cell jail. A cell LaMar frequented more than any man in town.

Since she and LaMar arrived here seven months ago, the 1600 or so people of Pleasant Valley had pretty much decided Annabelle was damaged goods. Thanks to LaMar and his big mouth. One night in the saloon, deep in his cups, he'd informed the patrons of his marital state, or lack thereof. A pregnant, unmarried woman didn't gain entrance into respectable society, she'd soon discovered.

She wiped her damp face on the sleeve of her heavy dress. Her hip joints hurt from the pressure of the baby. Her backside ached from the jolting it had received on the drive into town to be married, and her head pounded from the merciless heat of the sun.

In her twenty years of life, tagging after sweet-talking LaMar Tucker and his promises of marriage for two years had been her worst decision—until today.

Impulsiveness and her temper had caused her more trouble than she cared to remember. Surely the number of beatings she'd received from her foster father for her rash deeds should have taught her the value of temperate action.

Frank Bodine's quick fist and thick boot had left many a bruise on her. Often, even his wife couldn't keep him from beating Annabelle nearly senseless. She had to admit he didn't treat his boys much better. They were a mean reflection of their father, and when Mrs. Bodine wasn't looking, they took out their frustration on Annabelle.

She remembered the countless times she had run to hide in the burnt-out Georgia mansion she'd never lived in. The home where her mother died shortly after Annabelle's birth. The ruined home that became a refuge from the violence and pain suffered at the hands of Frank Bodine and his rebellious sons.

She reached into the pocket of her dress and fingered the small square of fabric she always carried with her. The scorched, faded green velvet had once framed the many tall windows in the ballroom of her family's home.

Annabelle closed her eyes and recalled the day she'd found the faded scrap of material. She'd been hiding from the tormenting boys behind a section of fallen roof, when her hand touched something soft. Her fingers had closed on it and stroked the silky nap as she conjured up visions of her mother dancing in the vast room.

When Annabelle felt safe from the boys, she'd pulled the fabric from the jumble of burnt wood and brushed dirt from the velvet. She'd held it to her breast and reached for an image of the woman who'd given her birth, a woman she'd never known.

She lost the battle against tears, wiped her eyes on her sleeve and silently scolded herself again; crying never solved problems. Weepy, timid action hadn't solved the problem of a name for her child. A gun in the side of a killer had. She shuddered, then felt a sudden burst of pride at forcing the gunman to her will. Lord knows, all the cajoling, demanding and tears hadn't brought LaMar to the altar. Until today, when it was too late.

The fact of her pregnancy had brought a guilty look to LaMar's face, but her panic at having an illegitimate child didn't move him one bit. After all, he'd said, he'd turned out all right and he was a bastard. He'd been that all right, she thought, a sweet-talking, lying one. Finally, she threatened to leave him, and he said he'd marry her before the baby came.

There was a time when his attention was sweet and fulsome. It was her own fault she'd mistaken his early tenderness for love. Her gratitude for her rescue from the Bodines' wore as thin as her blue cotton dress. When LaMar's dreams turned to dust, his tender feelings for her took last place after whiskey, bragging and sleeping.

She had given him two years of her life and that was enough. She shook all thoughts of LaMar from her mind, took up the reins and prepared to leave the heat-baked streets of Pleasant Valley for home.

A few doors away she saw the town's most influential women huddled in earnest conversation. Most likely they were planning some new strategy to get her out of town now that LaMar was dead.

The Tuesday Club was determined to turn Pleasant Valley into a "decent family town." They'd run off nearly every loose woman before she and LaMar hit town.

Since then, a man had to ride clear to Nevada City to satisfy his lustful urges. Now they saw Annabelle and Emma Rooney, who owned the "boarding house," as their final challenge. Weary of the fight, Annabelle sighed, knowing she couldn't avoid them.

Had she really felt a begrudging gratitude to those women? They'd cornered LaMar outside the saloon one day and presented him with their ultimatum: marry his "pregnant harlot" or get out of town. He'd been too drunk to argue and too lazy to pack. When she'd threatened to leave him, LaMar had gone to see the preacher. Being the lesser of two evils had finally established Annabelle's place in LaMar's affections.

Dressed in dark colors, the women reminded Annabelle of a flock of noisy crows squabbling over a choice ear of corn. Frowns in place and noses raised righteously in the air, they advanced on the wagon. Grouped tightly for added strength, they came to a stop in front of Annabelle.

They were all there. Mrs. Fillmore, wife of the owner of the general store, weighed two hundred and fifty pounds and looked like fully risen bread dough. Felicity Whitehall taught in the one-room schoolhouse. A spinster, she was so skinny a faint breeze off the Sierra would waft her into Placer County. The preacher's pinch-lipped, gray-faced wife, Hepsaba Mills, would most likely have a few things to say to her husband for marrying the "harlot" and the gunfighter.

Annabelle felt some disappointment at seeing Mrs. Cummins with these women. With her round cheery face, Martha was the only female in town who'd ever spoken so much as a "good morning" to her. Early on, responding to Annabelle's attempt to be neighborly, the woman promised to drop by for a cup of tea and a visit. Somehow, after word of her pregnancy got around, that never happened.

Mrs. Jennings, the banker's wife, her tall figure held with rigid confidence, stepped forward. A sick feeling gathered in Annabelle's stomach. Judaline Jennings, traces of her former beauty ruthlessly subdued beneath tightly pulled-back hair and black dresses, had been after Annabelle ever since she discovered that Pleasant Valley's newest residents were living in sin. Banker Jennings's hand on the money gave his wife an authoritative voice in the town's affairs.

"*Miss* MacDonald," Judaline said, her thin, screechy voice emphasizing Annabelle's unmarried state. "Since your *intended* husband lies in the back of the barbershop awaiting burial—for which you're expected to pay—we want you off that disgraceful ranch and out of town within thirty days." Her faded hazel eyes flashed her dislike.

Annabelle straightened her back and looked down at the women. Only Martha refused to meet her eyes. The others silently dared Annabelle to object to their demands. These women ruled the town, but they didn't rule her.

She made a silent vow to keep her temper from erupting. Right now, her biggest worry was how she'd pay for burying LaMar. "I'm not leaving," Annabelle said, her voice soft but firm.

"Oh yes you are." Judaline's small eyes narrowed with determination. "I'll have my husband get the sheriff to throw you off that property. Only decent women will reside in Pleasant Valley. We will not tolerate *your kind*." She turned to smile at her cohorts. They vigorously nodded their approval as though they were puppets and Judaline held their strings fast in her bony fist. "You can't marry a dead man and we won't tolerate a pregnant whore living in our town."

"I keep wondering, Judaline, why you're so all fired interested in the moral behavior of others. Seems mighty suspicious to me. Maybe your own bedroom needs tending."

From the sweep of scarlet that rushed over Judaline's face, Annabelle feared the woman would pop her stays. Her chest heaved and she seemed to have a terrible time finding her breath.

Judaline strode nearer the wagon. "You cheap little tramp—"

"Get out of my way," Annabelle said, emphasizing each word. Deep inside the insult drove painfully into her heart. She wasn't a tramp! She was just another stupid woman lured by a lying, beguiling man. She snapped the reins against the back of the mule. "I'm going home and you can't stop me."

Felicity, a spiteful expression on her ruddy face, grabbed the mule's halter. "Oh yes we can!"

The jangle of spurs arrested the reckless action of the townswomen and riveted their attention on the approaching gunfighter. Leading his horse, he walked unwaveringly toward the group, his eyes locked with Annabelle's.

The fear that had settled in her stomach when LaMar challenged the gunman stole up again and clenched her heart. She had nearly succeeded in putting him out of her mind. *My God! He's coming after me!* she thought.

She lifted a trembling hand to shade her eyes from the hot sun and observed his progress nervously. An intimidating, hard-looking man with a confident, arrogant walk. Tall, rangy and broad-shouldered, he wore a full, golden-colored mustache that nearly covered his upper lip.

The brim of his trail-worn hat held his eyes in shadow; she'd been too angry inside the saloon to take notice of their color. He stopped a few feet away and pushed his hat back on his head and she saw his eyes were a clear, brilliant blue. His gaze resolutely held hers.

She sighed and her shoulders slumped in momentary defeat. With the furious women in front of her and the threatening gunfighter to the side of her, she felt completely trapped. What made her think for one moment he'd let her get away with that shotgun wedding? What gave her the idea that she could best a man? Any man.

Lord knows, her life had been filled with men who had beaten her, threatened her, lied to her. Now here stood another. One to whom she had firmly and legally tied herself by marriage.

Clint stood quietly and looked her over. An honest-to-God redhead, he thought. Her hair was bright and wildly out of control. The unruly sight of it made a man want to smile. Out in the sunlight he could see she was covered with freckles. From the look of her, she most likely had them over her whole body. Not that he was interested in finding out. He didn't find a woman pregnant with another man's child appealing.

Why, he wondered, would a woman want to marry the gunfighter who shot her man? A name for her kid? He guessed a woman would do most anything to protect her child. He recalled his mother's passionate defense of him to his father. Yes, this desperate woman would do anything for her child. He would use her need to his advantage. If he moved in with her... a good cover for a gunman, to be settled down with a wife and a baby.

Clint looked at her life-promising body, at the desolation in her eyes and the fear in her rigid posture. In that instant the impulsive decision he'd made in the bar became logical. She wanted a name for her kid? She'd gotten one. He needed a refuge? She would provide it. How could she object? They would solve each other's problem.

He glanced at her fists, white-knuckled around the reins, and at her heartbeat fluttering at the base of her throat and felt the pull of her vulnerability, an inexplicable enticement that was almost sensual.

He pressed the bridge of his nose between his thumb and forefinger; he had to be crazy. This woman was pregnant and off limits. She was trouble and *in* trouble, that was the lure. A woman needed rescue. Always a weakness for him. One that started him on this lonely trail he rode.

She's terrified, he realized. She'd been so stridently brave in the saloon. Now he could almost smell the fear on her. It was in command and he would take advantage of that. He felt a tug of guilt at his willingness to use her this way, but she'd used him, hadn't she?

"You having a problem here, Mrs. Strand?" He tipped his hat farther back on his head and sent a fierce glare in the direction of the curious women, who backed off a little before his condemning expression.

"Mrs. Strand?" Judaline Jennings cried, a stunned expression on her face.

Annabelle's eyes snapped wide, then narrowed. What the devil was he up to? Anger over her past treatment at the hands of men boiled to the surface. Her fear evaporated and she nearly choked on her words. "My problems aren't any of your business."

"Well now." Clint lifted his good arm and rubbed the soft nose of his horse. "I'd say your problems are my business, since you're my wife." He glared again at the women clustered in front of the wagon. "It's of great concern to me if someone is causing you trouble."

"Wife?" the women questioned in one unbelieving voice.

"Wife!" Annabelle exclaimed, astonished at his public announcement.

Ignoring the bewildered look on her face, Clint walked to the rear of the wagon and tied on the reins of his horse. He bent down to undo the cinch then threw his saddle into the back of the wagon. He briefly closed his eyes from the pain the effort caused, then walked around to where his new wife sat, looking tense and confused. "Move over, Mrs. Strand. I'll drive."

"You're not...I'm not taking a killer home with me."

At the word "killer," the women of The Tuesday Club gasped in unison.

Clint stepped into the wagon and gathered up Annabelle. Disregarding the throbbing pain in his arm and the shocked women in the road, he moved her over on the seat.

"Sure you are. Where else would I go except home, with my sweet bride?" He slapped the reins across the back of the mule and the wagon lurched forward, scattering Judaline and her companions.

Annabelle's jaw dropped in amazement. This man's a foul, despicable murderer, she thought. *And also my husband.* There he sat, staring straight at her, waiting for her to say something. Looking into his eyes she saw they rivaled the color of a clear summer sky and held an unexpected softness that sparked an answering tenderness in her heart. Oh Lordy, what would she do with him?

Clint nodded in the direction of the group of stunned women clustered a short distance from the wagon. He brought his hand up to his hat brim in a polite salute. "Ladies."

Annabelle held her breath and watched with fascination as he raised his lean hips, reached into a pocket of his tight-fitting trousers and withdrew a five-dollar gold piece, which he tossed at the women. Judaline, ever knowing the value of money, automatically reached out and caught it. "Take care of my wife's friend," Clint said.

Out of pure meanness, Annabelle nodded haughtily at the women as the wagon passed them. She felt secretly grateful for this man's unexpected defense of her.

"You haven't heard the last of this, Annabelle MacDonald!" Judaline bellowed, determined as always to have the last word.

Clint looked over his shoulder at the indignant woman. "That's Strand. Annabelle Strand."

When they'd left the town behind them, Clint turned to the silent woman by his side. "Tough bunch of old biddies. They make life hard for you?"

"That's only half of it." She sighed. He might as well know everything, she thought. Maybe then he wouldn't be so eager to come with her. She told him briefly of the warning the women had given LaMar, sparing herself nothing in the telling.

"Are you a harlot?" he asked, his amusement evident.

"No!" A heated blush flooded her skin, blending with her freckles. "And you needn't look so hopeful."

Clint shrugged. "Hard for a man to tell sometimes." He glanced pointedly at her swollen belly and bare ring finger. "How'd you get yourself in this mess?"

"That's none of your business, either."

"You crying back there, was that for your, uh, friend?"

"I wasn't crying and he wasn't my friend," she stated, her voice flat and empty sounding.

A look of surprise widened his eyes. "Then what was he to you?"

"A born disappointment." And he fulfilled his birthright today, she silently added.

"I'm impressed by the depth of your grief and your inventiveness in getting another man." Clint's sarcasm was barely hidden.

"Since you don't know anything about it, except that you shot him, I'd suggest you shut up." She prayed he'd do just that. She didn't want to think or talk about lying LaMar Tucker. And the very last thing she wanted was another man. This whole business made her so tired she feared she'd fall off the wagon from sheer exhaustion.

"Could the bank do that?"

"What?" His sudden switch of topic made her dizzy.

"Kick you off your land."

"If you're behind in your mortgage payments and the bank president's wife is the leader of that bunch of hateful women. And they dislike my condition." Her voice trailed to a whisper.

"You're married now," Clint reasoned aloud.

She fought back the hysteria rising in her throat. "To a gunfighter! I'm sure that elevates me in their estimation." The bitter tone of her words revealed the depth of her pain.

He studied the country around them. The well-protected valley, the defiant Sierra, the thick forest of pine and mountain oak—all guaranteed a degree of isolation that suited Clint's needs perfectly. This was the ideal place to heal and make plans. Maybe Mexico would provide a place to start a new life. A place far from Docker and the men who would follow him. Rootless, restless men searching for the dubious fame of a gunfighter.

They rode in silence for about a mile before Clint decided it was time for a family conference. His shoulder hurt like hell. No doubt he was bleeding again. "How far's this home of yours, Mrs. Strand?" All he could think of was getting off the hard seat of this damned wagon and into a comfortable bed.

"Now this is right pretty country," he said, drawing out his words. "I've had a mind to see it, but I don't think this old mule has what it takes to go more than a couple of miles." He paused, hoping for a reply; none came. "What do you think, Mrs. Strand?" When he spoke, she didn't even turn her head and look at him, just sat there lip-locked and stiff as a fence post. He smiled inwardly at her stubbornness.

"Stop calling me Mrs. Strand!" She spat the words at him like buckshot.

Clint nodded. He'd rather have her anger than her fear. A scared woman did crazy things—but then, so did an angry one. He could bear witness to that fact, as this day had proved.

He eased the reins to the right and guided the mule and wagon under the welcoming shade of an ancient oak tree. He felt the sweat roll down his face and back. His jacket was far too heavy for the midday heat. "Whoa, mule."

He turned carefully on the high-backed seat and pushed his hat back on his head. "Seems to me we have a few things to straighten out here." He cupped her chin in his fingers and forced her to look at him.

The warning message of her rigid posture conflicted with the lost look in her eyes. She puzzled him as no woman ever had. One minute defiance, the next defeat rounded her shoulders. She posed no feminine wiles, yet he was drawn to her. In town, when he'd let those women know she was his wife and under his protection, she'd looked at him for a moment, with grudging appreciation. Now she was frozen in contempt for him and his touch. He decided to push her a little more, find the limits of her control. He'd need to know that as the days passed.

"Your neck's as stiff as that old mule's hind legs." He moved his fingers against her skin and he allowed the soft feel of her to register only briefly in his mind.

Annabelle had enough. She didn't want the strong touch of his callused fingers on her, didn't want the feelings his nearness generated in her middle.

She slapped his hand away from her face and glared straight into his bold blue eyes. "Keep your blood-stained hands away from me and get the hell off my wagon." His expression darkened and conveyed a determined purpose she didn't want to dwell on. "You heard me," she said. "Get down and get going."

He pulled his hat over his eyes and slumped down in the seat, leaning against its hard, slatted back. His shoulder throbbed and he felt light-headed. If he didn't get care soon, he'd be in trouble...more trouble, he amended. He needed to get her moving.

"As you can imagine, I'm not a man versed in legal refinements." He tipped his hat up a little and mockery gleamed in his eyes. "But if I recall it correctly, what's yours is mine. Still, I'm inclined to be more generous. I'll settle for what's yours is ours. Let me know when you're ready to head for home. Meanwhile, I'll just take a little snooze." He shifted in his seat to ease the strain on his shoulder and turned away from her. God, he hurt. The idea of resting on this barely-held-together wagon almost made him laugh.

He needed to close his eyes against the increasing dizziness; he was afraid he'd pass out cold. He'd been shot before, but somehow the strain of this day made him more conscious of the pointless, risky life he led; it made him more aware of his pain.

He wondered why, this particular day, his thoughts turned so often to his home in Philadelphia. The fine three-story house along the lakeshore with its large airy rooms and the smell of lemon and beeswax and fine cooking. His mother, so serene and capable in her care of her family. He purposely shut down his memories when they turned to his father. Stern, unforgiving, wanting things from Clint he couldn't give.

The continued silence of the furious woman beside him caused him to wonder at his decision to come with her. She didn't look all that ready to come to terms with him. Serenity didn't make up any part of her demeanor. She bristled like a thistle, all sharp and itchy for a fight.

Anger at the gunfighter and at herself simmered inside the woman across the seat. Well, Annabelle MacDonald, you've gone and done it again. It wasn't bad enough you ran off with that no-account LaMar Tucker when he offered you the moon. Trailed after him like a crazy woman, you did, believing his golden words and promises of marriage. Well, he lied—and now look where you are. Worse off than ever. A dead, good-for-nothing almost-husband, a fatherless child on the way and married to a murdering gunslinger who won't leave you alone—all in one day. What's worse, you asked for it!

Annabelle risked a peek at the dozing man. He had wide enough shoulders. Lord knows, she thought, he's

handsome enough, and she could use his strength in the
orchard, caring for the horse, mule, the cow and
chopping wood. *No! That's just crazy. I don't need
him, don't want him.* And handsome didn't count for
a thing.

The baby chose that moment to punch her low in the
belly. *But I sure need somebody.*

Clint sat up carefully. He yawned and glanced at
Annabelle.

She glared at him. "I told you to get off my wagon.
I don't want you here."

"You married me, now you've got me. Like it or
not."

"That's crazy! I was scared and mad. It was a fool
thing to do, I know that. Not for one minute do I expect you to be a husband to me. Dammit, I don't even
want a husband!" She took a shuddering breath. "I
just didn't want my baby to be a . . . nameless." Gathering a handful of the skirt of her dusty wedding dress,
she wiped the sweat off her forehead.

"Well, you've got that and more." He reached out
and blatantly patted her very pregnant belly. "And it
seems to me you need a husband more than any lady I
ever saw." He grinned inwardly at the furious cuss
word she spat at him. "You sure do swear a lot for a
female."

"Get your hands off me! You've no right to touch
me!" The shock of his intimate contact drove her
struggling to her feet, rocking the wagon. "And how I
talk is none of your business."

He pulled her back down onto the rickety seat and
blinked away the sudden wave of dizziness that over-

took him. He had to get her under control and home before he passed out.

"Hold on there, Mrs. Strand. I've got every right to touch you, and touch you I will," he said, deciding to forgo further comment on her vocabulary. "Let's get this settled right now." With a firm grip on her stubborn chin he forced her to look at him. *"I'm going home with you."*

"No!" She gave a mighty heave and shoved him.

Her move was so unexpected, Clint couldn't save himself from falling off the wagon. He landed heavily on his wounded shoulder and he thought he might vomit from the intensity of the pain. He thanked God for the heavy padding of his jacket. He reached out, grabbed the wheel and levered himself up.

Holding his injured arm close to his side, he climbed back onto the wagon and jerked her around to face him; he swayed, light-headed with the effort.

Her eyes widened when she looked at the spreading bloodstain on the sleeve of his jacket. "You're hurt!"

"Take the reins and get this wagon moving."

"No!"

"Listen, lady. I'm real tired of this sniping. Now get this through that wild red head of yours." His nose practically touched hers. "I'm going home with you and we will be husband and wife—" he glanced pointedly at her ripe belly "—and mother and father."

"No," she whispered.

"Yes!" He let her go and handed her the reins. "Move it—now!"

Chapter Two

Annabelle roasted in her heavy wedding dress. She hated the homemade gown. Somehow it symbolized all her failures at the hands of men.

She closed her eyes and let the mule take them down dusty Mosquito Road on the way to the ranch. She saw again her last day at the Bodines' home in Georgia. She felt the rasp of the bushes against her face as she raced away from the Bodines. Father and sons, drunk and crazy with the idea of rape.

She could still feel the damp earth beneath her back as they tore at her clothes and jabbed and poked at her body, slobbering and arguing which one of them would have her first. Her foster father and his three sons holding her down, their hot, foul breath on her face, their filthy hands spreading her legs. Laughing at her screams until Mrs. Bodine, a rifle in her hands, told them to move off Annabelle.

Mrs. Bodine had dragged her, naked and crying, back to the hovel the Bodines had called home. There she told her to dress and get out. Annabelle had been shocked at this unfair treatment by the woman who had shown her the only kindness she'd ever known.

The woman who had taken Annabelle from her dead mother's arms. A woman who had treated her like a daughter when the men weren't around. Taught her how to cook and sew a fine seam.

She'd thrown a few things into a bundle and hurried away, scared but relieved to be gone from those awful people who had hated her for reasons she'd never understood.

LaMar had found her hiding in the brush beside the road, scratched, bruised and crying. He'd comforted her, promised her a new life, and in her desperation she'd followed him.

She sighed and let go of the memories. At least LaMar hadn't beaten her. For a while, she thought, he had loved her a little. But disappointment in his abilities to obtain his dreams had soured him on life...and on her. Unfortunately, by then she was pregnant and in need of a name for her child.

LaMar kept promising marriage. *Soon.* Soon never came. The gunfighter came instead.

Annabelle pulled the wagon to a stop in front of the most unstable cabin Clint had ever seen. At the sight, he swore silently and thought perhaps she was right: he ought to get the hell out while the offer still held, while he could still sit a saddle. How in blazes did she expect to stay here alone? There looked to be more work than five men could handle, let alone one.

Clint glanced at Annabelle. She had a sweet smile on her face as if she had come upon a castle in the midst of the forest. He shook his head in disbelief. What kind of life had she lived if this place put that look on her face? "Home?"

Still smiling, she nodded. Stretching, she reached around to rub her lower back. "Yes," she said with a contented sigh. "This is my home." The only one she had ever had. She couldn't count the Bodines' place as home. Or the remains of her family's plantation.

She and LaMar had worked so hard for the money to buy this land. For four months she had stayed alone in Omaha, in the back of the seamstress's shop where she worked, while LaMar cowboyed on a ranch twenty-five miles out of town. Every cent of that money went into her tin box for safekeeping.

The time in San Francisco brought more money. But that was where LaMar had lost his job. She had refused to give him the money for yet another of his crazy schemes, so they'd ended up here, in Pleasant Valley. Most of the money had gone for this land, for the materials to start the cabin and to buy the cow, the horse and the wagon.

Annabelle knew the moment she saw this property that she wanted it. The acres of meadowland surrounded by tall pines and oaks would be a wonderful place to raise children. And the peach trees. Seventy nearly dead peach trees reminded her of those on her family land in Georgia. They were a sign; this was her home.

She worked so hard all summer to bring those trees back to life. She hauled water from the stream, pulled weeds, cut back dead branches. Her reward had been lush, ripe fruit.

Now the money was all but gone and LaMar was gone, but she had her baby and her house. She would build a future for herself and her child, somehow.

Clint got down and walked around the wagon. Since her waist wasn't available, he put his hands under her damp armpits and lifted her down, wincing at the effort. She'd be crazy to live unprotected in this wilderness, he thought. "You actually planned on living here alone?"

She drew her dark red brows into a frown. "What's wrong with living here?"

"First thing, this place looks ready to give up and fall down." The motion of his good arm encompassed the house, the barn and the peach orchard. "Nothing about it is squared. It's built from bits and pieces of wood, tin and heavy paper, for God's sake. A hefty spring breeze would scatter it over half the state." Why was he arguing the point? Shack or not, he needed to get inside and take care of his injury.

Clint shook his head in disgust at the pathetic-looking shelter before them. It looked ready to topple into the surrounding heat-scorched weeds. It seemed an affront to the quiet meadow and the giant pines and mountain oaks bordering the cleared land on which it sat.

"Second, I'd say that man of yours didn't know a hell of a lot about putting up a house."

Annabelle drew nondescript pictures in the dirt with the toe of her worn boot.

"He did build it, didn't he? Or was it already here?"

Ignoring her stiff silence and sensing her discomfort, Clint pressed. "Well? Did he build it?"

"Some." She looked off toward the scraggly peach orchard.

Suspicion rose rapidly in his mind. "How much?"

"What difference does it make? He built some of it! Leave me alone." She started to walk away.

Clint grabbed her arm. "How much?"

She sighed. "He sort of framed it."

He took her by the shoulders, the action reminding him painfully of the wound in his arm. "Sort of framed it?" She didn't want to talk about this, he thought, any fool could see that. He took a wild guess. "And you sort of did the rest, right?"

"Yes!" She pulled free and started for the sad, tired-looking shelter, stomping all the way.

Who did this man think he was to criticize her home? Did he have to face the hostile people in town to ask stupid questions about how to build this cabin while LaMar spent his days in the saloon? Did he drive in those hundreds of nails?

When the money ran low, Clint Strand wasn't the one who shifted through the leavings behind the lumber yard for scraps of wood and then bartered with the old bachelor who owned the yard—homemade bread for rusted tools.

It was her vision of a peaceful future for her child in this valley that had built her home, not the furtive nightmares of a hunted man. He had no rights here, none at all. Especially no right to find fault with her home.

What of her hopes now that this day had so completely changed her life? She looked at her small home, the place where a family was to live, and felt the steady pounding of fear in her chest. The uncertainty of the days to come scared her so much. Her throat tightened with the need to just sit down where she stood and cry until she had no more tears. To what purpose? she asked herself. None, except for appearing a weak fool in front of this man.

"We can't stay in this wreck of a place!" he hollered after her.

"I can and I will!" she yelled back. "Nobody invited you, so get out!"

Clint took off his hat and wiped his brow on his forearm. Damn, he'd really gotten himself into a mess. In that moment he realized how desperately he'd yearned for a place to rest and remake his life. What he had was an about-to-fall-down house, the most forlorn peach orchard he'd ever seen and a stubborn, temper-ridden, redheaded, pregnant wife who looked to drop her kid any minute.

Swearing under his breath, he strode past her and climbed the unsteady steps to the porch. When he turned the door handle, it came off in his hand. In disgust, he threw it as far as he could.

"What do you think you're doing?" she cried, and took off in search of the worthless knob.

He glared at her departing figure then went inside. It was awful. A single room, except for a kind of curtained lean-to for the bed. On a tilting table he noted heat-wilted flowers stuck in a jar. Two loaves of freshly baked bread sat on a clean but faded towel. She'd hung once colorful feed sacks to frame the one window and a faded catalog picture on a rough wood wall.

The room was as clean as anyone could make it. The window was large enough to let in plenty of sunlight. They wouldn't have to use a lantern in the daytime, except maybe in the winter. Her valiant efforts to make a home out of this shack touched him as nothing had in years.

He moved out onto the porch and studied her as she walked slowly to the house, the rescued handle in her hand. She looked so exhausted, as if all hope had deserted her. He leaned against an upright supporting the roof and wondered if he had it in him to bring back some light into her eyes.

It seemed too many years since his life held a promise of any real future, let alone one with a wife and family. Dare he allow hope to be a part of his life again?

He nearly smiled at her wrinkled, sweat-stained dress and the total disarray of her hair. She wasn't the kind of woman who would wear out a man with her vanity, yet there was something about her looks that promised more: that with care and rest and maybe love, she would shine with a wholesome beauty. "You look as wilted as those flowers on the table."

She brushed some dust from her ruined wedding dress, then looked up at him, green eyes flashing. "It's a real shame my appearance doesn't please you."

Clint looked down at his dusty boots and felt the unfamiliar burden of responsibility settle on his aching shoulders like a harness on a mustang. "Well, if we're going to live here together, I'll have to do something about this place." He stepped off the porch. "Burn it down seems the best solution," he said as he passed her on his way to the wagon.

Annabelle followed him, her skirts trailing in the dirt. "Listen here, you fool of a man. You don't want to be here and I don't want you here. So get on your stupid horse and ride out." She turned her back on him and trudged toward the house, her anger evident in each step.

Clint jerked his saddle from the wagon and threw it onto his horse. A searing pain bit at his shoulder and he groaned. He felt the fresh flow of blood run down his arm.

He'd rather take his chances with a gun. He'd done it for more years than he cared to count. Maybe he'd head for the northern border; most likely no one had heard of him up there. Certainly Bull Docker wouldn't hunt for him in the Canadian wilds. That was exactly what he'd do. Head out for the north country and begin a new life.

He turned and looked at Annabelle sitting on the wobbly porch steps, her shoulders slumped in dejection and a lost expression on her freckled face. He rested his forehead on the saddle, fighting off the light-headed feeling overtaking him. He wanted to laugh at the unexpected turns life sometimes took; he knew he wasn't going anywhere. He'd made a personal, private commitment to this woman even if she didn't realize it. Crazy as the whole thing was, he knew he'd see it through...at least for a while. Besides, he needed her as much as she needed him.

The dizziness increased and buzzed through his head. He needed her for sure, right this moment....

"Annabelle!"

"What now?" she hollered from where she sat hunched on the porch steps.

"Come here!"

Something in his voice commanded her to her feet. She stumbled tiredly to his side. When she glanced up at him, she saw his skin had lost its healthy color and his lips were pulled tight across his teeth. Gone was the tough exterior of the gunfighter. She allowed the realization to penetrate her brain: he was taken by such pain it left him exposed, vulnerable—and he hated it.

She reached out to touch his arm and saw the widening wet stain of blood on the sleeve of his jacket. "Dear God, you're bleeding bad." She wiped his blood off her fingers with her skirt.

"Now you notice?"

"Let me see." She eased his jacket off his arm and removed the filthy rag from beneath his shirt. She threw the blood-soaked cloth to the ground. "You've been . . ." Her eyes widened in disbelief. "LaMar shot you?" She couldn't believe it. LaMar couldn't hit a tenpenny nail with a twenty-pound hammer.

"A lucky shot," Clint muttered.

She unbuttoned his shirt and gently moved it aside to better view his injury. It was worse than he knew, worse than she'd hoped. "You're right about that," she said, trying to keep the panic from her voice. She pulled the shirt back in place, clearing her throat as she did so. "Come inside. I'll fix it up the best I can." Knowing in her heart he wasn't going anywhere now, she put her arm around his waist to help him into the house.

He stepped away. "I can manage."

"Fine. Manage." She left him to do just that.

Inside the cabin, she lit the lantern and hurriedly tore a clean but ragged sheet into strips. *This man's turning out to be the curse of all time.*

She put a kettle of water to boil on the tiny wood stove. She would fix his arm and send him on his way, out of her life, she decided. A worthless hope, she knew. Clint Strand was days away from leaving her home.

She removed a bottle of whiskey from behind the flour bin, a bottle she'd hidden from LaMar. "Men, men, men!" she chanted derisively.

When she heard Clint's boots on the porch, she turned. He leaned against the doorframe, his growing weakness evident in every line of his tall body. She walked quickly over and took him by his uninjured arm. She guided him to an apple box, which served as a chair at the wobbly table. "You've proved you're big and strong, now sit!"

Carefully removing his shirt, Annabelle shook her head in amazement. The wound was bad. The bullet had drawn a deep, uneven, bloody gash in his flesh, leaving a torn, filthy track before exiting. How in the world had he held out so long? She felt her face grow hot with shame. She'd been so mired in her troubles she hadn't given a thought to the seriousness of his injury.

"It needs sewing up," she said. "Most likely you need a doctor."

"You do it." He swayed and she reached out to steady him.

She swallowed hard. The sudden thought of pushing a needle in and out of his flesh left her queasy. "Let me clean it and sew it up, then you can lie down for a while. A minute or two more and you'll be flat on your face. That foul rag you put over—"

"Fine. Quit nagging and just get it done."

She glared at him. His fight against the pain drew his pale skin taut over the hard, rugged planes of his face. He's in agony, she thought, and doesn't want me to know it. Reluctantly, she found herself admiring his courage.

She washed his arm with clean warm water, then carefully picked out pieces of his shirt material that had stuck in the wound. It was ugly and filthy. A sickening, inflamed red spread out from the torn edges. She quickly finished and poured the whiskey over his cleansed flesh.

"Damn! You trying to kill me off?" He knew he was close to passing out. If she didn't hurry, he'd be on the floor.

"No!" Horror filled her at the thought of killing anyone, even a murderer like him.

"It sure feels like it." He grabbed the bottle from her and and took several swallows of liquor. "Some on the outside and some on the inside. Works every time." He grinned at her, momentarily erasing the painful tension from his face.

Annabelle stood still, dumbstruck. His smile was so beautiful it nearly stopped her breath. She placed her hands between her breasts in an unconscious effort to feel for her heartbeat.

"What's wrong?" He took another large swallow of the whiskey.

"N-nothing!" Everything was wrong. Fluttery little feelings tiptoed in her belly, feelings that had nothing to do with the child resting there. Feelings a woman had for a man. Oh no, she vowed, not this one.

"Finish up, will you? That bed's looking mighty damned good." Weakness invaded his voice. "And I'm not getting better just sitting here."

Obviously alone in her tender feelings, Annabelle stiffened her spine, threaded the needle and began the grisly job of sewing his injured arm. Bile rose and seared her throat each time she pushed the needle through his flesh. When she saw the muscles in his jaw quiver with his effort not to cry out, she bit her lip and concentrated on fitting the ragged edges of his wound together.

Just like sewing a dress, she told herself, trying to ignore the feel of his heated skin beneath her fingers. The scent of him, warm and pungent and male, filled her nostrils and made her breath quicken.

Finished at last, she wrapped his arm in the clean cloth and put in some stitches to hold it in place. "There," she said, satisfied with her work now that her stomach had settled down. "That's more than a flesh wound."

"I think I'd better try that bed." He looked paler than before.

"Over here." She put her arm around his waist and he leaned against her. Accepting her help this time without complaint, he let her lead him the short distance to the bed.

By the time she got his boots off he had passed out; his long, muscular legs hung over the edge of the thin mattress. She silently cursed the turn her life had taken and the new problems this man presented. With considerable effort, she moved him around and covered him with the quilt.

She wiped her damp face with a piece of the sheet she'd torn to dress his wound and gazed at his long body, stretched out on her bed. He took up nearly the whole space. In repose, the hard lines of his face softened and she realized what a fine-looking man he was. His thick tawny hair lay damp on his forehead. His heavy brows, a darker gold, arched over his closed eyes. His lashes, even darker, were so long a woman would envy their length. She sighed and wondered how a man this strong and handsome had come to live such a terrible life. A woman would—

Annabelle brought her startling thoughts to a halt. She didn't care about his appearance, the life he led or his appeal to the female persuasion. She wanted him gone. He'd have to leave when he came around. She wouldn't have him staying a minute longer than necessary.

She took the bowl from the table and threw the bloody water out the door. She watched it soak into the dry soil. She rotated her tired shoulders and rubbed the back of her neck. Looking off toward the high Sierra, she allowed their towering beauty to calm her weary body and soothe her ragged nerves.

This hundred acres was to be the beginning of her dream of home, husband and children. The inadequate cabin, the nearly roofless barn, the struggling peach orchard were hers—nothing or no one would drive her away. Not the bank, not Judaline Jennings and her small-minded friends, not the winter or the gunfighter. This place, this land, belonged to her and her child. Together they would build a new, safer life.

The bellowing of the cow jarred her serenity and she went back inside for the milk bucket. She glanced at Clint; thankfully he still slept.

The barn smelled of dusty hay, warm animal flesh, old leather and—she wrinkled her nose—manure. The stalls needed mucking out. A low ache in her belly reminded her that heavy work was beyond her capability now. She glanced up at the roof and prayed that what was left of it would hold out against the coming winter snows.

The barn had been the only building standing when she and LaMar had put their precious two hundred dollars in the hands of Banker Jennings. Now she stood in danger of losing even that. The four hundred dollars owed might as well be four thousand. She suppressed a sob and rubbed her tired back.

The cow's insistent lowing reminded Annabelle why she stood in the middle of the barn. "Hush up, you miserable old thing," she said. "I'm coming."

With her foot, she scooted the milking stool next to the complaining cow. Once seated, Annabelle spread her legs, leaned out over her distended belly and pulled the teats of the cow's swollen udder.

"If I didn't need you so bad, I'd sell you so fast it would sour your milk," she told the still-noisy animal. "Can't you see I'm doing my part? Stop bellowing at me." She pulled harder and watched the warm milk foam in the bucket.

"I'd think you'd be on my side, being another female. But no, you're just like everyone else, devoting your life to making mine as difficult as possible."

It seemed difficulty had been the cornerstone of Annabelle's life right up to and including this day. The War had taken the lives of the grandfather and uncles she had never known. The family plantation—a burnt-out reminder of a gracious past—lay dead in the ashes. Her mother—vulnerable to a roving soldier—gave birth on the floor of a sharecropper's hovel, then gave up her sad life, leaving her daughter alone.

Growing up among the Bodines, the former "croppers" on her family's land, hadn't held one minute of happiness for Annabelle. She didn't remember ever having a full stomach as a child. Hunger seemed as normal to her as the beatings and the shouted curse words. Even the uncertain and occasional kindnesses of Mrs. Bodine didn't make up for the miserable treatment from her husband and sons.

When she thought of the gunslinger's surprise at her swearing, she laughed bitterly. Perhaps, she thought, it would be a good thing to try to tone down her speech. But life hadn't taught her the value of sweet words.

She thought of the injured man lying on her bed. There was a difficulty. What would she do with him if he decided to stay? She felt sure he'd go as soon as he was strong enough. In several days he'd be healed and off down the road.

She vowed she wouldn't traipse along after this one the way she'd done with LaMar. She tightened her hold on the leathery teats and the cow complained. "Sorry, old girl," she said. "That man can leave anytime. I got all I want from him." A scuffing sound behind her startled her and she shot milk over her feet. "Damn!"

"Annabelle?" Clint leaned heavily against the frame of the barn door. "You in here?"

She knocked over the stool in her effort to get to his side before he slumped to the straw-covered floor. "What in blazes are you doing here?" She braced him against her side. "Are you crazy?"

Clint made a feeble attempt at a laugh. "Yesterday I would have said 'no.'" He rested his head on top of hers. "Lord, girl, I have a thirst that could empty a beer barrel."

She pulled his healthy arm around her shoulders and started toward the house. "Don't get hopeful. Water's the only thing you'll drink around here." He stumbled and she grabbed him tighter around his lean waist. "Hang on, we're almost there."

Close to the porch she nearly fell and he groaned loudly. "It'll be a miracle," she said, straining to hold him upright, "if we both don't end up sprawled in the dirt, you passed out cold and me too tired to move." Under his weight, she staggered up the steps and half dragged him back to the bed. They were both soaked in sweat.

When he was seated on the bed, she eased him down against the pillows. His wound bled profusely and stained the bandage. "You've gone and pulled out some of my stitching."

"Sorry... thirsty." Sweat poured off him, the effort of his little walk to the barn too much for him in his weakened condition.

She dipped water from the crock and he gulped it down. A good share ran down the sides of his face and over his chest, finding a path through the heavy mat of golden hair and soaking into his trousers.

"Can you sit up for a second while I get the things to take care of you?"

"Yeah... I... yeah."

Annabelle propped him against the head of the bed, then set about getting clean bandages, hot water, the bottle of whiskey and some toweling. When she turned he was flat on his back and out cold again.

Good, she thought. At least he wouldn't feel the pain of her stitching. She quickly cleansed, sewed and rebandaged his arm. Pulling off his damp clothing and ignoring the look and feel of the strong, naked masculine body, she sponged him with cool water.

When she finished, she stood back and looked at him. *Lord above, he is one fine-looking man.* While caring for him, she had discovered a long, thick scar hidden in his chest hair. This wasn't his first brush with a bullet.

Her gaze followed the curling trail of hair down his flat, hard belly and to the powerful mark of his manliness, resting in its nest of dark gold. Blushing with shame, she covered him again with the quilt.

Annabelle pulled the curtain closed and began to unbutton her filthy wedding dress. "Stupid thing, looks like a fancy bed cover. All it needs is tassels." Wiggling out of the hot gown, she let it drop to the floor and then kicked it into a corner to lie in a pool of late afternoon sun.

Bending over the limp gown, she pulled a small, scorched square of velvet out of the pocket. She brushed the nap, then ran the soft fabric over her cheek. Eyes closed, she tried to picture her home in Georgia before the War. A tall, stately, three-storied mansion with soaring columns and wide verandas. *Stop it,* she scolded herself. *That life is gone, past. It's a life you never knew, so stop pining for it. This is your life now.* Reaching up to a small shelf, she drew down her tin box, placed the velvet inside and firmly closed the lid. *Foolish dreams shut away.*

She poured cool water into a basin and washed off her own dust and sweat. She put on a light cotton gown, holding its fullness away from her body. Everything she owned would fit that cow.

Exhausted from her labors, Annabelle drew back the curtain and moved Clint's legs over on the bed. She desperately needed rest and this was the only place to get it. Practicality overcame caution; she stretched out beside him. "You leave precious little room in this bed, gunfighter," she mumbled to the unconscious man. Rolling to her side, she looked around the room where she had lived since her arrival at the end of winter past.

She sighed and silently agreed with the gunfi—her new husband. It wasn't much of a house. All things considered, she'd kept it as clean as possible. The window was without glass and plenty of spaces in the walls had allowed the dry August dust to blow through.

Even with LaMar doing odd jobs around the valley and Annabelle just beginning to bake for some of the unmarried men who worked at the lumber mill, there'd been barely enough money to make the mortgage payments. Certainly none for frivolous things like paint or curtain material. The feed sacks over the window fought a losing battle against the vagaries of the weather.

She angled her body and rose from the bed. Grabbing the wilted flowers from the table, she opened the door and threw them outside. The gunfighter's remark irritated her, mostly because he was right; the flowers looked too much like she felt and she couldn't stand the sight of them.

She knelt awkwardly in the middle of the floor, pulled up three short boards and reached down into the cool space where she kept milk, butter and cheese. She drank the milk straight from the jar, then realized she'd left the pail of fresh milk in the barn. No doubt that fool cow had dumped it by now. And if she wanted more, she'd have to go out and milk her again.

She got up and went to the sink board and swished a clean rag in cool water. Sitting next to Clint on the bed, she ran the cloth over the relaxed planes of his face. In his sleep, he looked younger and more approachable.

Annabelle quickly suppressed the unbidden longings seeping into her mind and heart. She could take care of herself. Two lessons hard learned from her tyrant of a foster father and lying LaMar: a man brought heartaches and a man brought worry.

When she stopped wiping the sweat from his face, he groaned. She rinsed the cloth and fanned it in the air to cool it. Yes, she thought, he is a fine-looking man. And the last thing she needed in her life was another man, fine-looking or not.

Chapter Three

The sound of impatient knocking dragged Annabelle from her exhausted sleep. She groaned as she hoisted herself carefully over Clint and climbed from the bed. The fading light signaled early evening and she turned up the lantern by the bed.

In all the months she had lived here, no one had ever come to call on her, thanks to LaMar's announcement in the saloon one night that they weren't married. There were weeks on end when she yearned for company, when she would have dearly loved having another woman to talk with, but not tonight.

"Open up, Annabelle MacDonald" came the strident voice of Judaline Jennings through the door.

Shock arrested Annabelle's hand as she reached for her worn shawl. What in the world is that woman doing here? she wondered. Trouble. That was the only thing that would bring her clear out to the ranch; she wanted to cause more trouble.

Annabelle released a weary sigh as she opened the door and saw the determined-looking Judaline standing on the porch. In front of the cabin, she had parked her fancy buggy.

"What do you want?" Annabelle brushed her mussed hair from her tired eyes. "Seems a strange time to come calling, if you ask me."

Judaline, never the shy one, pushed her way into the room and sat down at the table. "I haven't come calling. I came to see if that killer husband of yours actually came home with you." She glanced at Clint and then ran her gaze over Annabelle's nightgown. The look of disgust on Judaline's face revealed her opinion of the situation.

"Why are you here?" Annabelle crossed her arms over her chest. "I'm sure it isn't to wish me well on my new marriage."

"I don't give a fig about your so-called marriage."

"It's real enough. Ask Reverend Mills. He looked ready to faint away through the whole ceremony."

Judaline got up from her seat and moved to the bed. "Got himself shot, did he?" She poked at his arm. "Probably the only thing LaMar Tucker ever hit besides a spittoon."

Annabelle grabbed Judaline by the shoulder and pushed her away from the unconscious man. "Don't touch him. I took care of his arm. It's just fine." She checked the bandage. He was hers to care for! She turned to look at the querulous woman. "What gives you the right to barge in here and snoop around?"

"I've got every right! You are one month behind on your mortgage payment. My husband may be soft-hearted but I'll see he gets some starch and throws you out before another month goes by. Married or not, within thirty days you and your murdering husband and all your worthless belongings will be out in the road."

"What good to you is my property?"

"None. I want you gone, out of this valley."

"Why? I don't under—"

"Why doesn't make any difference. You and all like you will not live here. I won't have it."

"Then I've still got thirty days so you just get out of my house," Annabelle said, backing a surprised Judaline out the door. "And don't show your sour face around here until you come to throw us out. Then we'll see." Annabelle marveled at her bravado. She was so tired she could barely throw out dishwater, let alone this hateful person. And Clint—a lot of help he would be.

A harsh cry broke through the tension shimmering between the women. "Anna... Annabelle?"

She glared at Judaline. "It puzzles me no end how a woman like you, with everything in the world, finds pleasure in hounding those who have nothing." She felt a good deal of satisfaction at the look of astonishment that flashed across Judaline's face.

Annabelle turned and rushed into the house, leaving Judaline standing alone on the porch. Stubbornly she followed Annabelle through the door.

Judaline stopped just inside and studied the spare interior of the cabin. She took in the sight of Annabelle's gown-clad body arched over the handsome gunfighter, worry on her young face.

Abruptly, long-forgotten memories assailed Judaline. Herself, as a young girl, bent over her mother's satin-clad body. Fever from an unspeakable disease eating away at her mother's brain and her paramour backing away, promising the frantic Judaline he'd be back with a doctor. Of course, he never returned and her mother died. This man who'd kept Judaline and her mother secreted in their lovely apartments, out of the sight of his wife and family and society. This man who had visited this horror on the woman he said he loved. This man—Judaline's father.

The soothing sounds of Annabelle's voice interrupted Judaline's painful reminiscence and forced her attention to the present and *this* woman, so like Judaline's own mother.

"What's wrong?" Annabelle knelt by the bed and caressed Clint's hot forehead.

"Water...I asked...hours...drink." He fell back on the pillow. "Thirsty..."

His face appeared flushed and beads of sweat glistened on his skin. "Men! Always demanding of a woman," she muttered as she pushed herself to her feet. When she turned to get him some water, she bumped into Judaline. "I told you to get out of here." She stepped around the interfering woman.

"He's running a fever." Judaline gave a satisfied nod.

Annabelle set the basin of cool water on the apple box beside the bed. She frowned and fought to keep the worry from her voice. "He is not," she said, knowing it was a lie.

She ran the cloth over his face. His skin felt hot as the midsummer sun. She placed her hands on either side of his head and shook him a little. "No! You can't get a fever!" He'd run a fever for hours, but she didn't want Judaline to be right.

"W-won't," he said, his voice faint and thready.

"Damn you! Don't you dare get sick on me." Useless words. She knew he was sick enough to die. Panic gripped her chest and she gasped for breath. How would she care for him? She pushed the unwelcome thought from her mind and vowed not to panic; she'd be useless to him if she did.

Judaline's irritating voice broke through Annabelle's panic. "A marriage made in heaven, I'd say."

"Oh, shut up, Judaline." Annabelle tightened her grip on Clint's flushed, stubbled face and yelled at him. "Wake up! I'll never forgive you if you pass out on me!"

"Won't," he whispered, and his fevered body went slack against the mattress.

Lord, she thought with dismay, he's lifeless as a dead calf. She put one hand at the small of her back and tried to rub away the sharp, shooting pain. She rested her aching head against her other hand. "What should I do?" she questioned herself aloud.

"Sponge him down." Judaline looked startled at her words of good advice. Recovering, she said, "Well, any ninny knows that much. You sponge him down and give him plenty of water."

"That's exactly what I've been doing," Annabelle declared.

"Keep doing it if you want him to live. Though why you would is a mystery to me." She tossed a blazing look at Annabelle. "You surely have a talent for picking up with trashy, no-account men."

Judaline marched to the door and threw her parting warning over her shoulder. "Thirty days, Annabelle MacDonald." The slamming of the door punctuated her words.

"Strand!" Annabelle yelled after Judaline.

The door opened again and Judaline stuck her head back in. She looked over at the desperately ill man. "He's going to die, you know," she pronounced, and closed the door.

Rage soared through Annabelle's shaking body. She stumbled to the bed and looked down at the unconscious man. "No you won't," she vowed. "I'll *make* you live!"

She leaned against the wooden bed frame and covered her face with her hands, striving for control. Straightening, she admonished herself that she didn't have time for tears. Clint needed her. She grabbed a bucket and rushed outside, down to the stream. Darkness threatened and soon she wouldn't be able to see her way to her source of water.

Two more trips and she'd filled two buckets and the basin. She had plenty of wood in the stove and set the coffeepot to reheat. She would need hot coffee to keep her awake this night.

She sat next to Clint, pulled the covers from his heated body and began to sponge him down. His skin felt as dry as old paper as she moved the cool cloth over his firm muscles. Discovering more scars, she spoke aloud to him. "Clint Strand, this strong body of yours is a sad testimony to the life you've led." He began to shake.

"Great heavens, will you make up your mind?" She threw the quilt over him then wrapped her arms around him. Through the covers she felt his tremors and absorbed them with her body.

"I can't keep up with your sweats and your shivers," she said as she eased away from him. She tried to spoon water past his cracked lips, but most of it ran down his cheeks and soaked into the already damp pillow. "You've got to take this water—you'll die—don't you understand that?"

Buried in a fevered nightmare she couldn't penetrate, he hit out at her and shouted, "Docker!"

Agitated, he tossed and turned. She pressed her tired body against his, holding him in the damp, rumpled bed. It seemed hours before he quieted. She fell into an exhausted sleep, her arms holding him close, their breath and the heat of their bodies mingling.

When he called out fitfully in his sleep, it seemed to her she'd just closed her eyes. She peeled the covers from him and reached for the cloth to begin cooling him again. His bandage had come loose. Dread filled her heart as she gently unwrapped the dressing to check his wound. She gasped in horror.

Bringing the lantern near, she saw ugly yellow pus oozing from the center of her stitching. Anger flooded through her. She wanted to hit him, shake him awake, for coming into her life and stealing away what little peace she had.

She slumped to the floor and wrapped her arms around her swollen stomach. She cried desperate tears for herself, for her unborn child and for Clint—and what lay before her for the three of them.

Clint's deep moan ended her weeping. Fear lumped in her throat as she steeled herself for the task that confronted her. She held out her hands and prayed she could still the shaking, prayed she knew the right thing to do for him.

Taking several deep, shuddering breaths to calm herself, she moved to the dry sink. She'd had few choices in her life; this was no different. She took a small knife and began to sharpen it on a whetstone. She tested the knife against the skin of her thumb and it left a thin, bloody line.

Numbing her mind to the feelings of uncertainty and fear, she washed her hands in strong lye soap and thrust the blade of the knife into the fire burning in the belly of the stove. When she couldn't stand the heat any longer, she pulled the knife out of the flames. She walked back to the bed and looked down at the sleeping man.

"Dear God, I can't do this."

Clint groaned and lashed out at some unseen enemy.

If he thrashed around, she could worsen his injury. She'd have to tie him down. Once again, she clamped down on her rising terror. Tearing more strips from the old sheet, she bound his muscular, healthy arm to the bedstead and tied the wrist and forearm of his injured arm to the frame. His size and weight made her work more difficult. It was impossible not to notice the strength of his masculine body. Satisfied she had done her best to immobilize him, she gathered up the knife, bowl, remaining whiskey and the lantern and put them on the apple box.

She placed her hands together and raised them to her trembling lips, sending up a rusty plea for help. *Dear Lord, please stay with me this terrible night. Help me to help this man. Take my hand in yours and guide me along the right path.*

She closed her eyes and whispered "Amen." The fear pounding through her body stilled. There was no one else to help. Clint's only chance lay with her and the good Lord. She had to be calm and sure—her hands steady and her heart quiet.

She took the knife and poised it over his fevered flesh. A shudder raced through her and she cried, "I can't do this!" He stirred. An agonized groan escaped his parched lips. She held her breath and hoped he would remain unconscious. He settled down once more and she released the air from her lungs. Yes you can, Annabelle Strand, she told herself, unaware she used her new name. You have no choice here. It *has* to be you.

She braced his arm against her hip and firmly drew the sharpened knife over the seeping wound. His anguished scream broke the silence of the room.

Annabelle bit her lip. "I'm sorry," she whispered. Tears flooded her eyes.

He fought the bindings. His skin seemed to cleave closer to his bones as every muscle strained against the shackles. The skin around his eyes seemed to darken as she watched, leaving deep hollows in his face. She wiped her eyes with the back of her hand. She couldn't cry; tears would obscure her vision and cause her to fail him.

Half-lying across his bucking body, Annabelle concentrated on her grisly task. She ignored his strident pleas, ignored the rank odor assaulting her, causing her stomach to heave and roil. "Please, Lord, we're almost there," she prayed.

She cut the festering tissue from his arm. Bile rose in her throat, but she kept cutting until she had removed the last bit of deadly corruption.

Finally, he collapsed, and she quickly completed her work. She poured the balance of the whiskey over the newly shaped gap and with a steady, determined hand, closed it with small, even stitches. She rewrapped his arm, then carried the bandages and the bowl of bloody water to the sink.

Lowering her chin to her chest, she said, "Thank you, Lord." At last she could surrender to her own needs and allow her tears to flow unguarded down her face.

Every inch of her body ached. Her legs trembled and the pain in her back radiated down her thighs. Never in her life, not even toiling over the huge, steaming washtubs full of the Bodines' filthy clothes, had she ever been so tired.

She dipped a cloth in the water warming on the stove and ran the rag over her face. She had to gather her strength. He would need her throughout this long night.

When he moaned, Annabelle pulled a crate over to the side of the bed and sank down, resting her fatigued body. "Lord," she said, once again addressing the Almighty, "I believe even my soul is played out."

She ran her hands over her belly and laughed weakly. "I even wore out the baby. He hasn't moved for hours." She laid her head against Clint's thigh and gave in to her urgent need for sleep.

The acrid stink of boiled-over coffee and Clint's incoherent mumblings awakened her. Annabelle set the nearly ruined coffeepot in the sink and returned to the bedside.

She eased the bandage from the wound and felt a swift spear of pleasure. In the time she'd slept, the bleeding had stopped. There seemed to be no recurrence of the infection.

"Watch out," Clint whispered in warning. "Watch...danger."

"The only danger here is me falling over in a complete state of exhaustion. The Lord is watching over you!" She wiped the sweat from his face and knew the fever still held him in thrall.

He thrashed as much as his bonds would allow and cried, "Look out...your back!"

"Not much I can do about my back, caring for you the way I need to." Annabelle moved him carefully to the edge of the bed and threw back the blankets, leaving him naked.

As she wiped down his muscled body, she talked to him, trying to calm him, ease him from his wild dreams. "That must be some fearful man chasing around in your deliriums." She ran the cloth over his sandy-haired legs, forcing herself not to look at the mark of his manliness, ignoring the unwanted yet beckoning feelings he aroused in her. "Who's after you, Clint Strand?"

She started when his weak voice replied, "Docker." She hadn't been expecting an answer, thought him too taken in his nightmare to respond.

Clint's eyes were half-open and he licked his dried lips. "Water."

She gently raised his damp head and placed the tin cup against his mouth. "Here now, take small sips. Won't do you a bit of good if it runs down your chin."

"Bossy...just like...Ma."

Annabelle detected a faint smile at the corners of his mouth. "Fine. You just pretend I'm your momma. Maybe you'll behave and get better."

"Ma...not Momma." He seemed to smile at some favored memory. "She...hated...name Ma." He slipped back into his fevered world.

When his body felt chilled again, she pulled the covers up and patted them around him. "You're a lucky man to have a momma. I'll just bet she loves you and would give the world to see you." She straightened, placing her hands to the small of her back in a frequent, unconscious gesture. "Some of us never did know our momma."

Sadness overwhelmed her. She wondered why the terrible feeling of loss came so strongly this night. Giving in to a need she didn't understand, she spoke again to Clint. "My momma died giving me birth. It was the last year of the War." She brushed the damp hair from his forehead. "I don't know what she looked like or how she walked...what she smelled like or how she smiled."

He stirred again and watched her through half-closed eyes. She sat beside him and carefully slipped her arm under his head. Holding the water cup, she urged him to take sips.

"So...sorry...Anna..."

Not hearing, she went on, old longings swelling inside her. "All I had was Mrs. Bodine, who was sometimes kind, sometimes not." A shudder raced through her as memories of her growing-up years surfaced. "And her nasty, drunken husband and her nine children. All a trial to me."

"Anna . . . ?" Clint whispered her name and turned his face to her breast.

"I'm here." She cradled his head close and caressed his damp hair.

His fevered voice sounded parched and rough. "Docker, he'll . . . find . . . I . . . don't want . . . kill anymore."

"Hush," she soothed. "It'll be fine. Nobody's going to kill anybody. You're safe here." She ran her fingers over his flushed skin and he pressed his head more firmly against her breasts. His breath penetrated her thin cotton gown and washed her nipples in its heat. She felt an answering warmth in the tips of her breasts and forcibly reminded herself of her condition, how improper her feelings were.

She concentrated on comforting him. "Hush now and rest. Docker won't find you here." The completeness of his vulnerability reached a place in her heart that until now held only longing and broken dreams. She clutched him close, rocking and telling him over and over, "Shh."

"He . . . get . . . you."

She closed her eyes and the vivid picture of whiskey-soaked Bodine chasing her through the woods poured into her mind. "No . . ." Her voice trembled. "Mrs. Bodine stopped him. He didn't get me."

The memory of that night made her sick to her stomach. Elva Bodine waving a gun at her husband; screaming at Annabelle to get her man-tempting soul off their property; shoving her few belongings onto a threadbare blanket; quickly knotting it and throwing it at her. Annabelle ran down the road and hid in the bushes until morning.

Clint's whispers broke into her reverie. "He's coming...find me."

She caressed his shoulder, lost in a reverie of the past. "That's where LaMar found me. Hiding in the brush, crying my eyes out, terrified of being alone and feeling glorious to be out of that hellhole I'd been raised in."

"It's...nightmare. He's..."

"No, LaMar was a dream come true. He was young, clean and full of laughter then. He wiped away my tears, pulled me to my feet and invited me on an adventure." She could still see him. Full of life and himself, spinning the future in front of them like a fairy tale. And she'd bought the story. Handsome prince and starry-eyed maid, hand in hand striding toward the rainbow. There'd been no pot of gold. Just more misery.

Clint began to shiver violently. Annabelle grabbed her old shawl and LaMar's woolen jacket and placed them on top of the quilt. She held the fevered man in her arms as he tossed and moaned. She knew he had to be in terrible pain, but she had nothing else to give him.

"Tell me, Clint Strand, tell me of this man who's after you. This Docker person." She wanted to know who kept his mind in such torment.

"Bull...Docker." Clint rolled his head back and forth on the pillow. "Won't...let...stop..." Tensing his muscles, straining against his bonds, he screamed, "No! We've got to run. He'll kill us." The sudden relaxing of his body told her he'd passed out again.

She rested her head against his hot chest and wondered if this night would end with his body cold, to be buried in the ground. She looked at his slack face and felt the old longing for someone of her own blossom stronger than before.

Under her seeking hands his body began to weep perspiration. Sweat ran in rivulets from his pores, soaking the bed and blankets. His hair clung to his finely shaped head in damp ringlets of dark gold.

She'd won! She felt triumphant. She and the Lord defeated the awful, deadly infection. He would live and she'd done it in spite of her fear. She touched Clint all over his body. He felt cool to her searching fingers. Her heart felt light and her head giddy.

Annabelle washed the wastes of his illness from him. She untied his bindings and carefully rolled him to change the bedding. She soothed him and crooned to him. "We'll be fine now."

The tight, agonized stretch of his lips over his teeth relaxed and his beautiful mouth softened in his peaceful slumber. Annabelle felt relief course through her body.

She wondered if she had saved him only to be shot down by this Bull Docker person. She would ask Clint about him later. Tonight she could only give thanks he lived.

After all the years of her loneliness this man had come into her life, reluctantly, unwanted. Forced at the point of a gun. Would he stay?

With the tips of her fingers she touched his mustache, marveling at its softness. She ran her hands over his chest, through the deep amber curls, over the flat, nearly hidden male nipples, and loved the feel of him under her hands. Would he stay?

No. When he healed, he would saddle his horse and ride out of her uncertain world and into the violence and danger of his. And, she supposed, that's what she wanted.

Getting to her feet, she moved her aching, ungainly body to the table and took a soft round peach into her hands. Somehow she must find a way to stay here. This small ranch with its rickety cabin and half-roofed barn and scrubby peach trees represented permanence and belonging.

With this man or without him, she'd survive here. Through the single window, the darkness of the night yielded to the first gray light of dawn. Annabelle calmly washed her hands and face, moved to the bed and crawled over Clint's unresisting body. She shoved her white knuckles against her trembling mouth, buried her face against his cool, bare chest and sobbed.

Chapter Four

Clint awakened with a bone-deep throbbing in his shoulder and arm. He shifted his head on the pillow and felt the heat of the sun cross his face. By focusing on the warmth trailing over his skin he could block out the relentless pounding in his arm. When the sun's brightness reached his right eye, he turned his head even more until he felt the soothing heat at his temple.

A moment later it occurred to him he shouldn't be feeling the sun. He knew he lay in a snug bed and suddenly he realized he had a soft female bottom resting against his hip. Lord, he thought, he must have tied on a good one last night if he couldn't even remember taking a woman to his bed.

His eyes snapped open and he turned his head toward the figure sleeping beside him. Tangled hair as red as a new brick sprawled over the pillow. Hell, he thought, it's Annabelle. Much as he'd like to be with a woman, he didn't need this one. No matter he was married to her.

He closed his eyes and forced his mind to concentrate. To try to find the sequence of what happened. The shooting...drinking in the saloon...Annabelle with a gun and a preacher. He tried to smile at the ridiculous image he remembered of her in that dusty white gown and the wilted flowers, but his dry lips cracked and he ran his tongue over them. He'd sell the remainder of his soul for a drink of water. How long had he been here? he wondered.

He remembered passing out, but after that just hazy recollections of pain and sweat and of Annabelle bending over him, talking. Always talking. Telling him he'd be fine, describing her life and demanding that he live. That was Annabelle, all right. Telling and demanding. He figured plain asking and suggesting weren't native to her character.

Well, he was alive, thanks to this woman who slept beside him. She'd saved his life and he owed her a debt he felt sure he could never fully repay.

The bandage on his arm stuck to the wound and pulled painfully against it. Clint eased the cloth away and assessed the damage. Closed with tight, neat stitches, the injury was healing well. Annabelle had done a fine job. The scar would be even and not too noticeable.

Moving his head again, he looked at the source of the sunlight. In the roof, a hole the size of an egg allowed a dusty shaft of light through. He'd have to fix that soon. Winter came early to the mountains and he knew he'd stick out the season with her; he had no choice in the matter. He wasn't a man to walk out on the woman who had saved his skin.

Annabelle stirred and he glanced over at her. Damn woman. She didn't want him and he'd figured to use her as cover for a few weeks, then move on. But he was stuck now. He was a man who paid his debts. He'd fix up this shack of hers then be on his way—in the spring. She would have her kid and Clint would be free of Docker.

She groaned, pushed the covers off her bared legs and sat up. Clint narrowed his eyes and glared at her from beneath his lashes. She rubbed her lower back and sighed a deep, already weary sigh. The motion pulled her worn gown tight over her full breasts and his mouth watered at the sight.

He clamped down furiously on his unworthy thoughts. Her breasts were for the nourishment of her child. Not for the hot mouth of a greedy man. She stretched her arms high over her head, then ran her work-roughened fingers through her hair. Clint wondered how she ever got a brush through that tangled mass of red.

He sighed his own troubled sigh and asked, "How long have I been here?"

At his words, Annabelle started and jerked down the hiked-up hem of her worn cotton gown. She reached over and felt his forehead. "Well, it looks like you're going to live. I thought that cruel fever would never break."

"Never mind the fever. How long?" He ran his furred tongue over his cracked lips. "God, my mouth feels like it could grow cactus and hide lizards."

Annabelle reluctantly smiled at the image he created with his words. She didn't want to like him, but now and then he did make her smile. She slipped off the bed and moved to the crock. She filled a cup with water and brought it to him. "Here, this should help."

Clint swallowed the cool water and closed his eyes with pleasure. He held out the cup. "More." She didn't move, just glared at him. "Well, what's wrong?" he asked. "I need more water."

She grabbed the cup from his outstretched hand. "You have the manners of a goat, that's what's wrong." She dipped another cupful and handed it to him.

He drank greedily then fell back on the pillow and smiled. A goat? "Thanks." She certainly deserved his gratitude.

She took the cup from him and huffed her way to the sink.

"The proper reply, Annabelle, is 'You're welcome.'"

She whirled and gave him a black look. "I don't need lessons in manners from a gunfighter. A person who in one day kills a man, invites himself where he's not wanted, passes out cold, then expects a strange woman to nurse him." She raised the stubbornest little chin he'd ever seen and damned him with her fierce look.

He couldn't stop his grin. "I'll go along with that. You are a strange woman all right." Her face grew so red he thought she just might explode like a Fourth of July firecracker. "How long, Annabelle?"

Confusion chased the anger from her face. "How...? Oh, how long have you been here?" He nodded and waited. He noticed her lips move in a whisper and she frowned in concentration. "This is the fifth day," she finally said.

"Five! Five days...?" His voice trailed off. "Unconscious five days?"

"Mostly."

"But who—"

"I did." She walked to the bed and pulled the covers over his bare, muscled chest.

Clint closed his eyes and grimaced at the picture of her caring for his inert self. Sponging him down, taking care of the wastes of his helpless body. Forcing food and water down his throat. He shook his head in an attempt to banish the image of what she had gone through trying to save him.

She turned away and he grabbed her hand. Groaning at the pain the effort caused him, he pulled her down on the bed beside him. The ache in his shoulder intensified and he fought to keep from crying out.

"Thank you, Annabelle," he said, a solemn tone to his voice. "I owe you a great deal."

His touch confused her and she needed to free her hand. She rose to her feet and backed away, out of his reach. "You don't owe me a thing. Just get well and be on your way." She pulled the curtain closed in front of the bed. "I have to dress. I'll thank you to give me some privacy."

Clint stared at the hole in the roof. The sun had moved but dust motes danced in the light. She had taken care of him in the worst of circumstances. She'd been alone, pregnant and weary to her soul. God yes, he owed her.

The opening in the roof reminded him of everything else on that pitiful ranch that needed a man's hand. Well, *he* was that man, for now. A large part of his mind tried to convince him to take off when he was stronger—just as she wanted him to do. The remaining part shook a judgmental finger at him, castigating him for ungrateful thoughts.

Hell. Who was he fooling? He needed the time. Time to get strong and time for Docker to move on to another part of the country.

He parted the curtains a little and nearly passed out again at a sight that made his dry mouth water. Annabelle stood with her back to him. Naked. Her body was firm and feminine and from his view he could hardly tell she was pregnant.

Her untamed hair reached just below her shoulders. Her back looked smooth and strong, evidence of the hard work she did. Her legs, lovely shapes that took up much of the tiny length of her. She *is* covered with freckles from head to toe, he thought, remembering back to that moment when he first saw her in the sunlight. Clint felt his desire stir.

She turned in profile and the rounded prominence of her belly testified to the fact of the baby there. She lowered her head to rest her chin on her chest and rubbed her stomach. He saw her whisper some words to her child.

The movement of her full, lightly freckled breasts tantalized him and he groaned inwardly.

Clint, man, he said to himself. Your goose is truly cooked. You're here for the winter. There's no way in hell you can leave little mother on her own to see the winter through and have that kid in this shack.

He watched as she rubbed her belly and spoke aloud to her child. "Wake up, little one. It's morning, get a move on." Clint grinned and suppressed a chuckle. Yep, a well-cooked goose. The chuckle grew into an ironic laugh as he closed the curtains.

Annabelle pulled her worn blue dress over her head and brushed it down over her body. She turned toward the bed. "It strains my imagination some to find anything funny about this situation."

His laughter increased. "That's because you don't have much of a sense of humor."

She jerked the curtains open. "I've had precious little to laugh at in my life, Clint Strand, and you taking up space in my bed doesn't strike me as funny."

He wrestled his grin under control. "Well, we'll just have to find your funny bone, won't we?" He had a sudden need to discuss the other part of her remark. "How come we're sleeping in the same bed?"

The color of her face fascinated him. He felt sure he had never seen anyone blush such a fiery red. Her freckles disappeared and her clover-colored eyes flashed.

"Look around this room, Clint Strand. Do you see another bed? Am I supposed to sleep on the floor? Or in the barn?"

Shame coursed through his body. He should be on the floor. "Spread out my bedroll. I'll sleep there."

"If you can only make suggestions that make my life more difficult, then keep quiet. Do you suppose I want to get myself up and down off my knees to care for you?"

Clint realized his life on the trail didn't train a man for living with a woman. He figured he'd make plenty of mistakes over the coming days. He didn't like the idea of always being in the wrong of it. "Well, what do you want, then?" His words came out more harshly than he'd intended.

"I want, and expect, you to be a gentleman. We've been in that bed together for five days without a problem. You going to cause one now?"

She was practical down to her bones, he thought. "No, Annabelle. I'm not going to cause you a problem. You have my promise." Neither of them needed to state in open terms what he meant. They both knew.

He smiled. "We still have to find your funny bone."

She loosed a disgusted sigh and moved to the dry sink to fill the blackened coffeepot with water from the crock. "You have to start getting up a little each day to get your strength back."

She carefully measured coffee and poured it into the pot. She cracked six eggs into a chipped brown bowl and dropped three of the shells into the coffeepot. "I'd guess it'll be a week before you can stay in the saddle." She wiped her hands on a towel and tied a flour-sack apron over her belly, pulling in the loose-fitting dress and creating a shelf under her breasts.

"Where you planning to go from here?" She took flour from a fifty-pound sack and measured it into a large bowl.

Clint watched her efficient preparation of breakfast and decided not to answer any of her questions. The minute she knew he planned on staying, she would pitch another fit. "I don't know where I'll head." That was true enough. He'd do his best not to lie to her.

"I love the mountains," she said while she stirred. "We spent some time in San Francisco. I sure couldn't live there. Too many people." She placed a griddle on top of the wood-burning stove. "Did you know there's people from all over the world in that city? I never heard so many different languages in my life. Chinese! Imagine, people all the way from China." She paused and looked off out the window. "I guess it's a long way from here." She seemed to shake off her thoughts and returned to her cooking. "Interesting place, San Francisco, but I like it here better."

Clint marveled at the unconscious grace of her movements in the small room. "I love the mountains, too. You chose a fine place to settle."

Annabelle stopped pouring pancake batter onto the hot griddle and glared at him. "Don't get any ideas."

He smiled. He'd moved beyond ideas right into plans. "I won't," he said.

She stared hard at him for a moment, distrust evident in her gaze. She grasped a pancake turner and expertly flipped the perfect, browned pancakes over onto a tin plate. She carefully eased the eggs onto the griddle, moved it off the hot stovetop, then walked the few steps to the bed. "I'll help you sit up."

"I want to sit at the table."

"Don't be foolish. You've been nearly dead for days."

"I can get up and over to the table, for God's sake. It's only a few steps." He didn't want her doing anything more than necessary for him. He already owed her too much. He pushed himself up on his good arm and tried to swing his feet over the edge of the bed. The room swam before his eyes and he sensed blackness closing in.

Clint fell back on the bed, a long string of foul words spilling from his mouth. She was right. It would be days before he felt strong enough to get out of bed, let alone start work on this wreck of a ranch.

"You are a stupid man." She jerked the covers over him. "Keep this up and your eggs will be as hard and flat as six-month-old cow chips."

A disgruntled expression on his face, Clint nodded his agreement and allowed her to plump his pillows and fuss with the blankets. Deep inside he found he liked this feminine attention. Not that he'd let her know; she would most likely dump his breakfast in his lap.

She dished up his food and handed him his plate. "Can you manage or do you want me to feed you?"

"No! I don't want to be fed." His stomach growled and he grabbed the plate and began shoving the pancakes into his mouth. They tasted wonderful. "Where did you get the eggs? I haven't heard any chickens."

"I traded my baking for eggs. The bachelors from the lumber mill dearly love peach pie. They buy eggs, then trade them with me."

She was a fine cook and he was hungry enough to eat old boot leather, let alone this fine fare. He watched her out of the corner of his eye as she filled her own plate and sat down at the table.

She mostly moved the food around, little of it going in her mouth. Clint frowned. "You have to eat more."

Annabelle shoved the plate away. "I can't. Lately I just seem to have lost my appetite."

"The kid needs nourishment." He recalled the slender look of her from the back. She seemed smaller than the day she marched into the saloon and demanded he marry her. He gritted his teeth. She'd probably lost weight nursing him back to health. The yoke of debt settled more firmly on his shoulders.

Annabelle placed her dish in a bucket. She looked out the window. "Be nice to have a pump. LaMar promised me one once." She turned to Clint. "Finished?"

He savored the last bite. "I sure could use a cup of that fine-smelling coffee." He smiled at her and wondered how far away the stream was or how far down water lay. A pump might be possible. "Please. I'd like some coffee."

This time she swallowed her disgruntled reply and returned his smile. She nodded and moved to the stove. She poured his coffee, then handed him the cup. "You have a fine smile, Clint Strand." She blushed, grabbed his plate and flatware and put it into the bucket.

She took her coffee cup and sat back at the table. Now that he felt up to it, she needed to know how much danger they faced. "Who's this Bull Docker you raved about in your delirium? Is he going to come through our door shooting?"

She had every right to ask about Docker, but he didn't want to scare the daylights out of her. Yet, he believed they were safe.

"Docker's after me. A year ago I shot his brother."

"Dear God!" Her face paled so that Clint knew he could count each and every freckle and not miss one.

"I last saw him in Tucson. I spread the word I was heading for Mexico. I rode out in the general direction of the border, then doubled back. I waited off the trail and saw him go on."

"Why did you shoot his brother?"

"He tried to backshoot me." He shrugged. "I'm faster and he was a poor shot."

"Do you think he'll find us?"

"I think he won't give up, but he knows Texas and New Mexico are where I've spent most of my time."

She looked out the window, a sober expression on her face. He'd give a gold piece to know her thoughts.

"What are you thinking, Annabelle?"

Lifting the bucket by the handle, she started to leave, then turned back to him. "I don't know yet. Seems like another worry to face down the line. You'll be gone by then anyway."

"Wait," he called. "Where're you going?"

"Out to the stream to wash the dishes, then milk the cow. Why?"

"How come you don't wash the dishes inside?"

"I love being outdoors. Winter will change that."

"I'll be able to help some tomorrow," he said, knowing wishful thinking when he heard it.

She laughed and shook her head. "Not tomorrow. You won't be strong enough." She closed the door behind her.

After she left, Clint threw back the covers and eased his legs over the side of the bed. He grabbed the bedstead with his good arm and pulled himself up. Dizziness whirled in his head and he nearly fell back against the pillow. He felt weak as a newborn calf.

The memory of another time came to him. He'd been in Dodge City. Joey "Boots" Coughlin had pulled on Clint and damn near did him in. God, he'd been sick. And alone. He looked around the small, forlorn cabin and felt the fullness of his gratitude for Annabelle's care of him.

With a decent man to look after her, she'd probably make a fine wife. If she cared for a man she'd most likely smother him with good food, a clean home, and in bed... His earlier reaction to her unclothed body told him that fiery, redheaded woman could turn that explosive temper into a passion that would take a man to his knees.

He shook his head against the pillow and told himself firmly he wasn't *that* man.

Determination etched deep lines on his sweating face. He might not be ready to repair a roof tomorrow, but by God, he would sit at the table like a full-grown man.

When she stepped out on the porch, Annabelle saw a wagon coming up the road. She prayed it wasn't Judaline returning to make life more miserable.

When it drew near, Annabelle recognized Jed Cummins, owner of the livery stable, Martha's husband. What on earth . . . ?

Jed pulled the wagon to a stop in front of the cabin and jumped down. He touched the brim of his hat in a polite salute. "'Morning, Mrs. Strand."

The use of her new name by a man who was more stranger than friend surprised her; she realized that everyone in the valley must know the story by now. She nodded. "Good morning, Mr. Cummins. What brings you out here?"

"Well, we . . . that is, Martha thought you might need a few things, what with your . . . husband laid up and it being difficult for you to get to town and all."

"Martha sent you?" Annabelle couldn't believe a member of the Tuesday Club cared one hoot about her.

"Yes'm, she did. She feels pretty bad about—"

"It seems Judaline spread the word pretty fast about what's happening here." Just like that woman, Annabelle thought, to rush about telling tales of the harlot and the gunfighter. She must have been in her glory all right.

Jed smiled. "That's true. That woman's mouth rivals the telegraph in speed." He moved to the wagon and started putting crates on the porch.

"I don't have the money to pay you, Mr. Cummins."

"This here's not for sale." He set a sack of flour by the door. "More like a peace offering, I'd say. Better still, an apology. Martha's too ashamed to face you right yet. She'll be over soon." He laughed out loud. "First time I ever saw that woman of mine back off from facing something down nose to nose. But you've got a pretty fierce tongue yourself, good as Martha's any day and nearly good as Judaline's."

He swung a burlap sack of potatoes next to the flour. "Be happy to take this inside, Mrs. Strand. Guess that man of yours isn't up to hefting."

Annabelle's chest felt tight and her throat nearly closed against her words. "I appreciate it, Mr. Cummins. I—" She had to take a deep breath to fight back the threat of tears. The idea of having friendly help was so unexpected she didn't know what to say or even how to feel.

She brushed quickly by Jed and opened the cabin door. He lifted the flour sack to his shoulder and followed her inside.

Clint scooted upright and looked at Annabelle. "What's going on?"

She gestured at the other man. "This is Jed Cummins. He owns the livery stables. He's brought some supplies for us."

Clint realized she held onto her emotions by a thin thread. This courtesy from a neighbor must have nearly knocked her off her feet. He stretched out his hand in welcome. "We appreciate your kindness, Jed. I'm sorry I can't be of help, but I can pay you."

Jed waved off Clint's offer. "Told the missus, it's an offer of friendship and not for sale."

Clint wanted to insist but recognized the truth behind the man's statement. He wouldn't insult Jed by forcing money on him, and Annabelle could use some friends in this valley. "Well, we thank you for your kindness, don't we, Annabelle."

"Yes . . . we do." She grabbed the bucket of crockery and rushed from the cabin.

Jed scratched his head. "Womenfolk are a puzzle, that's for sure."

"Annabelle's not so hard to figure out. She hasn't been treated so good in this valley and can't quite believe what's happening."

Jed nodded and brought the rest of the supplies inside. "Martha feels pretty bad. She'll be over as soon as canning's done."

Clint held out his hand again and the two men traded firm grips. "You're both welcome, anytime."

Jed smiled and pulled a small bottle of whiskey out of his back pocket. "Care for a pull before I go? Clears the dust out of a man's throat."

"I don't think so. Annabelle doesn't hold with drinking."

Annabelle hurried down to the stream, swinging the bucket of dishes. The sudden offer of friendship and the gift of supplies had her so perplexed. Could marriage, even to a gunman, make this much difference? Or did Martha Cummins truly feel contrite and desire to make amends?

How wonderful it would be to have a friend. Never in her life had she had a friend. Annabelle wanted to trust this gesture but knew it would be hard for Martha to stand against Judaline. Well, wait and see seemed to be the best path to follow. No sense getting hopes up yet.

Annabelle slowed down her pace and took in the sight of the land that made up her home. She remembered how she felt when she and LaMar first saw this valley. She'd known at once this was home. This was the place where she'd settle and have all those things she'd missed growing up—a real home, a family of her own.

By the time they'd bought the property, she'd known LaMar would never be the husband she'd dreamed of. But she had made up her mind to make the best of an unhappy situation.

Like most young girls, she'd hoped for a strong man, a man who would love her and take care of her. She would care for him and give him fine, strong children.

A man more like Clint. He showed a tenderness and a playful humor she hadn't expected. She just knew if he loved a woman— She quickly pushed away the traitorous thought. She couldn't believe she'd been thinking it was possible for a man to care for her or she for him. A man is a burden, she told herself, not a pleasure and this one is no different.

Annabelle shaded her eyes and gazed toward the mountains as if she could see the fragile beginnings of her stream in the faraway snowcaps. She believed she drew strength from the mountains. Perhaps they had some magical quality that gave a person hope. *Foolishness!*

Kneeling beside the clear water, she scrubbed the tin plates with sand. She'd bring his shirt here and let the icy water soak away the bloodstain. She cupped her hands and lifted the cold water to her face, sloshing it over her skin. Refreshed, she drew in a breath of crisp mountain air. She felt its coolness deep in her lungs.

She would never leave here. Her child would be raised in this beautiful, peaceful place, so different from her own upbringing in Georgia. There would be no drunk man or beaten-down woman here. In her small valley she would create a safe, loving home.

She and her child would care for their animals, harvest their peaches and sell them in town. Maybe as far away as Placerville.... Standing, she brushed damp sand from her skirt and vowed to talk with Banker Jennings this very week.

Somehow she'd convince him that she would find the money for the mortgage payment. She was a good cook. Maybe she could sell her pies to the tea shop or bake bread for the lumber camp. She could take in sewing once more or— Relentlessly, she shoved all thoughts of "how" from her mind. She would do it!

Annabelle started toward the barn, then changed her direction when she saw Jed Cummins's wagon head down the road to his ranch. She'd take the plates to the cabin and check on Clint. Annabelle opened the door and dropped the bucket, the tinware rattling onto the floor.

Seeing him naked in bed, weak with fever and nearly dead, was different from this. He stood bare as a winter oak, spare and strong-looking in spite of the lost weight. His shoulders seemed broader than she'd remembered and his height almost reached the low ceiling.

In the bright light from the open door, the mist of hair on his body shone like gold and called to her to run her hands over him. Her mouth dried like the parched ground outside the cabin and she thirsted, hungry for something she'd never known.

She felt the hot blush rise from her breasts to her hairline and in her embarrassment shouted at him. "Are you determined to kill yourself?"

His head snapped up and he forced his grimace into something resembling a smile. "I thought you were down at the stream." He swayed a little and she rushed to his side. He was drenched with sweat.

"Men! Fool, fool men."

Wrapping an arm around his firm waist, she helped him into the bed. The feel of his warm, damp skin through her clothes forcibly reminded her that she was a woman and he a man. Her heart beat in an unfamiliar rhythm and her breath quickened. She settled the pillows behind his damp head and drew the covers over him, then sighed in relief that his naked body was covered. "You couldn't wait until I got back—you needed something that bad?"

"Yes!" he shouted in return. His fierce look almost made her laugh.

She reached under the bed and handed him the chamber pot. "Save yourself the walk." She turned her back and headed for the door.

"I don't want to use this!"

She turned and leaned against the door. "Clint, I've taken care of all your needs. You're too weak to make it to the privy and I'm too tired to help you get there."

She pushed herself off the wooden door and took the handle in her hand. "I'll be back soon."

Eight days since he'd passed out on her bed and she still treated him like a sickly child. Today would see the end of that, he vowed, and buckled his belt. It felt good to be dressed and out of that bed. He rotated his shoulder and felt relieved that the stiffness was much less this morning. The stitches would come out tonight; she'd promised.

Clint walked to the sink, pulled aside the curtain and looked out the cabin window. He watched Annabelle trudge toward the barn. She stopped, lowering the milk bucket to the ground, and placed both of her hands to the small of her back. An increasingly familiar gesture, he realized.

She is so damned mule-headed, he thought. He'd offered to milk that noisy cow. Would Annabelle let him? "No. You've only been out of bed two days," she'd told him.

He narrowed his eyes as she picked up the bucket, walked a few steps, then leaned against the barn. Her body seemed to fold in on itself with weariness. *She's stubborn as a stump.* Clint grabbed his hat and slammed it onto his head. He jerked his jacket from a hook and eased his injured arm through the sleeve. Leaving the cabin door open, he strode for the barn, muttering curses against all those of the female persuasion.

The lowing of the cow welcomed Annabelle into the dim interior of the barn. She smiled at the sound. "Old cow, you're the only pet I've ever owned," she said as she placed the bucket beneath the swollen udder. "And

I've never even named you." Rubbing her fingers over the softness of the cow's nose, Annabelle was reminded of the square of scorched fabric in her tin box. "That's what I'll call you. Velvet."

Pleased with her choice, Annabelle lowered herself to the milking stool and patted the cow's bony rump. "There, there, Velvet. I'm going to relieve you of that burden."

Adjusting the bucket, she began to coax the milk from the warm udder. "I just wish my burdens could be so easily relieved." Velvet made a contented sound. "I've got this child lying like a heavy stone in my body and that man plaguing my life. Feels like I've got a gun at my back and a sheer drop into the Lord only knows what in front of me."

She heard the crunch of dried straw and straightened on her stool.

Clint walked up behind her. "I told you I'd milk that damned cow. Now get up and go into the house and rest." He waited for the argument he knew was coming.

With remarkable grace, considering her exhaustion and pregnant state, Annabelle rose from the stool. He stood too close and towered above her. His nearness made her feel defenseless, though she was pretty sure by now he wouldn't hurt her. She had to tip her head back to see his eyes. She poked a finger on his hard chest. "Don't you come storming out here telling me what to do. This is my ranch and I do as I please."

Clint ran a shaking hand over his face. "You are the most cussed, balky female it has ever been my misfortune to come up against." He turned his back on her and struggled to bring his temper under control before he hauled off and laid her out flat. Never in his life had he thought of hitting a woman, but this one tried him as no other had.

Swearing, he swung back to her and took her by the shoulders. "Annabelle, look at it this way. You helped me, now I help you. It's as simple as one plus one makes two."

"What the devil does that mean? One plus one makes two."

Clint pondered her through narrowed eyes. "Simple arithmetic." He paused, a suspicion entering his mind. "You know, the numbers you learned in school."

She turned her face away from him. "Oh. Of course."

"Annabelle, look at me." He gently took her chin in his hand. "Did you go to school?"

She pulled her head back. "You have a way of poking your nose into matters that do not concern you."

"It's a simple question. No reason to be ashamed— or mad. Most people in this country didn't go to school." He forced her face back so he could see her eyes. They gave away much more than she'd have liked. "Did you go to school?"

The negative shake of her head was so small he felt it against his hand rather than saw it. "You can count. I've seen you cook, and measure feed for the animals."

Her firm little chin nodded against his hand. Lord, she puzzled him so. "Then how?"

"I paid attention when Mrs. Bodine did things. She showed me some about cooking. I watch other people and remember." She shrugged as if it were no feat at all.

Mrs. Bodine's name sounded familiar to him. He'd ask later. Right now he would use this chance to break down a little of the wall she'd erected between them. They had to find some ground to build on, even for the short time he'd be here.

How could he help her? He bent over and picked up some straw from the barn floor. He held one out to her. "How many pieces?"

"I am not stupid, you know. Any fool knows it's one piece of straw."

He fought a grin at the indignant look on her face. He held out the other piece. "And how many is this?"

"Clint Strand, you'll be lucky if I don't leave those stitches in your arm till they grow clear to the bone." She brushed her hair from her eyes. "That's one more piece of straw, you great ox."

He lost control of his grin. "You're doing fine. Now, how many pieces of straw altogether?" His patience came easy now as he watched her labor to hold hers.

She closed her eyes and let out an enormous sigh. "Two!"

"Right! One plus one makes two."

Her eyes flew open and he could see them fill with the dawn of discovery.

"It wasn't that I didn't know," she said. "I'd just never really understood before."

A beautiful, stunning smile lit her face and her green eyes danced and sparkled. She reached out and touched his arm. "If you really want to milk her, it's fine with me if it's all right with her."

Clint's jaw dropped as he watched Annabelle walk from the barn, her step lighter than he'd ever seen. He snapped his mouth shut and grinned. He wasn't certain how being allowed to milk a cow constituted a thank-you, but that's just what this peppery little woman had done. He laughed out loud and sat down on the milking stool.

"Ouch!"

"Hush up. This can't hurt anywhere near as much as it did putting them in." Annabelle held her tongue between her teeth as she carefully removed the stitches from Clint's arm.

"I was half drunk and half conscious, so it doesn't count." He knew she tried not to hurt him, and in reality she didn't. He just couldn't help goading her. Her temper rose so satisfyingly to his teasing.

She caused such contradictory feelings in him. One minute he wanted to protect her and care for her...and the next? He wanted to put a gag in her mouth to shut her up. He chuckled at the vision of Annabelle without the use of her blistering tongue.

"Well," she said, "I appreciate you not flinching like I'm killing you, but laughing seems overdoing it." She wiped his wound with clean water. "You're nearly healed. A few days and you should be able to leave here."

Clint frowned and tipped his head in curiosity. "You're a strange little filly."

She threw the rag into the bowl and water splashed onto the table. She glared at him, then stepped over his sprawled legs, giving them a meaningful glance.

Grabbing a towel, she began to furiously wipe up the mess. "I'm not strange. I'm just not one of those weepy women who can't live without a man cluttering up the place." She glared at his legs again.

"That's why you think I'm strange. I'm not on my hands and knees begging you to take care of me." She crossed her arms over the shelf of her stomach and gave him a firm nod.

Clint stood up. "If you want me to move, Annabelle, all you have to do is ask." Lord, he thought, she can rile me as easy as a breeze blows dust. He kicked his apple-box chair away. "And...I'm staying." With angry gestures he put on his jacket and slammed out the door.

Annabelle sank down on the apple box and felt the lingering warmth of his body against her bottom. She got up quickly and brushed off the back of her skirt as if to remove his mark. "Two minutes," she said aloud. "Two minutes is the amount of time we can speak decently with each other."

She shook her head in despair. It was mostly her fault, she thought. He was trying to help and she kept pushing him away.

The sudden need to apologize to him drove her to the door. She reached for the handle as Clint shoved his way in. He carried a bucket of water.

His big, strong body filled the doorway and she felt the floor shake as his boots struck the loose boards. He seemed to take up all the space in the small cabin, leaving little for her and the child to come.

He took up her thoughts more than she liked, and those thoughts were a confusing jumble of needs and wants and sensations she wished she didn't have. Her experience told her not to trust her changing feelings for him. A man could turn against a woman when she least expected it. Yet even though he had a healthy temper, he seemed able to control it.

"I washed your bloodstained shirt," she said. "If you'll give me your jacket I'll wash it, too. Then you can be on your way." She hoped he'd take her hint. Well, more than a hint and less than an order.

He stood quietly and looked down at her from his great height. His lips were drawn across his teeth and his eyes drilled her with a fierce glower. Gently but firmly he moved her out of his way and went outside.

Temper boiling, Annabelle followed. Nearly running to catch up with him, she hollered, "Clint Strand! You stop right now and listen to me." He stopped and she slammed into his hard back.

Blowing her hair out of her eyes, she said, "You could have let me know you were stopping." That her demand was unreasonable escaped her.

Clint, his thumbs hooked in his pockets, waited for her to continue.

"You have to go."

He noted the pleading tone in her voice and the anxious expression in her eyes and the way her hands nervously twisted the faded blue cotton of her wide skirt. If ever a woman sent out confusing signals, it was this one.

He knew in that instant, even if she went down to her knees to beg him to leave, he wouldn't. She needed him, and deep down some part of him treasured that knowledge. He suspected he needed her, pregnant or not, in ways he'd thought hopeless for a long, long time. He turned and went into the barn, closed the doors and dropped the board into the notch.

Annabelle pounded on the door. "Clint Strand! You let me in this barn!"

Clint grabbed the pitchfork and concentrated on putting fresh straw in the stalls. Soon he would go to town and begin the preparation for winter and a stormy life with his wife.

Chapter Five

Over the next few days Clint eased into work, testing his arm. Using the poor tools available and bits of wire and rusty nails, he made a few temporary repairs to the cabin. He spent most of his time deciding which major jobs had to be done to the cabin and the barn before winter. The trip to town couldn't be put off much longer, now that he could sit his horse. He made a long list of the materials and supplies they would need for the bitter season to come. He figured they had maybe a month or so before the first snow fell.

He needed to pick up tinned goods, also. Annabelle's efforts at a vegetable garden produced some puny-looking produce. A few radishes and scraggly carrots would not take them through the long cold months ahead.

He paced off a sheltered area next to the barn best suited for a chicken coop. When the peaches were gone, Annabelle would have nothing to trade for eggs, and he'd formed a passion for Annabelle's baking. They could start the chicks in the cabin and move them to the coop later. If the winter was too severe they could stay in the barn, if he got the roof repaired before really bad weather set in.

He walked the rows between the peach trees. He felt sure more than half of them could be saved. When they went dormant he would replant most of them. Some would never make it and would have to be replaced. With good care the remaining trees would produce a cash crop or good trade. They were the only peaches in the valley.

He knew Annabelle watched him, but in her determination to appear uninterested in his activities, she refused to ask any questions. She wanted to know what he wrote on the square of brown paper he'd found in the barn. He saw her looking at it one morning, but she just frowned and said nothing. Suddenly he felt like a fool. Of course, she couldn't read.

If she'd been able to, the list of lumber, nails, roofing material, wire and foodstuffs would have prompted a hundred questions and a demand to make decisions about what went on at her ranch.

He wanted her to be part of what he was doing, but he also didn't want the endless arguments that would bring about. Better for now to figure out his projects, go to town for the supplies and have it all out with her at once. It would save time and wear and tear on his patience.

He spent hours absorbing the beauty and silence of the valley. The peace he'd found worked a kind of magic on him. He felt really alive for the first time in years. With every footprint he left in the rich soil, with every nail he drove into the fragile walls of the cabin, he claimed the ranch as his own. Not that he had the right. Not yet, but soon. Sooner, he suspected, than

Annabelle would like. He'd claim it with work and sweat and money.

Clint couldn't put his finger on the moment when he began to think of the ranch as theirs, not just hers. He found himself making plans for a new barn to be built next spring. He walked east of the orchard to a rise overlooking the stream. It would be a fine location for a new house. The slope of the land would drain well; he wanted an inside bath and commode.

The rise was big enough for a large kitchen garden, a flower garden and a fine place for children to play. He shook his head, dazzled by the wonder of how deep his need went for this kind of life. A life that would wipe from his soul the violence and blood of his past.

He could just hear Annabelle sputter in anger over his plans for her future. She would throw him out on his ear so fast he'd get to town without his horse.

Annabelle peeled the last of the carrots for the rabbit stew and thought over the past days. They were certainly different than the time she'd spent with LaMar. Not that he'd been around that much.

Without so much as words, she and Clint had formed a shaky but almost friendly truce. He puttered around, doing things his arm allowed. He cleaned the stalls, repaired harness, drove in nails until the constant pounding gave her a headache.

She cooked and mended. Washed and cleaned and cooked some more. That man has an appetite that surpasses a fast-growing colt, she thought. Still, things were beginning to look better and she felt rested for the first time in months. She felt a blessed relief knowing the barn doors would stay on through a blizzard.

She glanced out the kitchen window and in shock dropped the knife to the floor. Clint led his horse from the barn. His saddle rested on the top rail of the corral fence. *He's leaving!* Alarm shot through her and she covered her mouth with both hands. He must have changed his mind, she thought, trying to ignore the fearful feelings in her stomach.

Well, this is what you wanted. Isn't it?

She threw her apron in the direction of the table and rushed outside. She slowed her pace as she approached him. She didn't want him to know his actions disturbed her. She didn't even want to admit to herself that his leaving wasn't exactly what she wanted now.

She walked slowly to the front of the horse, rubbed his soft nose and glanced up at Clint. "Are you leaving?" she asked, her rapid heartbeat contradicting the casual tone of her voice.

"It's what you want, isn't it?" He tossed the saddle on the animal. The smooth action belied the three-week-old gunshot wound.

Her thoughts skittered around in her head, her confused feelings making her hesitate. They'd settled into a fairly comfortable routine. Together they discussed—and argued over—the needs of the ranch. They even slept beside each other, not touching. But often she'd awaken in his arms and lie quiet as a deer, listening for danger, savoring the warmth and strength of his body, feeling safe, pretending their life was normal. When he stirred she'd ease away and he never knew she had been cuddled up to him like a real wife. She had to admit she would miss all that.

His heavy jacket was strapped to the back of his saddle and buckled around his lean hips were his guns. She had the strongest desire to jerk loose his gun belt and throw his weapons into the stream.

She wanted to shake him until his teeth rattled, to scream at him that his way of life would kill him someday. A slow, squeezing pain encompassed her heart. Visions of him lying dead in some far-off town filled her mind and brought tears to her eyes.

"That's what you want, right? For me to leave?" He pulled the cinch tight and with a firm stroke of his hand soothed the restless horse. Then he looked at Annabelle.

She raised her eyes from their determined study of the guns and sighed. "Yes," she whispered. A lie if she'd ever told one.

Clint's laugh had a certain smugness to it. "Don't look so dejected. I'll be back this afternoon."

All sympathy for him and his perilous future left her mind. Annabelle glared at him. She wanted him off her place as fast as snakes struck mice. "You take joy in trying to rile me, Clint Strand."

He nodded, his grin full of masculine arrogance as he continued outfitting his horse. "Yep. It's so easy to do."

His deep chuckle caused her anger to bubble. "I'll just go inside and get your damned bedroll. You can be in Placerville by nightfall."

She did make him smile. More than he had in years. She bred a volatile mixture in him. She made him so mad sometimes he wanted to paddle her, then he found himself teasing her, pushing her to find the humorous side of things. It wasn't hard to figure out she hadn't had an abundance of laughter in her life. Someday he'd get her to tell him about her past.

At times it disturbed him to know he had let her find the soft spot in his heart. A spot he'd thought frozen over many years ago. He needed to tuck those feelings away. They made him vulnerable, exposed him to real danger. If he decided in the end not to stay here, he couldn't let her too far into that soft place. It would hurt too much when he left her—if he left her.

For now, he would concentrate on preparations for the winter. Thoughts of the future? He pushed them from his mind. Come spring, he'd decide what course to take with his wife.

Annabelle stomped all the way into the house. She reached under the bed and hauled out his scruffy bedroll. Tears stung her eyes and she pushed herself to stand straight. She forced a smile—she was getting her way. This was what she wanted.

She put the bedroll on one end of the shaky table and quickly assembled the makings for two venison sandwiches. She paused and sliced two more pieces of fresh brown bread. Better make him three, she decided. He's a big man with an even bigger appetite.

She wrapped the sandwiches and the last piece of peach pie carefully in a clean towel. She smoothed the cloth over and over while she looked at the offending bedroll.

To her, it symbolized the impermanence of his life. Never staying in one place to gather the common goods that made for a home. Just a jumble of blankets to keep him warm in the cold outdoors, a tin cup and plate and enough tough jerky to ward off starvation.

She sighed again. Yes, it was best he leave now, before... Impatiently she shook off the beginnings of the errant thought. She tucked his meager belongings against the fullness of her body and left the suddenly bleak cabin.

He leaned against the uncertain support of the small corral and waited for her. She shoved the bedroll and the towel-wrapped food at him. "There's sandwiches and pie in there. You'll get hungry before you hit Placerville." Abruptly rage exploded inside her. "Now get out," she shouted.

She turned to leave. His strong hands closed on her shoulders and he pulled her against his body. She could feel each of his fingers burning into her skin. His warm breath brushed against her neck and her heart kicked up its beat. At his touch, fear and anticipation skirmished in her stomach. She turned and looked into his beautiful eyes and saw them snap wide in surprise.

He lowered his head a little and she held her breath. *He's going to kiss me!* Her eyelids felt heavy and they began to close. Her mouth parted and she ran her tongue over her dry lips. She wouldn't lie to herself. She wanted his kiss more than anything she'd ever wanted before.

Suddenly, he gasped and pushed her away. Gripping her firmly by the arm, he led her at a near run to the newly-repaired porch steps and eased her down. "What time of year is it, Annabelle?"

"Dear Lord, don't tell me we're going to have another lesson for stupid Annabelle." An angry flush masked the freckles on her face and disappointment slowed her reckless heart.

Clint let out a disgusted sigh. "We both know you're not stupid. Just bear with me a minute. Please," he added, in hopes it would coax her cooperation.

"All right! It's fall."

"Right. And after fall comes winter." He waved at the dark clouds approaching from the mountains. "The first signs are clearly there. Are you going to be able to repair the barn roof so it doesn't come down on that cow's head?"

"Velvet."

"What?" She would drive him crazy, he figured.

"I named her Velvet." Annabelle smiled sweetly at him.

He knew better than to trust the smile. It was as false as fool's gold. "Fine. Just how are you going to protect *Velvet* from the heavy winter snow?"

He watched as Annabelle twisted her skirt between shaking fingers. She looked up at him. He suspected she knew he had the right of it, but she'd die before admitting it. Surely she was the most stubborn woman he'd ever met. Also one of the strongest and brightest and, though she would cut her tongue out before owning to it, the most needy. She didn't even suspect how much she needed him.

"I don't know," she said softly.

"Maybe you can find room for her in the cabin. She can take my place."

"Don't you talk to me like I'm without any sort of a brain. Of course I can't keep her in the cabin."

He bent over, his nose nearly touching hers. "Right again. And how will you haul water through hip-deep snow for you and that kid?" She was mad as the devil. Good. He couldn't stand it when she looked fright-

ened. It ate at his heart and urged him in directions he
didn't want to go. Made him want to hold her and kiss
away her fear and worry. Enough of that! he told himself. It was a road that led to trouble for sure.

She looked off toward the stream, then at the cloud-
shrouded mountain peaks, and knew she was bested in
this argument. "I won't be able to. I know it." She
hadn't lived through a winter in these foothills, but
stories she'd heard in town gave her a good idea how
deep the snows could get.

He continued relentlessly. "The stock has to be fed
and the feed's nearly gone. There's two more holes in
the cabin roof and the seams in the walls need caulk-
ing. The tar paper has to be pulled off and replaced
with boards. The privy needs to be shored up before it
topples over. Supplies have to be brought from town.
Can you drive the wagon through the snowdrifts or
convince a horse to go home through a blizzard?"

It was all she could do to get up and down the porch
steps. Sitting a horse was impossible, and finding her
way to town through deep drifts of snow a joke. She
pictured the long, jarring ride on the buckboard, saw
herself lost and alone in the dead of winter. She shook
her head and fought the bitter tears stinging her eyes.
She would not cry.

He reached out, grabbed a porch support and shook
it hard. It seemed to her the whole cabin trembled under the strength of his hand. She covered her head as
the accumulation of summer dust fell, turning her
nearly colorless dress a dingy brown.

Clint strode away and began pacing before her. He
felt driven to prove his presence was necessary to her.
This was his second chance and he knew he didn't want

to lose it, even if it meant building a life with this difficult woman.

"If this cabin is to carry the load of winter snow, somebody better get up there and do some serious repairing. I've just done enough to keep the sun out of my eyes in that damn bed." He walked over and brushed dust from her freckled nose and her shoulders. "You going to do that, Annabelle?"

She gave up the fight and tears trailed down her dusty cheeks. She shook her head. She hated this helpless feeling.

As if to reinforce his words, a cold wind blew off the Sierra. She shivered and wrapped her arms around herself in an attempt to throw off the biting chill that stole clear to her very marrow. She closed her eyes against the bright morning sun and wondered where its warmth had gone.

Clint went to his knees in front of her and pulled her against his shoulder. "You see, I can't leave the lady who saved my life to the dangers a hard winter can bring. The lady who cajoled me and demanded that I live." He patted her back and inhaled the wonderful smell of fresh baking that lingered on her. Homey. She smelled homey. His touch turned into a caress.

Annabelle relished the feel of his arms around her. She drew in his warm, masculine scent with each breath and held it a moment, savoring its uniqueness. She wanted to rest here, in the safety of his embrace, and forget everything but this moment. He shifted a little and placed a kiss on her damp neck.

A little moan escaped her lips and he dropped his hands away as if she had turned into a hot ember. She got up from the porch and turned her back on him, embarrassed to her toes at her brazen reaction. He'd think her a fallen woman for sure.

She wiped her eyes on her sleeve and decided to make one more try, even though she knew it was hopeless and not too bright to push him further. "You aren't leaving then, even though I don't want you to stay?" She fleetingly wondered how many lies a body had to tell to find the pearly gates firmly locked against her?

"No I'm not. And thanks for the food. I'll be back in time for a late supper." He whirled her around to face him. "We aren't going to have this conversation again." His words were forced through tightly clamped teeth. "I'm here to stay, get used to it." He let her go. Furious, he strode to where his horse stood. His fury came from his loss of control when he held her. What the devil had he been doing? Kissing a pregnant woman. She should have slapped his face.

As if giving in to the inevitable, she called out none too graciously, "I guess you can stay."

"Thank you very much. I'd have stayed anyway. A man doesn't desert his—*a* helpless woman in the middle of winter."

She sensed his avoidance of the word *wife* and she wanted to be sure he knew her own feelings about it. "Don't get any fancy ideas about being a husband to me."

Clint looked at her child-swollen body and grinned. "Not much chance of that."

"It's not winter yet and I'm not helpless," she shouted at him. She turned to go back into the cabin. A sudden thought about men caused her to stop and call out to him. "And stay away from Emma Rooney's boardinghouse. I don't want people to think you're cavorting with loose women while you're married to me." She nearly choked on her words. Good Lord, what was she saying? What did she care what he did? She did care, and that worried her even more than being alone.

Clint laughed out loud. "People already think that, since I went home with *you.*" Still laughing, and with a considerable degree of arrogant, masculine grace, he mounted the animal and rode to the steps.

Intending to give him one last piece of her mind, she turned and muttered to herself that she hoped he fell off and broke his neck. How he continually outmaneuvered her was truly a mystery.

Clint leaned over and cupped her furious face in his large hand. "I think you want me here, Annabelle, you just won't admit it." A movement of his heels against the horse sent him galloping down the road.

She stood with her fists on her hips. *Want him! The last thing in the world she wanted was Clint Strand in her life.* Trudging back into the cabin, she swore she didn't want him. She vowed she would run him off before the snow fell.

When she went inside, she decided the place needed a good cleaning; he'd shaken dust all over everything. She stripped the bed of its mussed sheets and gathered them to her, nuzzling them; she could still smell the musky fragrance of his body. She quickly tossed them onto the floor near the door. She'd boil that smell out and hang them in the sun.

She took the dishes from the one narrow shelf and removed the latest accumulation of dust. Carefully, she placed them back, then covered them with a clean cloth. What she would give for a real cupboard with doors.

Annabelle spent the next half hour scrubbing and cleaning. Anything to keep from thinking of Clint and his parting remark.

Finally exhausted, she sat at the table and looked at the bowl of fruit. She counted the peaches in the bowl. Three. Not enough for anything. *He'd* eaten most of them, had even left one half-eaten in the bowl. She decided to bake him another peach pie and try not to think it strange behavior for a woman who wanted to run a man off her land.

Giving in to the need to do something nice for him for a change, she got up, left the cabin and went to the barn for the ladder.

"He's staying." She said these words over and over as she dragged the rickety ladder to the last row of trees. She said them again as she placed it under the tree with the most remaining fruit. She said them once more as she tied the bottom of her apron around her waist. It made a perfect sack to hold the peaches.

The remaining fruit clung to the highest branches. She went farther up the ladder than she had before. The birds had made a fine meal out of most of the peaches. She breathed in the heady scent of ripe fruit and hoped there was enough for the pies she wanted to bake for him.

Perched on top of the ladder, she gazed around her fifty-acre ranch. She barely saw the dizzy cant to many of the trees or the woeful inadequacy of the cabin with its peeling roof and gaps in the thin walls. She saw home.

For the first time, she saw the promise of a future.

He was staying.

She spotted a large golden peach the birds had missed. Perfect and blushing with ripeness, it was one she wanted for Clint. Blast, she thought. It was just beyond her reach.

She carefully eased herself up on the top rung and touched the peach with the tips of her fingers.

"It's too beautiful to leave for those greedy birds." She stretched out as far as her belly would allow. "If I lean out a little more—"

A sharp, shooting pain struck her lower back and drove its way down her thighs. She grabbed a branch and held on, gasping for breath. She must have stretched too far for someone in her clumsy condition. When she was able to breathe easier, she cautiously reached again for the tempting peach.

Suddenly, her belly cramped viciously and hardened like stone. Fearful of letting go of the branch, she waited out the dizzying pain and clamped her teeth against it. Dear God, could it be the baby? It wasn't due for more than a month.

Before she could gather her senses and go down the ladder, she was hit again. The pain ripped through her, took her whole body in an agony so terrible she swayed and stiffened on her unsteady perch. She fought the scream rising in her throat, then let go of the branch with one hand to wipe the tears from her eyes.

In that instant she lost her footing on the ladder, a blood-chilling emptiness gaping beneath her. Instinctively, Annabelle gripped her stomach with her arm, crushing the ripe peaches against her belly.

Frantic and terrified, she reached out to grab one of the bigger branches to save herself and her child from sure injury.

She missed.

As she fell, sharp twigs caught in her hair and scratched her face.

Thinking only of the safety of her child, Annabelle used all her strength to twist her body so she landed on her back, forcing her breath from her lungs in a great, painful whoosh.

The back of her head hit a corner of the ladder. She thought of the pies she wanted to bake and the pleasure of Clint's smile when he took that first bite flashed absurdly through her mind. Then, a foreboding darkness closed in on her.

Her cry for Clint went unheard.

Chapter Six

Clint walked into the quiet elegance of the bank and thought it too ostentatious for the small California town. Though considerably smaller, the Pleasant Valley Bank resembled his father's institution in Philadelphia.

While the floors weren't marble, they were well-cared-for oak. Polished mahogany railings and brass bars at the cages separated the public from their money. The same atmosphere pervaded—one of money and power—a life he'd willingly abandoned and would be wholly unsuited for now. Just being in this building brought back the unhappy memories of the never-ending arguments with his father. How many times had Clint fought for his freedom from the world of finance?

He finally got that freedom, but at a terrible cost. Total estrangement from his father. Clint hadn't seen him in fifteen years, years he bitterly regretted.

A dark-suited gentleman approached, eyeing Clint's dusty clothes, worn boots and his guns. "May I assist you . . . sir?"

Officious little bastard, Clint thought. "I want to see Jennings."

"Do you have an appointment to see *Mr.* Jennings?"

"No. Tell him Clinton Strand of Philadelphia is here to see him."

By the look on his face, Clint knew the clerk was not impressed. The man nodded and hurried off toward an office at the rear of the building.

Clint took off his hat and ran a hand through his damp hair. He brushed some of the dust off his trousers, thinking he might as well make the best impression he could. He grinned and stopped his paltry efforts at grooming; his money would make the impression he desired.

The clerk returned and led him to a conservative but expensively decorated room. Behind a highly polished teak desk sat a well-fed, well-groomed man of about fifty. He didn't rise when Clint entered the office.

"You wanted to see me—Mr. Strand, is it?" A condescending, tolerant smile barely bent the banker's lips.

Clint threw his identification on the man's desk. The depositor's book on his father's bank in Philadelphia hit the wooden surface and scattered papers to the floor. "I think you may want to see *me*—Mr. Jennings, is it?" Clint hooked a chair with the toe of his boot, sat down and waited.

Jennings frowned and opened the small book. His eyebrows nearly disappeared into the carefully barbered, thick white hair covering his head. His eyes opened wide and he looked at Clint. His expression changed rapidly. A calculating light sparked in his pale blue eyes. He placed the depositor's book on his desk and leaned forward. "My wife and I came here from Philadelphia seven years ago. Am I right in assuming you have some connection to Clinton Augustus Strand, owner of this bank?" He tapped a chubby finger on the green passbook.

Clint smiled. "I am Clinton Augustus Strand, Jr."

"But—but you're a . . ."

"Gunman? Is that the word you're searching for, Mr. Jennings?"

"Ah . . . well, I . . ." His words faded away as his complexion turned a deep red.

Clint's voice hardened. "Yes. An unfortunate turn of events that has nothing to do with why I'm here."

"What can I do to help you, Mr. Strand?" Jennings grabbed his glasses and shoved them on his nose.

"I want you to wire my bank and transfer half that money to an account in this bank. I want to pay off the mortgage on my wife's—*our*— ranch. I want that—" he motioned to the passbook "—placed in a safety deposit box. And I want your wife to treat mine with respect and dignity. I want her and those biddies she runs with to be courteous. I don't expect them to bow down to Annabelle, but by God—" he slapped the desk surface for emphasis "—*they will behave.*"

The banker looked at the book and Clint knew Jennings was trying to determine if half the balance would buy Clint what he wanted. He knew it would buy that and a lot more.

Jennings frowned and tapped a diamond-ringed finger on the bankbook. After several seconds of silence, he gazed up at Clint. "I won't be foolish enough to tell you to take your money and leave. I'm happy to have your considerable account and you know it. But my wife is my problem, just as yours is to you."

He reached into the bottom drawer of his desk and pulled out a bottle of fine brandy and two small, cut crystal glasses. He poured and handed a glass to Clint. He raised his in a salute. "To your health."

Clint savored the excellent liquor. "It's been a long time since I've had brandy this good."

Jennings nodded. "Let's get down to business. I've known for some time your... Annabelle and that man she hooked up with would never find money for that place. It was inevitable they'd lose it. LaMar was a loser."

"What were your intentions, after the shooting?"

"Didn't have any. Judaline's been after me to run the—"

"My wife."

"Yes, of course—forgive me. To run your wife off that property." Jennings leaned forward and looked Clint straight in the eyes. "My wife does not run my business, Mr. Strand. I'd have given ... Mrs. Strand every chance to find a way to keep that land."

Clint relaxed in his chair and studied the man across from him. He couldn't pair him up with that crotchety woman who had challenged Annabelle outside the saloon. "Why does your wife dislike mine so?"

"That is my affair and I'll take care of it. As I said, my wife is my problem. She takes some understanding."

Clint knew he'd learned all he would from this man and he admired the way he stood up for his wife. "Fair enough."

The banker rose and smiled for the first time. "I think we can do business, Mr. Strand."

"That's Clint. I agree, Mr. Jennings."

"Call me Herv." He held out his hand.

Clint put on his hat and pulled it low over his eyes. He offered the banker his outstretched hand and a final nod and moved to the door. He turned and looked back at Jennings. "One more thing. I want every merchant in this town to know my credit is good."

Jennings nodded. "I'll take care of it."

When the door closed behind Clint, Jennings sat back in his chair.

Damn Judaline and her Tuesday Club. If she'd had her way, Annabelle MacDon—Strand would be in the street. He shuddered at the thought of what would happen now if he tried to put that woman off her worthless ranch just to satisfy his wife and her friends.

The time had come to talk straight with his wife. He had been too easy with her. His tolerance and pampering of her had created a social monster. Well, today would see the end of it. He loved her, but enough was enough.

The banker grabbed a telegraph form and hastily scribbled the message that would increase the bank's deposits by a healthy amount. "Wilson!" he hollered. "Get in here."

The clerk stuck his head through the door opening. "Yes, sir?"

Jennings waved the paper at Wilson. "Take this to the telegraph office, then send for my buggy." He stopped the departing clerk. "And find my wife. She's likely at the general store or that tea shop down the street. Tell her to get herself over here immediately."

After Wilson left, Jennings relaxed in his chair. Strand would be his biggest depositor after the lumber and mining companies. He wondered how the son of C. A. Strand had become a gunfighter.

Hervey Jennings was a businessman to his bones, but he liked to think he had a heart. He'd give these young people his hand in friendship. So would Judaline. Whether she wanted to or not.

The door flew open and in high dudgeon Judaline sailed into the office. He grimaced at the angry look on her face. This would not be easy.

"What do you mean, dragging me away from my Tuesday Club meeting at the tea shop?" she demanded.

Jennings glanced again at the passbook, then up at his furious wife. "Hush up, Judaline, and sit down!"

Astonished at the first harsh words her husband had ever spoken to her, Judaline nearly fell into the chair. "Herv, what—"

"I'll tell you what, my dear." He sucked in a deep breath and released it. "For years I've allowed—"

"Allowed—"

"Yes, allowed you to run roughshod over every woman you disapprove of—men, too, on occasion. Every poor soul who doesn't meet your particular idea of a 'good soul.'" He held up a hand to stop her when she attempted to interrupt him.

"Now, I understand why. I know all about your mother and—"

Judaline shot out of her chair as if she'd sat on a tack. "How do you—when did you—" She fell back in her seat. "Herv, you never told me you knew."

He came around and knelt by her chair. "I always knew. Everyone in town knew, my dear, except perhaps your father's wife. He was an important man and she was a shrew who held the purse strings."

"He left my mother to die, left me alone."

"He was a coward."

"My mother was a whore." Tears tracked down Judaline's face.

"You're too harsh on her, dear. She loved your father and he wasn't strong enough to leave his wife and the power her money gave him. He did love her, you know. And you."

"I . . . can't believe that."

"Well, it's true nonetheless. But we have to talk about it here and now. Clint Strand just left here—"

Judaline stiffened and drew back. "That woman is just another—"

"Another unfortunate woman who cared for the wrong man." He watched his wife closely. She had to see the truth of the matter.

"But she let him—"

"Make love to her?"

"Yes, just like my mother!"

"Women and men don't always make the right choices in their partners. Circumstances often dictate our actions and you know that."

"What do you mean?"

"You didn't love me when you married me, Judaline. You were alone and needed someone. You took me."

The still moments grew between them. Finally, Judaline spoke. "You've known that all this time?"

"Yes, my dear."

"Oh, Herv. I'm so sorry. You know I love you now, don't you?"

He gathered her into his arms. "Yes. I've always loved you enough for the both of us." He moved away and put a stern expression on his face. "We are going to the Strand place and you are going to make friends with that young woman. She's been treated pretty badly by folks in this town, and that's mostly your fault. Some mine for letting it go on this long."

"I don't want to be her friend, Herv."

"Fine. Just be kind."

"All right. But she'd better hold that tongue of hers."

Herv laughed. "I think you're both well matched in that department."

At the livery, Clint admired the new wagon he'd just purchased. He felt more than satisfied with his day's work. The lumber and tools he'd bought would be sufficient to repair the barn and make the cabin habitable for the winter.

He'd arranged credit at the general store and had two good-size flour sacks filled with supplies tied onto the back of his horse. Additional supplies would be delivered with the new wagon tomorrow.

He'd even bought some fancy-smelling soap for Annabelle. He'd like to smell something on her besides yeast and flour. He thought of the wonderful, homey scent of her and smiled. It didn't come from Paris, but he sure did appreciate the reason for it—her good cooking.

Thinking of all the work to be done in the short time before snow fell, he decided he needed some help. It was a toss-up who needed the shelter more, he and Annabelle or the horses and dear old Velvet.

He checked the security of the sacks on his saddle then turned and spoke to Jed Cummins. "I'll be needing some help. I've got more work than time." He looked up at the heavy clouds in the sky. "If the snow hits before I'm done, it will be a tough winter for us. Know anyone around here who's looking for wages and found?"

Cummins nodded his agreement. "There's a fella doing odd jobs around town. Seems to be a real handy type." Jed paused and looked at the ground, then up at Clint. "He's a colored."

Clint pulled on his gloves. "Not a problem for me."

Jed nodded. "If he's willing, I'll have him come with me tomorrow when we deliver the rest of your supplies."

Clint tipped his hat. "Much obliged."

He stepped into his saddle and turned his horse toward home. Home. He liked the sound of that. It had been so long since he'd been home. Ten years...a quick night visit with his parents. He hadn't even had time to see his little sister. Lord, she was married and had kids of her own now. Inside, the ache for the sight of his family grew painfully.

Would it be possible, after all these years, to make peace with his father? His mother would open her arms to him, welcome him home with love and tears. Ma. How she hated being called Ma. She insisted that the wife of a banker should be called Mother. Clint would tease her and laugh, then call her Ma and run when she took a loving swat at his behind.

Banking had never interested Clint. He'd been too fond of the adventurous life. He remembered, at eleven, deciding on being a sailor on a whaling ship. When he turned sixteen he wanted to be an explorer and travel over the world to new and exciting lands. The blood-rushing excitement of the gunfight drew him as nothing else. He'd practiced and practiced with his father's pistols—until he was caught and the guns taken away.

At seventeen he'd bought his first guns. At eighteen he'd been a deadly shot. At nineteen he shot his first man and at thirty-four he prayed he'd shot his last.

He slowed his horse to a walk and took a deep breath of the clean fall air. He liked this valley. The air was so clear the mountains seemed close enough to touch. The fragrance of pines and parched grass filled his nostrils. Yes, he thought, this is a good place.

He hadn't eaten in town and his rumbling stomach reminded him of that fact. It would be almost dark when he reached the ranch. The filling breakfast Annabelle had cooked at dawn was a long time gone and he had eaten her "goodbye" meal at noon. The thought of one of her meals made his mouth water. She did wonders with short supplies. He smiled, imagining her happy surprise at what he brought on the back of his horse.

She was a puzzle, that girl. She had a tongue sharper than a bowie knife and a temper to rival a she-cat defending her young.

She kept a spotless house, cooked better than a man could hope for and worked as hard as a man until he insisted she rest more. Then there were the revealing little touches; a jar of wildflowers on the table, a well-mended but colorful quilt on the bed, new patterned flour sacks on the window. Trifles that let a man know there was a woman around who wanted softer things in her life.

He remembered the time after the arithmetic lesson in the barn. He'd come into the cabin to find she had the table covered with things in pairs and threes and fours. She was moving them around, grouping them, then counting them. He sat down and wrote out all the numbers and she traced them over and over, then made her own.

She soaked up that new knowledge like a desert does the rain. She wanted to learn more, so they'd spent the day writing numbers. Every day now, she spent some time practicing, working on sums. Yes, she certainly was a puzzle. He would learn more about her, ask some questions soon.

His stomach growled again and Clint kicked his horse into an easy canter. Yes, home. And maybe a peach pie.

When he turned his mount onto the ranch road, Clint felt the threat deep in his marrow. Instincts he had honed over the years were sharp and true. Spurring his horse into the barn, he leapt from the saddle.

He tipped up his head like a wolf who suspected invasion of his territory and sniffed the air. No smell of strange horses; no odor of cooking coming from the cabin. He could always smell Annabelle's cooking, even in the barn.

He ran his gaze over the ground inside the barn for signs of footprints or hoofprints but could find nothing. If Docker had shown up, his horse would be near. Docker always needed a quick getaway.

If he was here and held her inside the cabin, Clint knew they were in real trouble. The only way out would be a bold challenge. Docker was a coward. He'd been trailing Clint for months, always searching for a back shot.

Discipline learned from years of defending himself took over his body. He held out his hands. Steady. He settled his hat firmly on his head. He checked each of his guns, whirled the chambers. Full and ready. He returned the weapons to the holsters riding low on his hips, then snapped them out twice to test his readiness. He retied the leather thongs around his thighs.

Closing his eyes, he cleared all thoughts of Annabelle from his mind and mentally prepared himself. Then, all senses alert, he left the barn cautiously, guns drawn. There were no signs in the dirt—no tracks. Slowly, he edged around to the side, crouched and made a run for the front of the cabin. He ducked down by the steps and waited for a sign, a sound. Nothing.

Easing himself up over the porch, he crawled on his belly to the door. It was open about a foot. Without making a sound, he rose to his feet and, hearing nothing from inside, kicked open the door. He lunged and hit the floor rolling, gun hand steady, eyes searching.

He was alone.

Where the hell was Annabelle? He examined the room for signs of a struggle, but everything was neat, orderly, the way she always kept it. A bowl of peaches, flour, sugar and a pie plate sat on the table, evidence she had been in the middle of pie making.

He relaxed a little, and returned his guns to their holster. If Docker had taken her from the cabin, it would look as if a tornado had come through. Even pregnant, Annabelle was a fighter. Removing her unwillingly would mean a battle. But where was she?

The stream. That's it, he thought. She's gone for water. He stepped from the cabin and glanced around quickly, still not convinced that his worry about Docker wasn't valid. He left the porch and stood in the open. A prime target, but taking chances made up the bulk of his life. If he could draw out Docker...

He stood, vulnerable, hands held at his hips just inches from his guns. Docker was dangerous, but he liked a show. He wasn't subtle. He would taunt Clint with Annabelle. But Docker wasn't there.

Where the hell is that woman? The feeling of danger remained heavily with him. He ran in the direction of the stream, all the time looking for traces of her. She still wasn't in sight when he reached the edge of the water. Taking off his hat, he wiped his forehead with a red bandanna, then, as he reached back to put the cloth in his pocket, he heard a low, moaning sound.

The orchard! The sound came from the direction of the orchard. He listened, his whole body in tune to his surroundings; he heard the moaning again. Fear tasted bitter in his mouth. His heartbeat pounded in his ears and he felt his control slipping. The idea of Annabelle in trouble wiped away years of professional mastery of his emotions. He raced to the orchard.

"Annabelle!" She lay pale and still beneath the tree, the ladder under her twisting her body into an unnatural position.

Clint eased his arm beneath her shoulders. Lifting her gently, he pulled the ladder away. Lowering her to the ground, he whispered, "Annabelle. Honey?"

Her eyes fluttered open and a small smile moved across her lips. "Clint," she whispered. "I knew you would come." Suddenly she groaned and pulled up her knees.

"Annabelle...what..."

A weak cry broke from her lips.

"Honey? Tell me what's wrong?"

She got the words out on another wave of pain. "The baby." She grabbed Clint's arm in a fierce grip. "It's the baby. It's coming."

"Oh God!" He slipped his arms under her knees and shoulders. "Hang on, sweetheart, I'll get you inside."

"No!" Her breath came in short gasps. "Don't...move me."

"Listen, Annabelle, I've got to get you in the house."

"Please...stay...no..."

"I'll go get somebody to help. Maybe Martha..."

Annabelle stiffened against him, then folded upon herself as once more the pain enveloped her; when it eased she reached up and took hold of his shirt. "I can't move. Please, don't move me." She panted and the perspiration rolled off her face.

"The baby's coming...I know it." She slumped back in his arms.

His fear of minutes ago was nothing compared to his feelings now. "You can't have this kid out here in the dirt! Please, let me go get somebody."

She rolled her head back and forth. "No," she whispered. "There's no...time." Another pain drove her nearly upright with its intensity. Clint supported her, and when it had passed, she went limp in his arms. Unconscious.

Clint held her close to his body and looked around frantically, hoping help would materialize from somewhere. He lowered his head and buried his face in her damp neck.

"It's okay, honey. We'll make it. I don't know for sure how, but we'll do it."

He maneuvered out of his jacket, then spread it beneath her and carefully laid her down. Drawing on the knowledge of caring for his gunshot wounds over the years, he prepared the best he could.

Removing a small packet of matches from his jacket pocket, he took the knife from his belt. He flicked a match with his thumbnail and held the blade in the flame. Spreading out his bandanna on the ground, he set the knife against the colorful red-and-black pattern.

Suddenly, Annabelle cried out and held her hard, distended belly in her hands. Clint pulled her into his arms and she whimpered at the movement.

"It's okay, honey. Just relax." That sounded stupid, even to him. "I'm going to the stream to wash my hands. I'll be right back."

"No! Don't leave me." Tears flowed from her eyes as she pleaded with him.

"Shh. I'll be so quick you won't even know I'm gone." As he eased her back down he wondered if he had time to run and get a blanket. She put her hand over her mouth to stifle a scream. He ran his hands over his face. No blanket.

At the stream he scrubbed his hands and, for the first time in years, prayed. Her scream broke into his thoughts and he ran back to her.

Her body arched and bucked as though some unseen force had invaded it and controlled her. "It's coming!" she cried.

Clint went to his knees between her legs and tossed her skirt over her belly. "Dear God." The head was already there.

Annabelle pushed and moaned.

Clint held the small head and shoulders in his hands. She cried and pushed again.

He eased one hand under the narrow little back.

Annabelle gave a mighty heave and a long, shuddering moan.

Clint held her son in his hands. Her stillborn son.

Annabelle heard voices whispering; the sounds faded and returned. She strained to hear more clearly.

"Doc...here tomorrow." A woman's voice. What's a woman doing in my house? she wondered. She tried to shift her body in the bed, but every muscle rebelled painfully against her slightest movement.

"Waking up, do you think?" Annabelle smiled. That was Clint. She frowned. He sounded worried.

Her eyes drifted open. She wanted to know what woman belonged to that voice. Her hazy vision cleared and she saw Judaline talking quietly with Clint. What the devil was that woman doing here?

"Clint?"

He nearly tripped over his own feet getting to her side. His clumsiness made her want to smile, but she felt too tired. Gingerly, he sat beside her on the bed. "How d'you feel, honey?"

She scowled at him. "Don't call me honey," she said, her voice thready. She attempted again to roll to her side; she hurt all over. She glanced up at Clint. "Why are you being so..." As memory of the morning returned in a rush, her eyes snapped wide open. "Where's my baby?" She grabbed hold of his arm. "Clint? My baby?"

"Honey, now calm down—"

"Answer me!"

Judaline stepped forward and laid a hand on Clint's shoulder. "Go on and take care of everything. I'll stay with her."

Clint nodded, got to his feet and left the cabin.

"Judaline, tell me." Dread coursed through Annabelle. She knew what she would hear. This woman always brought bad news.

The other woman dragged a box to the bedside and settled herself. "We know these things deep in our hearts, don't we, Annabelle?"

Annabelle swallowed to ease the pain in her throat from the need to cry. She released a hard, shuddering sigh. "Was my baby born dead? Did it live at all?"

"No." Judaline hesitated, then reached over and held Annabelle's hand.

"Was it a boy?" Tears began to run down her cheeks.

"Yes. I'm sorry. He never drew a breath." She squeezed Annabelle's hand.

Annabelle nodded. "In my heart I knew it," she whispered. "I've known it for days. He hadn't moved in so long." Ignoring the ache of her tired body, she turned toward the wall. Her shoulders shook in deep, heaving sobs.

Judaline patted her back and spoke softly. "That's right, cry it out." She sat quietly and watched while the distraught girl cried and eventually fell into an exhausted sleep.

She closed her eyes and remembered how many times she had cried those same tears of loss, how often she'd greeted pregnancy with happiness and great hope for the future. Until, at last, she and Hervey took separate rooms. Finally, Judaline rose and went outside to find the men.

Hervey Jennings sat on the steps. He looked a far cry from his usual well-groomed self. Jacket off, shirtsleeves rolled up and smeared with damp earth, he seemed more a working man than she'd ever seen him.

Judaline sat beside her husband and repressed the desire to link her arm with his. She felt uneasy with the new knowledge between them, unsure of how to act. "Where's Mr. Strand?"

"Putting the shovels in the barn." A forlorn ring sounded in his voice.

"Brings back memories of a sad time," Judaline said.

"Several sad times, my dear." He paused, then took her hand in his.

Startled at the endearing gesture, Judaline looked up at him. "It's made me too hard, I think, Hervey." The image of four small wooden caskets flooded her thoughts.

He nodded and squeezed her hand. Judaline vowed to be a gentler wife.

She saw Clint, head lowered, slowly walking toward the cabin. "It's going to be hard times around here for a while."

"Maybe we can help." Hervey rose to meet Clint.

Clint took off his hat and slapped it against his thigh. He straightened his damp hair with a hand, then pulled the hat back down over his forehead. He looked at Judaline and cleared his throat. "How is she?"

"Hurt. Sad. She's sleeping now."

Clint nodded.

Judaline touched his arm. "It's going to be...difficult for her for a while. She'll need your help and support."

Clint tipped his head back and watched the clouds drift across the late afternoon sky. "If she'll let me."

"Give it to her anyway," Judaline said, some of her former crust returning.

Clint gave a hard, short laugh. "Annabelle isn't the easiest person to give to. She thinks she can beat most of the world with one hand and bamboozle the rest with the other." At the memories of her determination to go it alone, he smiled. "Maybe she can."

"Then you're leaving?" Hervey asked.

Clint rubbed the back of his neck in an effort to ease the tension and tiredness that claimed his body. "No. I'm staying. She needs me and I need her. That's not the worst place to start a marriage." And, he thought, that was the first time he'd really thought of what they had as a marriage instead of a convenience, a way to get what he wanted without considering her needs at all.

Judaline wrapped her shawl about her shoulders and turned to her husband. "Come on, Herv. Even with a full moon it'll be difficult to get home." She looked at Clint. "We'll stop by Martha's on the way back. She'll be glad to come by tomorrow and help with Annabelle. She...one of us will come by every day for a bit."

"Thanks," Clint said. "I appreciate the help." He shook hands with Hervey. These people certainly surprised him. Never would he have expected this kind of help from them, especially Judaline.

Hervey turned the buggy around and tossed a salute to Clint. He stood and watched until the buggy disappeared down the road.

He had never felt so alone.

Chapter Seven

Clint stepped out onto the porch the next morning and watched Martha and Jed Cummins drive up the road to the cabin. Riding beside the wagon was a giant of a black man.

Jed brought the wagon to a halt in front of the house and helped Martha down. "Clint, this is my wife, Martha. She's come to help out with your missus."

The image of the group of women haranguing Annabelle that first day came into his mind and he frowned. "I saw you in town."

Martha blushed. "I'm not proud of that day, Mr. Strand. Sometimes a body gets carried away with Judaline's plans." She looked him straight in the eye. "I'm not offering that as an excuse. Once in a while, I'm just as stupid as the next person."

Jed laughed. "Not often, that's for sure." He gave his wife a warm, loving look.

"Hush up, Jed Cummins," she admonished fondly, then turned back to Clint. "How's she doing?"

"I don't know," Clint said. "I'm not sure what to do for her." He turned and looked at the cabin and worried about the woman inside. "She's quiet. Hell, she's more than quiet. It's like she died with that baby. She just faces the wall and cries or sleeps."

Martha reached out and patted his arm. "Don't fret, Mr. Strand. She'll be fine. Takes a good while for some to get over a shock like this. Especially with a first child."

Clint quickly changed his initial feelings about Martha. Her round, friendly face promised comfort and wisdom. He figured Annabelle could use both and he sure felt uneasy about offering it to her. "I appreciate you coming to help. She needs a female around, I think."

Martha smiled. "You'd be surprised how a woman needs her man in these circumstances."

Clint frowned. "I'm not her man in this."

Martha tipped her head to one side, then smiled. She nodded her head as if she liked what she saw. "You could be."

He gave a grim laugh. "You don't know Annabelle."

"Well, I intend to." Martha hustled into the cabin.

Jed cleared his throat and scratched his chin. "This here's Aaron Parker." He gestured to the big man still seated on his horse. "Brought him out to help you."

Clint walked over and stretched out his hand in greeting. "I'm mighty pleased to have you here, Aaron."

With amazing agility for a man his size, Aaron dismounted and clasped his hand in Clint's. He towered over Clint by a good four inches.

"More a pleasure for me, Mister Strand."

"Clint."

"Yessir, Mister Clint." Aaron's grin spread over his face and revealed bright white teeth.

Clint smiled back, knowing "Mister Clint" was as informal as Aaron would allow.

Jed slapped Clint on the back. "What say we look this place over. I brought your tools and supplies in the back of the wagon. One of my sons will be along with your new wagon and the lumber. I'm not against giving you a hand while the womenfolk get acquainted."

Clint gave a sigh of relief. These people were the kind he'd wanted to settle among all his life. Warm. Open. Honest folk. A man could find a good life in this place. "Follow me, Jed, Aaron," Clint said. "I've got enough work to last us a year, easy."

Martha opened the door and surveyed the primitive room and the small huddled figure in the bed. She shook her head; this would be a troublesome day, she knew.

After filling a pan with water, she set it on the stove. "Annabelle. It's Martha Cummins." She went to the bed and gently shook the sleeping woman awake. "Come on, now. Let's get you out of bed and washed up. I'll help you to the privy."

Annabelle moved closer to the wall.

"I'm not going away, Annabelle Strand, so you might as well turn over and face me. I'm here for the day."

Annabelle rolled over and glared at Martha. "I didn't invite you."

"No. As a matter of fact, Judaline did, if you can imagine that." Martha plumped the pillows behind Annabelle's head. "Have you got a robe?" She looked around the room but saw only two faded dresses and a light woolen shawl hanging on some hooks. She took down the shawl. "Here, put this on and we'll go out to the privy."

Annabelle turned back to the wall.

"Oh no you don't, young lady. You need to get out of that bed and move around. You stay laid out like that, you won't be able to move easy at all in a few days. More like a goat with rheumatiz." She tossed back the covers and held out the shawl. "Come on."

With a resigned look on her pallid face, Annabelle eased her legs over the side of the bed. She grabbed her belly and her face turned even more ashen.

"I know, it hurts. From what I hear, you had a time of it."

"How do you know?" Annabelle asked.

"Judaline and that man of yours told me."

"He's not my man."

"Don't be foolish," Martha said. "'Course he is. You married him."

Annabelle frowned at the mention of her marriage. "A misguided decision."

Martha gave a hearty laugh. "I have to tell you, Annabelle, everybody in town has heard the story of how you marched into that saloon and faced down that gunfighter. Yessiree. I'd say you made an...interesting decision when you stuck LaMar's gun in that man's side."

She tucked the woolen garment around Annabelle's shoulders. Martha saw a bleak look roll over the young woman's face. "No sense taking yourself to task now, it's too late. Besides, that man out there seems to be the kind to stick it out no matter what."

"There's no reason now. A useless woman, a ranch that looks as if it were abandoned fifty years ago. What man in his right mind would want to stay?"

"A man who needs to change his life?" Martha suggested. "A man who's sick of looking over his shoulder every minute of the day. This place might seem pretty good to that kind of man."

Martha ignored the disbelieving expression in Annabelle's eyes. "One who wants a woman who works hard and is faithful even to a worthless man." She eased Annabelle off the bed and toward the door. "If a man is smart enough, he might want that. We all need a place to put down roots."

The cold air hit them hard when they got outside. Annabelle shivered. Holding the trembling girl close to her, Martha said, "We'll send a warm coat by Judaline tomorrow. You can't spend the winter dressed for summer." She fussed with the shawl collar. "Now, put those cold hands in the pockets. Land sakes, girl. You trying to freeze yourself to death? We'll be putting you in the ground..."

Annabelle stiffened and stopped. Tears pooled in her eyes and she turned her face into Martha's soft shoulder.

Martha patted the weeping girl's shoulder. "There, there, child. Sometimes my thoughtless tongue just rolls on without a sensible direction." She hugged Annabelle to her breast. "It seems as if the good Lord has tossed you out, right?"

Annabelle nodded.

"Well, he hasn't, child. He's given you a mighty test. You'll be fine. Come now, let's get you to the privy and back to that warm bed."

From the barn Clint watched the two women walk to the privy, then back to the cabin. The sight of the normally strong and feisty Annabelle bent over and weeping struck his heart like a mighty fist.

It would be tough, he thought as the women disappeared through the cabin door. She would fight and toss cusswords at him like wood chips flying from an ax. But they needed each other.

Annabelle took a sip of the hot milk and honey Martha had prepared and relished its sweetness. She looked at the woman curiously. "Why're you here?"

Martha didn't answer right away, just kept cutting potatoes in chunks for a stew. Finally, she put down the knife and turned to Annabelle. "Lots of reasons. Mainly, you need help for a bit." She poured herself a cup of coffee, spooned a liberal amount of sugar into the cup and sat at the table.

"Then there's the mean treatment. You know, snubbing you, judging you to be a worthless person, trying to run you out of town." She gazed down into her cup. "I don't know, Annabelle. My papa was a kindhearted, caring preacher. He'd have had a thunderous fit if he'd seen how we treated you. Believe me, I was better raised." She looked hard at Annabelle.

"Sometimes we let ourselves be taken over by a stronger person. Even when we know it's wrong." She sighed. "Judaline's got a soft spot somewhere. I just keep trying to find it."

Annabelle leaned back against the pillow. "It would be easier to find gold in Velvet's milk bucket." She cleared her throat. "I don't recall a preacher ever giving me a kindness."

"Don't you have any faith, child?"

"I've got faith, just not in preachers. They don't hold much with children of fallen women, let alone the women themselves." Preacher Dennis back in Georgia had run Annabelle from the church one day, saying she was unfit, a bad influence for his flock. She found it mysterious how drinking, swearing, wife-beating Bodine was fit and she wasn't, just because she was the child of an unmarried woman who'd been raped.

"Preachers are good for marrying, burying and baptizing. Beyond that, I don't care for them and they don't care for me."

Martha smiled. "My papa would've. There was a man who lived by the good part of the Good Book." She stood up and moved to the bed. "Are you hungry, child?"

Annabelle shook her head and eased herself down. She turned her back to Martha.

Martha sighed and decided to let Annabelle sleep. She thanked the Lord she and Jed had never lost a child. Seven healthy young ones raced through her kitchen every day. Even so, Martha knew the devastation Annabelle must feel. On behalf of the desolate girl, Martha sent another prayer heavenward.

She finished the fixings for the stew, made corn bread and vanilla cookies. She looked at the laundry piled in a box and a crafty smile lit her face. She would leave the dirty clothes for Judaline. Served her right!

She felt sure the Lord would agree.

At eight o'clock the next morning, the door slammed and Annabelle woke with a start. She rolled over in bed and groaned. Judaline stood there, a fierce look on her face.

"Well, I see Martha left me the laundry. Just like her. All sweet on the outside and mean as a skunk on the inside." She scurried around gathering up the wash. "I should have brought my house girl out to do this," she mumbled. She would take it home and have it done there. She would not stir dirty clothes in a tub of hot water and lye soap.

A weary sigh left Annabelle's already weary mind and body. "Put that down, Judaline. I don't want you washing our things." If anybody was skunk-mean it was the banker's wife, Annabelle thought.

"I suppose you're going to hop right out of that bed and do it yourself?" She stuffed the clothes in a pillowcase. "Good! I could use the help."

Annabelle turned her face to the wall. "Go home, Judaline."

"Not on your life, young lady. We are stuck with each other. Land sakes, even my Herv is here offering his help to your husband and that man."

Judaline watched the figure huddled in the bed. She hoped her conversation would arouse Annabelle's curiosity. She held a grudging admiration for what Annabelle had done in that saloon. The woman confounded her. She lived her life unburdened by the rules most people followed like sheep.

All her life, Judaline had followed convention, had played by the rules. But with the loss of each child it seemed the juices of her life dried up. There had been a time when she'd been soft and womanly. She and Herv...well, they had been close. Judaline felt her face blush with old memories.

She wondered how Annabelle and her new husband would face the vagaries of life, the unexpected and cruel happenings that cooled passion and stripped the body of eagerness for the next day. Suddenly, Judaline felt a longing for times past. When Herv had kissed her with sweetness instead of duty. When she had held her friends by caring instead of intimidation.

Judaline shook her shoulders and straightened. "Humph! Meanderings of an old woman!" she said aloud, and left the cabin to dump the armful of dirty clothes in the buggy.

When she returned, Annabelle's back still presented itself to the room. "You planning on spending your life in that bed?"

Silence greeted her question.

"Fine. Feel sorry for yourself. Grieve for your child. Then get up and get on with your life, Annabelle. Nobody has time or patience for a whiner."

Annabelle turned over and glared at Judaline. "I suppose calling me a whiner is better than naming me a harlot in front of the whole town."

In amazement she watched a deep crimson creep over Judaline's face. This woman embarrassed? She didn't believe it for a minute. "You'd better sit down, you look a little discomforted."

The banker's wife sat and toyed with a wilted flower in the jar. "I'd like you to accept my apology for calling you those names. Also for my... unkind treatment of you these past months."

Annabelle scooted up in bed, mindful of her tender body. "You want my forgiveness for trying to run me out of town like some criminal? For calling me terrible names? For causing most of the town to turn its back on me?"

Judaline closed her eyes and thinned her lips. She nodded.

"All right."

"All right?" Judaline rose from her seat and clutched the folds of her skirt. "Just like that, you forgive me?"

"Forgiveness is or it isn't, Judaline. Not halfway. I forgive you. I'd be glad to be your friend."

Judaline walked over to the bed and glared down at Annabelle. For several moments her struggle with the ease of her absolution was obvious. Finally, she burst out, "I didn't ask for your friendship, just your forgiveness."

"Sometimes they are one and the same." Annabelle smiled and treasured this victory over her enemy— she'd ask for her own forgiveness later for her unchristian feeling.

Judaline whirled and slammed out of the cabin.

The moment passed and Annabelle ran her hands over her stomach and felt an emptiness in her soul she knew would never be filled.

She turned and faced the wall.

Outside, Clint and Herv turned when the cabin door slammed and Judaline stomped down the stairs.

"Your wife is a clever woman."

"Now, Judaline," Herv said. "Did you apologize to that girl."

"Of course. And do you know what she did?"

"What?" Clint asked.

"She forgave me!"

Herv patted her on the shoulder. "Well, now that's just fine."

"She had the nerve to offer to be my friend!"

Clint rubbed his chin. "I'm confused here. Is there something wrong with an offer of friendship?"

His statement clearly upset her more. "Just like that? Straight out? So easy? Humph!" She turned and marched to her buggy, climbed in and sat rigid as whalebone.

"I'm not sure what's going on here," Clint said.

Herv smiled, put his hands in his pockets and rocked back and forth on his heels. "Judaline is a strong believer in penance. It appears your wife isn't demanding any and my wife is madder than spit."

A feeling of relief washed over Clint. His Annabelle wasn't the only puzzling woman in Pleasant Valley.

Annabelle felt Clint leave the bed. She lay quiet and still. She heard him pull on his trousers, then his boots. She knew all the little noises he made while he tried to dress without waking her. For nearly a week she had listened without speaking a word to him.

What could she say? Thank you for bringing my dead child into the world? Thank you for burying my son? She felt helpless to find the proper words to talk with him. She just didn't know what to say. If it came out wrong he might leave, and she admitted now she didn't want that to happen. Her tongue betrayed her so often; perhaps if she just kept quiet things would work out.

Now he was putting wood in the stove; he filled the coffeepot and set it on the stove with hardly a sound. She should get up and fix his breakfast while he fed the animals. She knew she was capable of doing at least that much for him. But, mind and body, she felt so tired.

Judaline's words kept circling in her head. "Nobody has time or patience for a whiner." No, Annabelle thought. I'm not a whiner. I haven't asked for a thing. Just to be left alone.

At the thought of rising from the bed, a heavy fatigue seemed to fill her and her eyes drifted closed. *Sleep,* she said silently. *I'll sleep a little longer, then maybe I'll get up.*

Clint bent down, lifted the board from the floor and removed the jar of milk. As he ate, he made plans. He'd give her a couple of weeks to recover and then he'd do something about their situation.

He'd use that time to fix the worst of the problems with the cabin and the barn. Aaron was a blessing. That man had talented hands, seemed he could fix anything. Between the two of them the place would be more than livable through the winter.

Maybe Annabelle would unbend enough to see how useful he'd be around the place. He felt sure she would try to convince him to go now that the baby was dead.

God, he'd never been so tired in his life. He felt out of control in a way he'd never experienced before. Even when facing some fool who wanted to kill him for the glory of it, Clint held control. He knew his strengths and weaknesses. This coil he found himself in now came close to defeating him.

Annabelle moaned and tossed in the bed. Clint moved to her side and pulled the covers over her shoulders. Her freckles stood out sharply against the paleness of her skin.

He reached out and brushed her hair from her face. She felt so soft. The texture of her skin was... He swallowed hard as the feel of her stirred his body and he jerked his hand away. Use your head, Strand, he told himself. She'd just lost a baby. This was no damned time for him to be feeling randy. But she did do that to him.

She opened her eyes and frowned.

"How d'you feel?" he asked.

Her hands moved to her stomach and she glanced down at the slight roundness. Tears rolled down her cheeks and she slowly turned her back to him and faced the wall.

What am I supposed to do about this? He'd never felt so helpless. She needed a woman with her now. Not a man whose only talent lay in a quick draw and a fast horse. But Martha and Judaline agreed it was time for Annabelle to take hold again. Time for him and his "wife" to begin their life without neighbors poking around.

In his uncertainty, he begged them to stay.

"No sir, Clint Strand," Martha had said. "The longer we're around the longer it'll take her to turn to you."

"Besides," Judaline had stated, "she's a lot stronger than you think. I can't believe that woman will loll around in bed for long. She'll want to be up and about ordering you and that man you hired."

Clint pressed his argument. "She isn't doing a thing to take hold of life again. How am I supposed to make her do that?"

"You'll know, Clint," Martha assured him. "Your heart will tell you."

"My heart?" What the devil did she mean? Clint wondered.

"You've got feelings for that girl, don't tell me you haven't. Just go with those feelings, you'll be fine."

"Humph!" Judaline had had the final word.

He noticed Annabelle shiver and he pulled the quilt over her. The cabin was cooling early. He'd better haul in more wood and keep the fire going. He opened the stove and shoved in several sticks of wood.

"Annabelle?"

She didn't respond.

"I'm going out for a bit. Can I get you anything? Water? Food?"

She shook her head against the pillow but kept her face turned from him.

"Do you need me to send for Martha? She'll come if you need her." He would jump at the chance to go for the friendly woman.

No movement from the bed.

He took his hat from the hook by the door. He looked at her one last time and left the cabin.

Clint admired the small room Aaron had crafted in the most sturdy corner of the barn. It held a comfortable cot, a three-foot-square table and a well-built chair. On a large flat rock, Aaron had placed the runty black stove Jed had brought by to stave off the cold of winter.

Dropping an additional blanket on the cot, Clint turned to where the big man mucked the stalls. "It's looking kind of homey in there. You've got a fine hand at working wood, Aaron. Where did you learn?"

Aaron leaned on the shovel and grinned. "I'm snug as an ol' boll weevil in a cotton patch, Mister Clint." He propped the pitchfork against the stall and walked over to Clint. "My folks left the South when I was a boy. We went north and I 'prenticed to a cabinet-maker. I had a feel for wood and that man weren't bothered by the color of my skin. He found joy in teachin' me. Jobs is easy to find when a man can use his hands to benefit the pockets of others."

"My pockets are fine. You'll draw a fair salary and a piece of land when we get to it."

Aaron nodded. "My thanks, Mister Clint."

"You sure you're going to be okay out here? Mr. Cummins tells me the winters are cold enough to freeze a man's—"

Aaron's laugh boomed through the barn. "Don't you worry none 'bout me. I got all my important parts. They's workin' just fine."

Clint grinned and silently appreciated the man's sense of humor. "We'd better finish the barn roof today and there's a few more holes in the wall to close up. Come hell or blizzards, I'm tackling the cabin tomorrow. I can't wait any longer for her to get up. Winter won't wait."

Aaron frowned. "The missus still grievin'?"

Clint shrugged. "I guess that's what she's doing. I am out of my element here." He glanced over at the other man. "Do you know who I am, Aaron?"

"Yessir, Mister Clint." He nodded and looked directly into Clint's eyes. "Mister Jed, he told me. Figured I'd better know before I come out here to your place."

"It doesn't bother you, then, that I'm a gunman?"

"I've had a gun in my hand a time or two. Sometimes a man ain't got much choice. That how it was with you?" Aaron wiped a large hand over his face and looked chagrined. "Sorry, Mister Clint. Ain't none of my business."

"That's all right. You've got a right to know the kind of man you work for."

"I'd say that's mighty generous, for a white man." Aaron's face wore a wry smile.

"Just two men, Aaron." He offered his hand to seal a pact with this strong, gentle person.

Aaron accepted and clasped Clint's hand. "Care to sit and have some coffee? I got a pot ready to go on the stove."

"I'd like that."

Clint sipped the strong, hot brew, tipped back his head and closed his eyes. Memories stored away and old longings rushed to draw pictures on his eyelids. His mother, full of love and forgiveness; his father; Lillian, his sister, as lovely as the Lily he called her.

His family. Full of love and kindness. Wealthy and charitable toward those who had less. This caring for others had led him into a life where people didn't care about others or themselves. Where life was a scratched-out existence of killing, hiding and running.

He leaned forward, elbows resting on his thighs, his tin cup between his hands. He swirled the coffee around. "From the time we first heard about gunfighters and the renegade soldiers tearing through the country, my friends and I practiced the fast draw." He looked up at Aaron and grinned. "We were something, all right. Little kids running around shooting, 'Bang! You're dead!' We had no idea what those bushwhacking soldiers really did, how much harm and destruction they caused.''

Clint set his cup on the table and shoved more wood into the stove. "By the time I was seventeen, I could hit anything I aimed at from two hundred yards." He sat down and emptied his cup.

"God, my father hated it. He'd seen so many men die in the War. He sent me off to Harvard with a prayer I'd straighten up and come to work in his bank. It's truly what I expected to do, even though I hated the thought of being cooped up all day behind the cashier's cage." He got up and paced over to the door of the room, pulling aside the blanket that helped keep in the heat.

"I was on my way home for the summer. The train had stopped in the middle of nowhere for water. Several of us passengers got off to stretch our legs." He ran his hands nervously through his hair. He hadn't talked of this in years. "All at once these two men stepped from the train. Later I found out they'd robbed a large payroll from the last car. Anyway, on the way out of the train they grabbed a woman as a hostage. They held a gun to her head and began to drag her toward some horses tied behind some bushes."

He stood before Aaron, the vision of that day blistered in his brain. "I didn't even think. I pulled my gun and began firing. I outshot them both. The woman didn't even get a scratch."

Clint poured two more cups.

"The railroad made a hero of me. Seems I'd killed two of the most wanted train robbers in the country. From then on, I was a marked man. It wasn't a week before I was challenged." A self-deprecating laugh rose from his chest.

"Obviously, I won. If that's what you want to call it."

"You supposed to stand still and let some piece of filth shoot you down?"

"No. I'm just sick of it all, Aaron."

"Yessir, I can see that. But you're here now."

"Yeah, but there's a man out there. He's been trailing me for months looking for a back shot. Same way his brother shot. He shot me as I turned, but I got him on my way down." He rubbed the scar on his chest. "Bull's been looking for me ever since."

Aaron stood up and stared down at Clint. "Bull Docker?"

"You know him?"

"Heard of him. He's a bad man, Mr. Clint. A real bad man."

"That's why I came here. I hope he won't look for me here in the mountains."

"If he does, Mister Clint, you got a man watching your back now."

"That gives me a great deal of comfort, Aaron." Clint meant every word. This man would be formidable as a friend—and an enemy.

"I said I'd handled a gun a time or two. There's plenty places that don't cotton to a black man risin' in the world. More than once I've defended myself and hit the road at a gallop."

Clint smiled and changed the subject. "I'm told you have a way with horses. Is that true?"

Aaron's self-satisfying grin told the tale. "I'll tell you true, Mister Clint. Ain't a mustang I can't break and ride. You buy 'em, I'll make 'em so sweet your missus will invite them to dinner and offer up dessert.''

Clint's laughter filled the barn. "When spring comes, you and I will ride to Sacramento and buy the best damn horses you ever saw.''

"I think, Mister Clint, the Lord is finally watchin' over me.''

"You better hope he's watching over all of us. We've got a hard winter ahead.''

Chapter Eight

"When you feel like getting up, Annabelle, you'll have to meet Aaron. Let me tell you, that man is a worker."

She could hear Clint rustling around, fixing his breakfast, stirring up the fire in the stove. Talking. He was always talking to her, ignoring the fact that for nearly ten days she hadn't said a word to him.

"We've got the corral fixed and the privy standing upright. Wait till you see the room we've enclosed in the barn for Aaron to sleep. He's staying here now. I've hired him." She heard him set the table.

"Don't you worry about a thing. We'll just work around you again today. The roof's nearly repaired—sorry about the dust on the bed—we've got some patching to do on the walls and Aaron's just about finished with the addition. We'll knock out the south wall, probably this afternoon."

Annabelle felt the strongest urge to throw something at him just to shut him up. She didn't want to hear about what he was doing on *her* ranch. She wanted him to leave her alone. Quiet was what she

wanted. Peace and quiet to mourn her dead child. To
mourn the pitiful state of her life.

"Soon as you feel like getting out of here for a bit
each day, we'll start on the floor."

She'd had enough. She twisted around on the bed,
took his pillow and threw it at him.

Clint ducked, but the pillow knocked his coffee off
the table and the tin cup fell to the floor. He calmly
picked it up and poured himself another cup. He
reached for a towel and tossed it onto the bed. "Best
clean the mess, honey. Martha and Judaline won't be
around and Aaron and I don't have time."

Annabelle fiercely suppressed the urge to question
him as to why the women had abandoned her. She
flopped down against her pillow and looked at the
ceiling. Why did she feel so angry? She longed for the
pain she'd felt yesterday. She searched for it in her
mind and heart, but all she could find was a roiling,
swelling anger.

Exhausted with her efforts, she turned to her favorite position—her back to the room and her face to the
wall.

Clint stood quietly and watched the changing expressions on her face. Before she turned away from
him, he'd seen in her the first signs of returning life. He
smiled and took a sip of the hot coffee. Good. She was
getting angry. Anger in Annabelle was a sign of life.

He slipped on his jacket and pulled his hat down on
his forehead. He glanced once more at her, then left her
alone.

At the sound of the closing door, Annabelle rolled
over. She looked at the mess on the table and floor.
Obviously, Clint wasn't going to do a woman's chore.

She eased out from the covers and stood, waiting for the light-headed feeling to leave her. In a matter of seconds she felt fine, a little stiff but fine.

Who did he think he was, ordering her around? Her husband, that's who, she told herself. Husbands ordered and wives did. That was the law of the land and she had better get used to it. Maybe not. He probably wouldn't even stay now that the...

"I'm sick of lying in bed, anyhow," she said aloud, skittering away from thoughts of her child. She moved slowly to the hook where her clothes hung. Lord, how she hated that blue dress. Well, it was all she had. She set the latch on the door so Clint wouldn't come in while she washed and dressed. For a belt she tied a long strip of flour sacking around her middle. She'd been considerably bigger around when she'd stitched this dress.

She fought back the tears that threatened. She was through with crying.

Pouring hot water into the basin, she marveled that most of the soreness had left her body. Granted, she still felt as if she'd been riding a horse for a hundred miles, but she was healing. She wondered if her bottom would ever feel normal again. Her breasts felt sensitive beneath the tight wrapping Martha had put around them. Three more days before the bindings would come off. Misery instead of milk.

Emptying her mind of all feeling, she wiped up the spilled coffee and cleaned the breakfast dishes. Satisfied with her work, she wiped her hands on a towel. The cabin needed a good cleaning, but that could wait for the men to finish whatever they were doing to it.

All at once slow tears traced their way down her cheeks. It seemed a strange sort of crying to her. No sobs, no shaking shoulders. It was as if the tears had their own life, deciding how and when to fall, no matter she'd made up her mind not to cry anymore.

She wiped her eyes with the faded towel and had a near-obsessive desire to be where her child rested. She'd never even set eyes on that poor baby of hers; at least she could pay decent attention to his grave.

Clint hefted a keg of nails from the bed of the wagon and prepared to swing it down to Aaron when he saw Annabelle, fully dressed, leave the cabin. She walked through the peach orchard to the baby's grave. Good, he thought, she's finally left her bed. "Heads up, Aaron," he said, and transferred the load to the man standing at the end of the wagon.

Clint jumped down and moved to the corner of the barn to get a closer look at Annabelle. Though she moved a little stiffly, he saw the slenderness of her figure and the perfect grace of her walk. There was a beauty about Annabelle that he had tried to ignore since his recovery. A loveliness that shone through even during her pregnancy. He had kept those thoughts from his mind. Now he couldn't. He had to face it, he wanted her.

The absolute realization that this disarming female was his wife, that he could have her, hit him like a blow to the gut and made his hands shake. Why would he want this woman as he had no other? She had a fierce temper, used her tongue like a whip and had little use for men. Certainly not the kind of mate he'd dreamed of through the years. A far cry from the serene presence of his mother and the quiet confidence displayed by his sister.

It didn't take a world of figuring to know she had been abused by men. Her respect for the male population rested somewhere beneath a snake's belly. Yet he knew he surprised her plenty. She must have expected him to take advantage of his position as her husband, though not as far as claiming his rights. Her pregnancy had stopped that. But he could have tried to lord it over her. Make her wait on him. Acknowledge his male superiority.

The only thing he was superior at was staying alive. He felt abundantly alive now. Especially behind the buttons on his trousers. He reached inside his pants and adjusted his unruly manhood and tried to settle this inappropriate flood of desire he felt for his wife. His wife. The words rolled silently over his tongue and tasted new and exciting. He had to wait, he knew that. She mourned her child now. But soon...

He watched as she smoothed the ground covering her child. He saw her hands move over the dirt in a slow, caressing motion. An uneasy feeling settled in his stomach and replaced the craving.

He heard Aaron's step crunch over the fallen leaves. "The missus is up?"

"Yes. That's Annabelle."

"She know about me?"

"Yes, I told her," Clint answered.

"All about me?"

Clint frowned, uncertain what the man meant. "What're you talking about?"

Aaron held out his hand and turned it over to display his pale, callused palm. Clint smiled. "Hell,

Aaron, she's from Georgia. She's used to colored folks.''

The tall, muscular man shook his head. "Mebbe that's good, mebbe that's bad.''

While he spoke with Aaron, Clint never took his narrowed gaze off Annabelle. "It'll be fine, Aaron,'' he said in a distracted manner. What the devil is she doing? he wondered as he watched her pull weeds from the ground about the grave. Then she rose and began hauling rocks, only to set them in a circle around the grave.

Aaron nodded his head. "She goin' to put 'em around her chile's restin' place, Mister Clint.''

Clint eased his hat off and wiped his brow with his forearm. "I hope that's all, Aaron.'' He couldn't rid himself of the apprehensive feeling in his gut. Annabelle always took things to the extreme. Why would she be different now?

He turned toward the wagon and climbed back up. "Well, she'll do whatever she wants, but we have a load of supplies to get under cover before the snow falls, the cabin wall to knock down and the flooring to fix.'' He tossed a sack of flour into Aaron's strong arms.

When the wagon was unloaded, Clint stretched his arms and rotated his shoulders. Lord, he was tired— and hungry enough to eat an unskinned bear. He looked over at Annabelle, sitting quietly beside the grave. She'd been like that for nearly an hour.

He walked up to her, wiping his face on a bandanna. "It's near noon, Annabelle. You hungry?''

She shook her head and reached out to pluck a small weed from the grave.

"You got to eat sometime.''

"I will," she said in a whisper.

"Aaron and me, we're nearly starving."

She looked up at him, then transferred her gaze to some far-off spot over his shoulder. "Well, best you go eat."

Clint clamped down on the fury rising in his chest. He had to shake her out of this lethargy. "Hell, woman, you're the wife." That ought to do it, he thought, and waited for her explosion.

She just gave him a small smile, turned her face away and looked off toward the mountains.

What in blazes is going on with her now? he wondered. Ordinarily she'd have jumped all over him for a remark like that. In frustration he ran a hand over his face. "All right, Annabelle," he said. "We'll do this for a while." He turned and strode away from her.

Annabelle found a sense of peace she had never experienced before. Over the past days, she felt closer to her child than when she'd carried him. Straightening one of the rocks she'd placed around the perimeter of the grave, she knew she would spend hours here each day.

For the first time in her life she had quiet time just to herself. No one made any demands on her. She glanced over to the cabin, where Clint and that man he'd hired scurried over the roof putting on a layer of heavy, oiled paper, and smiled. Bless Clint. He gave her this wonderful gift of time. Time to move from constant tears to this warm feeling of serenity.

Each morning she rose and fixed breakfast for him, listened patiently while he explained about their readiness for winter.

"We've put in all the feed we'll need unless we have the worst winter in history."

"That's fine, Clint. Best not to have to worry about the animals."

"We have plenty of flour, sugar, cornmeal and coffee. I think we won't starve. Meat's hanging in the barn."

She patted his hand. "You've done a fine job, Clint."

He stood quickly and grabbed his hat, shoved it on and strode to the door. He looked back at her. "Hell, Annabelle, wake up." The slamming door rattled the dishes. She surely didn't understand his problem. She had certainly been complimentary about the work he'd done.

Just this morning he and that man finally knocked out the south wall and she marveled at the additional space they had created. Yes, Clint was a good man, though a puzzling one. And she worried about where the money had come from for all the supplies.

She had run to her tin box to see if her last fifteen dollars was there, then chided herself. Her meager funds wouldn't begin to cover the expense of his labors. Besides, she didn't think Clint would steal from her. She had sensed his honor from the minute he climbed onto her wagon and threw the gold piece at Judaline. He might steal the money from a bank, but not from her. She tried not to believe he'd stolen the money at all.

Annabelle reached over and straightened one of the white rocks bordering the grave, then patted the earth back into place. She thought she'd plant flowers in the spring. Maybe petunias; they were so colorful and gay.

She brushed dirt from her hands. With a contented sigh, she leaned against the peach tree. Something cold whispered against her cheek. Snow. She tipped her head and let the first chill winter flakes fall and melt against her skin. Winter had arrived and she felt content.

On the roof Clint swore. He watched Annabelle sitting beneath the tree with a stupid smile on her face. Didn't she realize that it snowed right down on her? Was she going to sit there all the damn winter long? No, by God! He wouldn't allow it any longer.

"Aaron!"

From the other end of the roof, Aaron looked up from his work.

Clint edged himself over to the ladder. "Come on down with me. I want you to go into town and pick up some more things we'll need to carry us through the winter." He disappeared over the side and Aaron scrambled down behind him.

Aaron looked doubtful when they reached the ground. "I don't know, Mister Clint. I thought we had everything. You think they'll give..."

"Ben Fillmore at the general store knows you work for me, and we have credit at all the shops. No one will give you any trouble. Besides, I think Annabelle could use a few more things. We might be stuck at Christmas. Go by Mrs. Cummins's. She can add to the list...women things." He looked at the darkening sky. "You'd better hustle. This is the first snow. It won't last, but it's best you get a move on so you can get back before dark."

Aaron followed Clint into the cabin. "I don't know about those women things, Mister Clint. If you want to go, I'll stay with the missus."

Clint completed the list and handed it to Aaron. "No. I've got a few things to say to the missus."

Aaron smiled and his beautiful white teeth shone against his dark skin. "Gonna pull that lady of yours back to this here life?"

"That's exactly what I'm going to do," Clint said, and left the cabin. He approached Annabelle with a determined stride.

"Annabelle."

She smiled sweetly at him and brushed the dampness from her face.

"Come in the cabin with me."

She shook her head. "Later."

"I said now, Annabelle. It's snowing."

She looked around her and her smile widened. "Yes. Isn't it lovely?"

"It's wet and it's cold. Now get in the house."

"No, Clint," she said softly. "Soon."

Clint studied her. She was in some crazy place where she thought she was safe from the disappointments of the world. There is no place like that, he said to himself, and the sooner she realizes it the better. He didn't want to spend the winter with this Annabelle. He wanted the fighter back, the woman who didn't let anyone push her around. Shoot, he just plain wanted her.

He whirled and stalked off to the barn. He'd jerk her out of the false dreamworld she'd created and he'd do it fast. He grabbed a shovel and nearly ran back to her, swearing all the way.

She sat leaning back against the tree with her eyes closed and one hand resting on the grave. That did it! He drove the shovel into the ground next to where the baby lay. With a cold, frozen look on his face, Clint began to dig.

Annabelle stirred at the noise and opened her eyes. "Clint? I think it's too late for flowers. We can—"

He flashed her a look he felt sure spelled out his fury. She shut her mouth and her eyes snapped open to follow his every movement.

Clint dug with a kind of silent frenzy. He had to wake her from this mental slumber and get her in out of the cold and back into the real world. He hadn't realized until this day how much he missed the feisty woman who'd marched into that saloon and bullied him into marriage. The courageous woman who'd stitched him up and cared for him when he was so ill. The stubborn woman who worked beside him right up to the minute she'd had her child.

He wanted that woman back. He wanted the swearing, fighting woman who scurried around cooking and cleaning that meager cabin. He wanted... Shocked at the sudden tightening in his groin, he jerked to a stop and looked over at her.

Her eyes were wide with curiosity as she watched him. Her soft mouth was parted and her warm breath fogged as it left her body and met the cold air. Her wild, unruly red hair was beaded with melting snow and Clint realized fully how badly he wanted her. But not lost in some fuzzy dreamworld. He wanted her alive and kicking and by God she would be—and soon. He dug with greater purpose.

She didn't say a word, just sat and watched him dig. Anxiety tingled in her stomach. The look on his face scared her silly. He'd never looked at her like that before. She forced away all thoughts of what that look meant and, wary, just watched him.

Even through the layers of his warm clothing she knew how the strong muscles of his back worked. Supple and bronzed from the sun, he was relentlessly male. She swept the memory of his naked body from her mind and tried to recapture her newly won peace.

It certainly was gone now. Images of his naked body rushed into her mind. The strong, sleek look of him, bare and helpless. She nearly laughed at the thought of Clint helpless. She'd probably never see that again.

It seemed hours before he stopped digging. Finally, he climbed out of the large hole and threw down the shovel. The snow had stopped some time ago, but the air was bitingly cold. In spite of that, he'd removed his jacket and his shirt was wet with sweat from his labors. Even with dirt on his face and arms and in his hair he looked wonderful. He had even taken off his precious hat.

"Ask me, Annabelle. Ask me about the hole."

"Wh-what's it for?"

"Not what, Annabelle. Who."

She didn't want to ask the question, but she instinctively knew he wouldn't leave her alone until she did. "All right. Who, then?"

"You." The word fell from his lips with a cold finality, the look on his face fierce and determined.

"Me?" What in the world...? Anxiety pulsed in her stomach. For the first time she felt afraid of him.

"That's right, you. Climb in the hole, Annabelle. Climb in there right next to that child. Let the snow fall on you and bury you."

His words nearly stopped her heart and her breath caught in her chest. She felt adrift and frightened. What was he trying to tell her? "Wh-what, Clint?" She needed his kindness now. Not this cold hardness that shut her out. She wanted his understanding. This man who stood before her was the one who killed, the man who had shot LaMar in front of the church. A man who most likely stole the money that purchased the supplies that filled her barn. She held out her hand to him in a pleading gesture.

"Don't look to me for help, Annabelle. You want to sit out here all winter and mourn, you go right ahead." He pointed to the hole. "Crawl in there and turn your back on life. Feel sorry for all the bad things that have happened to you. *Don't make even the smallest effort to reach out for the future.*" He started to walk away from her, then turned back. "Go on, Annabelle, crawl in that grave. You're already dead."

If he had reached out and slapped her across her face she couldn't have felt more shocked. Even when he'd been delirious and in pain he hadn't spoken so cruelly to her. How could he do this? Didn't he realize how much she had needed her child? How her whole life had spun around her plans for the two of them? How empty this life was now, without her child to live for?

What did he want from her? To cook his supper; any fool could see to that. But to dig a grave for her over a missed meal?

Deep inside a small voice tiptoed into her thoughts. *Wake up, Annabelle. Take hold of your life again. Stop feeling sorry for yourself. Stop whining!* She shot to her feet and reached out her hands, for what she didn't know. She wasn't a whiner. What did these people want of her? She turned rapidly in circles groping for a firm foundation, something solid to stand on—to begin again.

Feelings of shame, hot and real, rushed through her. Clint was right. She couldn't spend the rest of her days dreaming of things she couldn't have. It *was* time to move on and figure out what came next. What place this man had in her life, if any at all. She fought to find her grief. It was there, but it inhabited a different part of her heart, her mind. Now there was room for life, her life—their life?

Clint had just filled the coffeepot and set it on the stove when Annabelle came bursting through the door, banging it against the wall. He wiped the smile off his face before he turned to her.

She stood before him, hands on her hips and fire in her eyes. She looked magnificent. Fury became her as no one he'd ever seen before. It brought a warm rose color to her cheeks and made her eyes sparkle like finely cut emeralds.

Her body had returned to its normal shape, and even in the too-large dress that shape was a temptation to a man. And this stormy, passionate woman certainly made him aware he was a man.

He decided they couldn't stand there all day and glare at each other. "You got something on your mind, Annabelle?"

Even though she suspected he had the right of things, she wanted to hit him for forcing her back to face the present—the future. Sock him so hard in the jaw he would carry a bruise for a month. "You bet I have, you miserable, unfeeling—"

"Watch your mouth, honey."

"Don't you call me honey." She walked right up to him and poked him in the chest. "And never mind about my mouth."

He stared at her mouth and the look in his eyes caused her to back off. "I was mourning my child out there when you came digging and throwing dirt around," she said, uncertain of her right to be angry.

"No you weren't. You were trying to create some protected place where bad things couldn't happen to you . . . where life couldn't happen to you."

Why couldn't he understand how she felt, that she wanted to be alone with her child? She pushed away those niggling voices in her brain, the ones that told her he did know. "That's not true," she lied. Something inside her didn't want to admit he knew her this well.

Clint knew exactly what she was doing. He took her by the arm and led her to the bed. He sat down and pulled her to his side. "Yeah. It is. Don't you know there isn't a safe place. We all have to have some of the good and some of the bad. That's what makes up life, Annabelle. Mourn your child. I'm not saying—"

From some deep well came her tears. She turned her face against his chest and cried; the sobs racked her body. "B-but all I've ever had is the bad." She burrowed even closer to his strength. He felt so warm and solid . . . and safe. She wiped her eyes on her skirt and glanced up at him.

He smiled that wonderful smile of his and she felt her heart jump around like a crazed jackrabbit. "It's true, you know.'' She hiccuped. ''I have lived a truly miserable life.''

''I suppose if we compared, we both could say we did pretty well in the misery department.'' He settled her more comfortably against his side. ''But think on it, honey. We have a chance, maybe, of something better right here.''

She leaned back to see him better. An uneasy feeling crept through her. ''What . . . what do you mean?''

''You picked good land here. The grass grows thick and rich. I suspect this little valley is sheltered from the very worst of the weather. Up behind the cabin on that rise is a fine place for a house.''

She jerked away from him and stood. Her tears evaporated like rain in the August heat and she shook like a leaf whipped about by the winter winds. He wanted to stay!

''Don't look as if I'd just proposed shooting your cow. I'm only suggesting that we try living together and see how it turns out.''

''No!''

''You just got through saying that you'd had a life of misery and pain. Why not try making a life here, with happiness as our goal?''

''You want to be my husband?''

''Hell, Annabelle, I *am* your husband.''

''You mean a *real* husband.''

She looked frantically at the bed, then back into Clint's eyes. The signs were there. The hot, wanting look. She shook her head. She didn't want him like that. She didn't want another man pawing at her, forcing a painful entrance into her unwelcoming body. Lord, she'd tried with LaMar, but it was awful.

"Don't look so damned disgusted. I won't be what you call a real husband until you want me to." He got up and paced around the room. "I mean to try and make something of the ranch. Build a herd of fine horses..."

Thank God he'd changed the subject, she thought. "All that takes money," she said, happy to leave the talk of the other. Yet the gnawing question returned: where did his money come from?

"I'll worry about the money."

"You going to rob a bank?" Sarcasm stoked her words.

"No, Annabelle," he said with great patience. "I don't need to rob a bank. I've got money."

"Where in the world would a gunfighter get money, unless he... You took it from someone else?" She could see his effort to control his temper.

"You finally getting around to asking me something personal?" He rose from the bed and went to stand by the sink.

"No. I don't want to know anything about you." Lord, lying was rapidly becoming a habit with her.

"Sure you do. Ask me. How many men have I killed? Go on, Annabelle. Ask me."

The grim expression on his face frightened her. She didn't want to know these things. She didn't want to think of him almost being killed. "How... how many?"

"Not nearly as many as you think. When you've got a reputation like mine, most men give you a wide berth. Only a few want to trade places with you."

It wasn't a complete answer, but it made sense to her. Still. "How much danger are ... ?" She couldn't bring herself to ask the question, to know if they could be killed.

"You've every right to ask questions of me, to know what we face." He stepped close and took her chin in his hand. "If I thought you were in danger, Annabelle, I'd go this minute. I left Docker a couple of states away, on a trail leading to Mexico. We'll be fine, I really believe that."

All of a sudden she felt so tired she wanted to sleep for a month. Talking with him just plain wore her out. Life with LaMar had certainly been simpler. She talked and LaMar ignored her. No chance of that with Clint.

She turned to get a tin cup off the hook and stopped still as a stone. Cabinets! There were brand-new wooden cabinets over the dry sink. Painted wooden cabinets. She whirled to face Clint. "Where did these come from?"

He looked puzzled. "What?"

"The cabinets." She turned back and ran her hands over the smooth, brightly painted surfaces.

"Do you mean to tell me this is the first time you've noticed them?"

"Yes," she said, feeling ashamed. For the first time she looked around the cabin and noted the changes. The addition gave them so much more room. A window with inside shutters to close out the dust and cold but let in the light had been installed. A simple but beautiful wooden chair sat near the window. She could make cushions for it out of rags and flour sacks.

For days she had been in and out of the cabin and hadn't really seen all the work Clint and the other man had done. She had been living in a hazy world of self-pity; she saw nothing but her own afflictions.

Clint walked over and opened the cabinet doors. "Aaron finished and hung them this morning. He brought the chair in last night. That man is really talented. With just a few tools, he coaxes miracles from wood."

Inside, the cupboards were three shelves high. Her tin dishes and supplies were neatly stacked. In her mind, she made a quick inventory of the ample stock of foodstuffs.

"Aaron and I have made several trips into town. We've got barrels of apples, sacks of flour and sugar. It's winter, Annabelle. We have to be ready. We'll go over everything and make sure we haven't missed something you'll need."

Here I go again, she thought as tears traced a path down her cheeks. "I'm sorry, Clint. I should have been helping you."

"Sit down." He gently pushed her down onto an apple box. "I'm sorry, too. It's fine you wanted and needed to grieve for your child. Any mother has to do that. I just feared you'd sit out there until you were covered with snow." He smiled, took her hand and gave it a squeeze.

"When I hurt myself, Ma would fix me up, pat my head and tell me to get on with my game. It's time to do just that, honey."

She sniffed, wiped her nose and considered all he'd said. She glanced over at the wonderful cabinets, the spacious room. She closed her eyes and a vision of acres of green grass and chestnut-colored horses filled her mind. And children. Suddenly, she didn't want it to be a game. She wanted it all to be real, wanted all those things he dreamed about.

She opened her eyes and looked into the brilliant blue of his. "That's what you want, isn't it? To get on with our lives, only together."

His intense gaze focused on her and he nodded.

She sighed and twisted the cloth of her faded blue skirt. Could she do this? Could she let another man fully into her life, into her body? She did want him to stay and continually fooled herself when she said she didn't. If he did stay, he'd want... Keeping her head bent, she asked him, "How soon...uh...do you want...oh!"

"That can wait. I think we need to see how long we can go without killing each other, don't you?"

When she looked up, he had *that* smile on his face. The one that made her heart flutter like a butterfly's wings. Desperately needing to change the subject, she said, "I don't hold with gunfighting."

"Believe it or not, neither do I."

His remark brought a dozen questions to her mind. Questions she wasn't ready to ask. "Aaron is the man who's been around here for the past couple of weeks?" she asked instead.

"Lord, you have been in a dreamworld. Yes, he is. However, he's been here over a month."

She felt stunned. A month? Shame drove purpose into her body and she stood up. "Well, I'd say it's high time I fixed us some supper. Where is this Aaron of yours?"

"I sent him into town for a few more supplies for the winter. One last wagonload."

"Seems to me you've got us stocked enough for two winters."

He took her hand and held it easy between his. She felt shy with him. They had seen each other in the worst of circumstances, and now she experienced a strangeness between them.

"I've got lumber and feed in the barn, along with barrels of potatoes and carrots. We've got meat hanging. It will keep fine out there in the cold. We should make it through in fine style."

She could see by the sparkle in his eyes he was excited and pleased. As well he should be, she thought. He'd been repairing the cabin and barn, caring for her, finding this Aaron person to help and stocking up for the winter. All this without any help from her. Any man would be rightly pleased.

"Thank you, Clint. I know I've been a trial to you."

Amusement curved his mouth. "Don't you know? That's part of your charm." He kissed the end of her nose, then left the cabin.

She touched the place he'd kissed and put her hand over her stomach to still those butterflies. Her finger drifted down to her lips and she wondered how it would feel if he kissed her there. Enough, she told herself. It's time to get to work.

When she heard the wagon return, she gave the rich soup broth a final stir. She drew in a deep breath. "Well, get yourself out there and apologize to that man." Shame came on her again as she thought that Aaron had been here a month and she hadn't even said as much as hello or thanked him for the addition to the cabin and for the chair and fine cabinets.

The men were unloading a crate of fresh vegetables onto the porch when she came out.

She stopped short at the sight of the huge man who stood before her, his arms loaded. "My Lord, you're colored!"

"For God's sake, Annabelle," Clint hollered at her.

Aaron gave her a wide, toothy smile. "Yes, missus. I sure am."

When Clint started toward her, a deep frown on his brow, she gestured him away. She stepped down from the porch and held out her hand to Aaron.

"Welcome to my—" she glanced over at Clint "—our home." She savored the stunned expression on Clint's face. However, it bothered her that he had expected less of her, but then they really didn't know much about each other. She could see she had some work to do—teaching her husband about Annabelle Strand.

She turned back to Aaron's dark face and twinkling eyes. "You are a sight. I haven't seen a black face since I left Georgia. Makes this place really feel like home."

"Thank you, missus. Makes me think of home, hearin' those soft Georgia sounds when you talk. I'm goin' to like it here just fine."

"I hope so. Lord knows, this place can use the muscles of two strong men." She glanced over at Clint and his returning gaze made the heat rise to her face. Why, she thought, he looks proud.

When his look turned to something more than pride, her blush deepened. She whirled and nearly ran into the cabin.

Annabelle shook out the damp dish towel and hung it on a hook near the new cabinets. Another little addition to make her life more comfortable. She sighed as she picked up the water bucket. That hadn't changed. She still had to haul water from the stream. She wondered how they would manage when snow made the trip impossible. She imagined the stream would freeze over anyway. She smiled and decided she would leave the problem to Clint. He would figure out something and it felt wonderful to know she wouldn't have to worry about it at all.

Having a real husband had advantages. All those difficult decisions she had dreaded making, he would make. She would have her say-so, but now there was a husband about to take on the hard jobs. Her husband.

The air felt cold and fresh against her skin. The first light snow had come and gone, leaving the oaks stripped of their bright fall foliage. The ripe grasses of summer were brown; only the tall pines rose green against the clear blue of the sky. Far in the distance, the jagged summits of the Sierra already wore a thick blanket of white.

She tried unsuccessfully to picture her land covered in snow. She was Georgia-born, and the image of vast snow-covered meadow wouldn't fill her mind. She swung the bucket and hurried to the stream.

A strong hand covered hers around the handle. "I'll go with you, Annabelle." Clint took the bucket from her.

Lost in her reverie, she hadn't heard his approach. Tamping down the need to tell him she could do it herself, she said, "Thank you." She tried to give him her sweetest smile.

"You don't fool me for a minute. You'd love to tell me to mind my own business, wouldn't you?" His grin rang little bells in her stomach and woke up those butterflies.

"Perhaps."

"Perhaps, hell." He put his arm around her and gave her a quick squeeze. "Believe me, I appreciate the effort you're making."

She sat on an ancient stump and watched him fill the bucket in the stream. He certainly was a fine-looking man. The muscles of his back worked under his shirt. She recalled the time right after their marriage when she'd looked at him and thought how useful his strength would be around the ranch. She had been right. *My husband.*

"I'd like to thank you, Clint, for all you've done around here. You and Aaron."

He set down the bucket and knelt in front of her. "You don't need to thank me. What I do, I do for both of us." He sat on the ground and pulled one leg up and wrapped his arms around it. "This place is like a dream come true for me." He glanced up at her.

"Since I was too young to have good sense, I've been . . . traveling—outrunning some fool who wanted to prove himself against every gunfighter out there." He made a wide sweep with his arm. "I'm lucky I've lasted this long. Gunmen have notoriously short lives."

"But that's in the past." She didn't want to think of the consequences of his dangerous life. He picked a long browned weed and stuck it in his mouth. She prayed he'd go on. Suddenly she wanted to know everything about him. "How did this . . . ?" She made a similar sweep with her arm to urge him on.

"Rescuing a damsel in distress." He pulled the weed from his mouth and with a disgusted gesture flung it to the ground.

She placed her hand on his arm. "Don't make a joke of it. Please tell me. I really want to know."

An uncertain expression on his face, he nodded and told her the story he'd told Aaron not so many days ago. She closed her eyes and listened, attempting to imagine him so young and untried. But the image of the man, strong and sure, dangerous, kept interfering. *Her husband.*

"You don't want to hear this, Annabelle."

She scooted down beside him. "Yes! Yes I do. Please?"

He shrugged. When he finished, he sat up and rubbed both hands over his face. A cold, vacant look came over him and Annabelle shivered.

"Everyone stood helpless. I'll never forget the lump of fear in my gut. The hell of it was, Annabelle, along with the fear was a terrible exhilaration." He stood up and walked to the edge of the stream, keeping his back turned toward her.

"I yelled at him to let the woman go. He shoved her away and turned on me."

"You shot him." Her voice trembled.

Clint jerked around, anger in his every movement. "Hell yes, I shot him. Once I'd challenged him he would have shot me." He paced along the streambed, then turned back to her. "He would have shot me."

She scrambled to her feet and went to him. Grabbing his hand, she held it to her breast. "I know. Of course he would have. You had to shoot. You saved that woman." She felt frantic inside that he might think she hated him for what he had done. "That's all in the past. You said we'd start over." She was half-appalled at her own words.

He looked down at her and his expression softened. "Is that what you want, Annabelle?"

She nodded, not sure at all it was what she wanted. But she couldn't seem to help herself. *He is my husband.* Her mind kept tossing those words to the surface, forcing her to concede the fact. To accept him as her mate. Dear me, she thought, where did that thought come from? Her mate.

"God knows," he said, "it's what I want." He gripped the bucket and then her hand. "Come on, I feel snow in the air and we have a day's work before us to get prepared for it."

She marched along beside him, conscious only of the warm feel of his hand around hers and the feeling of safety that surrounded her when he was near. *This man is my husband, and I am his wife.* She tried not to think what all those words really meant.

Chapter Nine

Annabelle stood on the porch and wrapped the heavy bright green shawl, a gift from Clint, over her shoulders. Winter had come with a vengeance and she welcomed the warmth of the soft wool.

She watched Clint and Aaron dig a wide path to the barn. During the night the snow had fallen steadily until a good foot covered the ground.

"Why are you making it so wide?" she hollered.

"Go inside where it's warm," Clint yelled back.

He always answered her questions when he was ready, not when she wanted an answer. Annabelle smiled. She realized she was becoming aware of his habits and sometimes understood the reasons for them. A man who had lived alone for so many years didn't explain himself much. When she asked questions, sometimes he looked so surprised that he even had to answer her, that she even cared or needed to know what he thought.

She swore he'd been avoiding her—not that it was easy to do in that small cabin. Each night as she lay beside him, she waited for him to fall out of the bed. He hung on the edge for dear life. If she touched him he jerked away as if he'd been burned. And lately she found she wanted to touch him a lot.

She wanted to snuggle against his warm body, to feel him spooned around her in the middle of the night. She loved the feel of the soft hair on his body. Often, she'd wait until he slept soundly, then ease her head onto his hard, muscled chest and rub her nose in the heavy pelt of gold.

But more often than not, each time she moved to get close to him he'd get up and make the cold walk to the privy. At least that's what he said he did. She suspected he just wanted to get away from her.

His actions belied his talk of wanting to be a "real" husband to her. Now that she'd about decided to give it a try, he ran away like a skittish colt. The older she got, the more men confused her. Older but wiser wasn't proving itself by her.

"Fine, Clint Strand," she murmured. "You just stay away from me and I'll stay away from you." Easier said than done, she speculated. Besides, she didn't want him to stay away from her anymore. She suspected being a real wife to him would be a whole different experience from the one she'd had with LaMar. The way Clint made her feel, all hot and shaky, certainly was different. Enough, Annabelle she scolded. Keep your mind off feelings you aren't sure of yet and sure don't understand—not completely, at least.

The men had only a few feet to go and the way to the barn would be clear. They'd feed the animals, then head for the warmth of the cabin. She'd better put on a fresh pot of coffee. They drank so much, it probably wouldn't even last the winter. She wondered why she felt so cranky and went inside out of the cold.

When she heard their stamping feet ridding their boots of snow, Annabelle took down cups and filled them with the rich-smelling brew.

When they entered the room, cold air swept in and she shivered. "Hurry and close that door."

Aaron grinned. "Can't get in without openin' it, missus." He hung his heavy jacket on a hook.

She smiled back at him. "Sit down, Aaron, and have some fresh coffee." She placed the cup before him.

"Do I get some of that, Annabelle?" Clint asked.

She looked at his strong, lean body and felt the rise of heat in hers. This reaction to him caused her no end of confusion and misgivings. "Is there much around here you don't get, Clint Strand?" She wished she knew why she felt so miserable. *You are fooling yourself again, Annabelle Strand,* sang that pesky voice in her head.

Clint raised an eyebrow and looked at her through narrowed lids. "Couple of things."

"Well, I'm sure I can't think of anything you want you don't get." The minute the words passed her lips, the heated feeling in her chest spread.

Clint continued to gaze at her speculatively and Aaron cleared his throat.

"I think I might give that good pine out in the barn a try at makin' a table." He laid his large hands on the old table and wobbled it back and forth.

Annabelle's heart beat frantically in her chest and she threw a desperate look at Aaron. "It's too cold in the barn. You need to stay indoors." She knew one thing absolutely. She didn't want to stay alone all day in the cabin with Clint. Not with *that* look in his eye.

"Now, missus, that barn is snug as can be now. I got that nice fat-bellied stove to keep me and the animals warm. No need at all for me to stick around in here." He glanced at Clint. "That right, Mister Clint?"

She could see Clint's efforts at controlling an arrogant male smile.

Clint nodded. "Right," he said with a smug look on his face.

Men! she thought. They will stick together always against a woman. Well, we will see, Mr. Smart. We will see. She would show him she could resist his efforts to charm her. She wasn't about to be led on by a handsome man who thought he could crook a finger at her and she'd fall at his feet.

She bustled around their sprawled legs preparing the midday meal while they made plans for moving the privy in the spring. She poured water off the beans she'd put to soak last night. Covering them with fresh water, she set the pot on the stove and began chopping onions and salt pork. There were plenty of apples for a pie and cornmeal for bread.

When Aaron left the cabin, she didn't look up. She was so engrossed in her work that she didn't hear Clint come to stand behind her. She felt his warm breath on her neck and nearly jumped out of her shoes.

She spun around and faced him, the knife between them. "Clint Strand . . . what do you want?"

He tucked a stray lock of her hair into the untidy bun at the crown of her head. "Why, not a thing, honey. I thought maybe I could help you." With a gentle touch he brushed his finger along her cheek and straightened the collar of her dress.

His tender ministrations had her trembling and she firmly reminded herself she was immune to his attentions. She worked the knife up and brandished it under his nose. "I don't need your help."

He crowded closer. "I think you do, Annabelle." He grinned that cocky grin.

She could hardly draw a breath. She touched the side of his face with the knife; she wouldn't hurt him and he knew it. "Back away from me." She didn't believe for a minute he'd let her get away with much more of this.

He reached up and plucked the knife from her hand and tossed it onto the sink board. "I thought you didn't like violence, Annabelle."

"I said I didn't like guns." She felt the edge of the counter dig into her back as he pressed against her. She wondered if she felt as hot against him as he did against her. Or if unhinged butterflies soared in his stomach as they did in hers. Or if the bones had suddenly left his knees and he feared he'd fall in a heap on the floor, as she did.

"I don't think you want me to back off, honey. I think you want to feel me against you just as bad as I want to feel you." He moved his hips in a downright suggestive motion and she felt the hard ridge of his manhood pressed against her belly. Some vain part of her feminine pride gloried in the evidence that he desired her so. But old, more believable fears surfaced, drove strength into her arms, and she shoved at him. He moved only enough to separate the lower part of their bodies.

He caught her by the shoulders. "Hold still, Annabelle." When she struggled, he slammed her against his chest and held her trembling chin in his strong hand. "I mean it, hold still!"

"What are you going to do?" Even to her, her voice sounded weak and fearful.

"What I'm *not* going to do is hurt you." He brushed her ever-wild hair from her face. "Do you trust me enough to believe me?"

Every instinct she possessed assured her he wouldn't hurt her or force her into...anything. He'd never raised a threatening hand to her or said vicious words just to make her feel bad. "Yes, but you make me feel such strange, new things."

"Good." He smiled and tipped his head to one side. "I'm going to kiss you, sweetheart."

She shook her head wildly. If he kissed her she'd faint, she just knew it. "No," she whispered. *Yes!*

"Oh, yes. That's all, just a kiss. All right?"

Oh my, did she ever feel uncertain about this. Just a kiss. A kiss would change everything between them. Nothing would be the same. Just as she was getting used to... He brushed his lips over hers. A little fuzzy feeling began at her toes.

Barely touching her, he ran his warm, wet tongue slowly around the outline of her lips. The fuzzy turned to heat and ran up inside her thighs to settle low in her belly.

He moved his lips back and forth and opened hers to him. A hot sensation shot up to her breasts and her nipples felt feverish, swollen and hard. She wondered where her breath had gone.

His arms moved around her and he pulled her tight against him and took her mouth fully with his. A lustful wildfire spread through her body and replaced her blood. A burning, throbbing sensation surged between her legs and she burrowed into him, trying to find relief.

He eased away from her and grinned. "Settle down, honey. We're going to take this a little further." His hand moved over her bottom and he lifted her against him. "Feel that, Annabelle. That's how badly I want you."

He was aroused and huge against her. She felt herself respond totally; a warm, liquid excitement fired the flesh between her thighs and scared the very devil out of her. "Put me down." She looked into his blistering gaze. "Please," she wailed.

"In a minute." He seized her mouth in a kiss that stripped her last defenses. She felt exposed clear to her middle. She wanted him to carry her to that bed and possess her completely. When he stopped and stepped back she swayed, unsure she could stand. He reached out to steady her.

He watched the pout form on her pink lips and the confusion build in her eyes. His satisfaction soared. She responded just as he'd hoped, more than he'd hoped. For a minute there, she'd been out of control, and that's exactly how he wanted her. Hot and ready. She wasn't quite there, but she would be soon. He wouldn't take her until he felt damn sure she wanted it.

"Why?" she asked. "Why did you do that?"

He thought carefully before he answered. If she knew how long he'd wanted to kiss her, to make love with her, she'd be so mad he wouldn't get close to her for a week. "It came over me today, Annabelle, that kissing is what we both need." He smiled. "A lot more than kissing, I think."

She tried to sort out her feelings. LaMar's kisses had never done this to her. Not that they kissed all that often. Kissing was not one of his strong points. But Clint's kisses unraveled her like an old sweater caught on a hook. Be honest, Annabelle, she told herself. You like his kisses and you want more of them.

She closed her eyes and tipped her face up for another kiss.

Clint grinned and placed an arm on either side of her, trapping her between them. He dropped a brief, soft kiss on her slightly swollen lips, then stood straight.

Her eyes flew open. "That's all?"

He laughed—a smug male sound—and strode to the door. He grabbed his hat and shoved it onto his head. "For now," he said, and left her in the middle of the room, fury building.

Supper was a silent meal.

Annabelle still felt angry and unsettled. She silently rebuked herself for her total surrender in Clint's arms this morning. She pushed her food around her plate and stared out the new window at the darkening sky.

Clint, content with the work done during the day and more than satisfied with his efforts with Annabelle, ate heartily and planned the next storming of her defenses. He knew she wanted him, so he held no guilty feelings at all.

Aaron knew he'd call it an early evening and get out of the range of the fire to come. He shoved down his food so he could leave.

He rose and took his plate to the dry sink. "I'm thinkin' to turn in, been a hard day."

Annabelle left her seat and reached for the coffee-pot. She didn't want him to leave. She wasn't ready to be alone with Clint again so soon. "Stay for another cup, Aaron."

"No thank you, missus. I'll just mosey out to my bed." He ducked his head and smiled.

Annabelle jammed her fists into her slender waist. "Well, if you 'mosey' out of here as fast as you ate, you'll be going at a dead run."

His shoulders shook with suppressed laughter when he reached the door. "Yep, missus, I 'spect you're right." With a smile and a knowing nod in Clint's direction he left them alone.

Clint piled his cup and silver onto his plate and moved to the sink. He leaned against it and crossed his arms over his chest. "You want to play some cards, Annabelle?"

At his words, she nearly jumped from her skin. She'd been expecting him to take her right to the bed and the thought scared her silly. Suddenly she knew why. She feared to be a complete failure at being a wife. She was terrified of disappointing him. She certainly hadn't built any great fires in LaMar.

She hustled to the cabinet and took out the deck of cards, thoroughly relieved for the diversion he offered. Clint had been promising to teach her a new game. She'd quickly grown bored with Old Maid; a stupid game in her mind.

"Teach me to play poker." That would take longer, she figured.

"Poker's a man's game."

"Well, I want to learn it anyhow."

He plucked the deck from her hands. "Fine with me. Sit down and relax, Annabelle. I'm not going to do anything with you but play cards." He grinned and pulled out an apple box and spread the deck out on the table.

Relieved and at the same time strangely disgruntled, she sat down and watched him arrange poker hands on the table.

"This is the value of the cards. The ace is high, the king is next, then the queen—"

"Of course," Annabelle interrupted.

Clint looked up, a puzzled expression on his face. "Of course what?"

"The king is worth more than the queen."

Clint laughed out loud. "Annabelle, you can't change a card game that's years old just to suit your feminine fancies."

"Well, somebody ought to. Isn't there a game where a woman is highest?"

"Yep. Old Maid." He laughed all the harder.

Annabelle jumped up and scattered the cards. She knew she acted like a spoiled child, but she couldn't seem to help herself. For some mysterious reason he made her furious. "You men. Can't even let a woman be first in cards unless she's in a position to...do you in."

Clint left his apple box and pulled her into his arms. "Honey, women have been doing men in for centuries." He hugged her tight. "Don't you know that most of the time it's the very best thing that happens to a man?"

She nuzzled his chest and inhaled the clean, male smell of him. She loved the feel of his arms around her.

It made her feel womanly and safe. She tipped her head back and looked up into his rugged, handsome face. "I'm sorry, Clint. I'm acting like a . . . witch."

He nodded his agreement and she brought up her fist and hit him in the ribs.

Laughing, he hugged her again and gently pushed her away. "It's okay, honey. I understand."

"How can you when I don't?" she cried. What the devil was the matter with her? She had never been so unsettled in her life.

He turned her around and gave her a gentle shove toward the bed. "Why don't you turn in? I'll tend the stove and have another cup of coffee."

She looked over her shoulder at him. Longing filled her heart and she wished she knew exactly for what. *You know, Annabelle Strand, you just don't want to admit it to him, let alone yourself.* How she hated that small voice inside her head that pointed out all the times she tried to lie or fool herself.

Later, when Clint climbed into bed, he thought she slept and he breathed a relieved sigh. He figured he had one more night in this bed before he had her ready and willing to be his wife in deed as well as fact.

"Clint?"

Hell, he felt so worn-out from work and sexual frustration all he wanted was to sleep and forget what he really wanted. Of course, Annabelle would sink those plans. "What?"

"Why did you dig the path so wide?"

Where did she come up with these questions? he wondered. "If we dig it too narrow it will fill with snow and we won't be able to find it. This way it will be a deep indentation in the snow and easy to follow when we have to shovel again.''

"Oh."

He felt her turn toward the wall. Lord, he hoped she'd go to sleep. Lying next to her each night was fast becoming, physically, a miserable situation. It usually took him a long time to find the peace sleep brought. Half the time he had to leave the warm comfort of the bed and pace outside in the cold air—an unhappy solution to his problem. He wanted to bury his "problem" deep inside her body.

"Clint?"

Oh God, he groaned silently. "What, Annabelle?"

"What's the matter with me?"

He laughed out loud at their crazy predicament. He reached for her and pulled her close, guaranteeing him a walk in the winter night. "Go to sleep, Annabelle. There's nothing wrong with you." He wished he could say the same thing about himself.

She snuggled against his chest and felt the wonderful safe feeling wash over her. Her mind and body relaxed and freed thoughts held captive in some guarded place in her brain.

He would never hurt her.

His presence made her feel secure against the world.

She trusted him.

He made her want to laugh.

She wanted to make a life here, with him.

She loved him.

She smiled and let sleep take her body.

He awoke to find his tempting little wife sprawled over him. Her white flannel gown was rucked up over her hip and she was plastered to him like library paste—one leg over his most needy part.

He knew he should wait until evening to give her the privacy of darkness for their first time, but he couldn't help himself. He reached down and ran his hand over her bare bottom.

Warm. Round and soft as peach skin. Lord! He had to stop this. Under her leg he felt himself growing hard as a stone. She shifted a little and brought that part of her he wanted above all things right next to his hip. Clint smiled. Wiry and full of life, just like the hair on her head.

He couldn't stand it any longer. He rose from the bed, looked down at himself and grimaced. "Well, what am I supposed to do with you?" he muttered. He ignored the surging need of his body and left the bed. He moved to the woodpile and shoved some small logs into the stove, then, freezing, he decided to climb back in beside Annabelle, just until the room warmed.

Her eyes snapped open. Memories of her thoughts just before she went to sleep last night rushed to her mind. She loved him and she no longer wanted to avoid being his true wife. "Are we going to talk about it now?" she asked, and put a hand over her mouth to hide a sleepy yawn.

"We aren't going to talk about a damn thing. We're going to do."

Her eyes grew wider and she frantically looked around the room.

"There's nobody here but you and me, Annabelle."

She gazed at him silently, then smiled. "Good."

"Why, you little baggage, you've been spoofing with me. You're as eager as I am."

Her blush obscured her freckles and she tucked her face into his neck. "I figured it out last night and decided it might be different this time." She had figured out a lot more than that but also decided he might not be ready to hear about it.

He raised her face and stroked her cheek. "I'll do my best to make it good for you, honey." He placed a fierce kiss on her parted lips and held her tight against him.

When the kiss ended, she tipped back her head and grinned. "I take it we aren't going to ease into this nice and slow." Her heart felt so full of love for him she feared it might burst.

"Hell, Annabelle, I can't even think when you're in my arms. I'm sorry."

She punched him in the belly. "I don't want an apology, Clint Strand. I want you to make love to me. I want something from you I've never had."

He felt confused and puzzled. "What do you mean, sweetheart?" He watched tears form in her eyes.

"I don't know. I just know I've never had it."

Clint smiled and hugged her close. Now he understood what she meant when she said she had strange new feelings. He eased her out of his arms and back onto the pillow. He stroked her out of her gown and marveled at the hundreds of freckles on her skin. He wanted to kiss every one.

She looked so soft and womanly. She was beautifully made. Her disorderly hair lay in a riot of curls around her face, her lovely freckled face. She was a complex mixture of temper and sensuality, of tenderness and stubbornness, sweet temptress and cool mountain lily. Now, in the chilly dawn light, he wanted everything she had to give. Most of all he wanted her heart.

"Can we start now?"

Clint nearly doubled over with laughter. "Hush up, Annabelle. We've already started."

"All you're doing is looking at me."

"My God, that is a pleasure to savor." He ran his hands lightly over her shoulders and down her arms. "That is, next to touching you."

She loved his touch. The feel of his hands on her bare skin made her shiver with delight.

"Are you cold, sweetheart?"

She shook her head, unable to find the simplest of words. This is what the touch of the man you love did—made you speechless.

There was a fineness and strength to her, Clint thought. Her neck was long and strong, easing into wide but delicate shoulders. Her arms were slender, yet firm from hard work. Her hands were capable-looking but at the same time feminine.

He caressed a path down her chest. "You have beautiful breasts, Annabelle. Full, round and pointing those pretty nipples right at me. And your waist." He stroked its indentation and brought his hands over and under her hips to her backside. "Nice, very nice. I do like a well-shaped bottom."

She pulled away, jealousy rising unexpectedly at the idea of him with another woman. "Never mind about how and where your preference in femininity came about."

"Why, sugar—" he grinned "—I just decided about bottoms." He glanced up and caught her smile.

"I choose to believe you." She grinned back at him.

The early sunlight shifted and caught the fiery curls covering the secret he most wanted to discover; gently, he ran his finger through them and felt his blood complete its race to his groin. She did set a fire in him.

"God, honey," Clint said, "this is going to be tough. I want to take it slow and easy, but I'm damn near crazy with wanting you." He slipped a finger into the heat of her and relished her readiness.

"I want you like that, too. Do you suppose we could sort of go fast now and maybe slow down later?" The sensation of his touch inside her drove her to the very edge of...something.

He laughed softly in her ear. Would she ever stop surprising him? He hoped not. "I think you've found the solution to a very critical problem." Never in his life had he been this full and hard, this needy for a woman.

Clint eased her legs apart and settled himself between them. He touched her with the head of his throbbing manhood and felt her hot and wet for him. Thank God! "Sweetheart, this is going to be short and I hope sweet."

"That's...fine." Her eyes were wide and her breath shallow and fast as he probed and found home.

She made sweet little murmurs as he slowly came into her body. Sweet heaven, that's what she felt like, tight and heated around him. "Am I hurting you, honey?"

She shook her head. "No," she whispered.

He pulled back a little. "You sure?" God, he didn't want to cause her pain, but he sure didn't want to stop, either.

She ran her hands down his back and cupped his buttocks, pressing him closer. "I said no."

"Your voice sounded so weak I—"

She raised her hips and took him fully into her. "I'm near speechless with pleasure, you fool man."

Clint laughed until he fell on her. Annabelle speechless was something he'd never figured to live long enough to witness. "Well, darlin', I'm about to get a week's peace and quiet." He lifted his weight from her and smoothed his stroke.

Annabelle lay quietly under his sprawled, sleeping body and figured he'd more than bought his seven days of peace and quiet. He'd given her a pleasure she'd never known or even imagined. She caressed his damp back over and over, loving the feel of his hard muscles and warm skin.

How could he sleep? She felt the fires of love surging through her body. Between her legs, where he was still joined with her, those fires gathered again and spread to the very surface of her skin. Sleep? Not for a second. She wanted to relive and savor every second of their lovemaking.

Her feminine instinct told her what they had found minutes ago was a rare thing indeed. This wasn't the hurtful, dry coupling done under the covers. Making love, that's what it was. Beautiful, wonderful lovemaking. She giggled. And fun. Lord, it was fun.

Clint stirred and she felt the sudden swelling of him within her. She even loved that part of him; his whole body gave her pleasure. As if reading her thoughts, he swelled even more. She smiled. This is a greedy man, she thought, and happiness filled her, for she discovered she was a greedy woman. She wiggled. When he opened one eye and glared at her, she laughed.

"Don't you glare at me, Clint Strand."

"You woke me up," he grumbled.

"Not me. It's that doo-dad of yours."

Both eyes snapped open. "Doo-dad?"

She nodded and her smile widened. He looked so insulted at this disrespectful naming of his manhood.

Clint raised himself up on one elbow and peeked under the covers as if to assure himself he was as he remembered. He frowned at Annabelle. "I'll have you know, woman, that doo-dad, as you irreverently call it, is a man's most treasured possession."

She laughed boisterously and pushed him over on his back. "I don't doubt it for a minute." She ran her hand down his belly to his treasured possession and gave it a little pat. She marveled at her playful feelings. Clint made it so easy for her to enjoy making love. There was nothing shameful or painful, only wonderful.

He grabbed her hand and held it over him. "Are you ready to pay the price for your lustful actions, woman?" Clint's wicked grin spread over his face.

Love for him filled her so suddenly she couldn't speak. His face, so handsome and flushed with desire for her, made her need for him so intense she wanted to shout her feelings from the very tops of the Sierra. "Oh, yes. Make love to me. Love me." Fearful her words revealed too much, she reached for a lighter tone. "That is, if you're not too tired."

Clint slowly shook his head against the pillow. "Not for days, my sweet."

The heated look in his eyes told her they wouldn't be out of bed anytime soon.

Annabelle lay sleeping on him, her arms tight around his neck. Clint smiled. She's still hanging on, he thought, remembering her wild ride atop him. Her soft breasts pressed against his chest and her slender legs fell on either side of his hips.

Her response to their lovemaking astounded him. He had felt all along she would be passionate. With her spirit for life, he'd been certain. But this morning had truly been a revelation. So had his own reaction. He knew now his feelings went much deeper than he suspected. He had wanted her heart. Now he wanted her to want his.

He wouldn't press her for the pledge he needed from her. Waiting wouldn't be easy, but he felt sure she wasn't ready to face his need for her love. For now he would settle for passion. Thoughts of his passionate Annabelle caused havoc in his body. His rapidly rising "doo-dad"—he loved her teasing name—was perfectly placed between her legs.

He shifted her a little. With his fingers he parted her sweet folds and gently, slowly, inserted himself inside her. God, how good she felt around him.

"Hmm. Did you really think to sneak around without me knowing?" She rubbed her nose in the dark gold hair on his chest. He smelled wonderful. Hot and musky. Manly.

He pulled her arms from around his neck and eased her up. "Slide down on me, honey."

She did as he asked. "My." She sighed the word and began to move on him. "My, my."

"Is that all you've got to say?" He knew he was grinning like some crazy man. A very satisfied crazy man.

"Mmm-hmm." Her eyes closed and a tiny smile tipped the corners of her mouth.

Clint grabbed her hips and arched up to meet her. "Hang on, sweet. You're about to get the ride of your life."

Annabelle awoke to find Clint tracing gentle circles around her nipples with the tip of his tongue. She yawned and looked at her pleased husband. *Now he really is my husband and I am truly his wife.* "Seems you have yourself a new toy."

He laughed and nuzzled her breasts. His breath felt warm against her skin and she thought she never wanted to leave this bed or this wonderful man.

"You're soft as peach skin," he murmured, and kissed her pebbled nipples, brushing his mustache over their tender surface.

She ran her fingers through his thick hair and turned his face to hers. "If I don't eat soon, all you'll have in this bed is a bag of bones."

He hugged her and whispered into the dampness of her neck. "Ah, but what a lovely bag of bones."

She scooted from beneath him and left the bed. "Get up. It's time to feed the animals and...oh my God! Aaron!" She hastily pulled on her nightgown and ran to the window. "Clint! It must have snowed all night. The ground is covered." She turned and watched him pull his trousers over his bare body. Desire for him rose so rapidly she lost her breath.

He glanced up and that satisfied male grin turned up the corners of his mouth. "You keep looking at me all needy and hungry like that, honey, and I'll have you right back in that bed."

She felt her blush to the roots of her hair. She wanted to swat him a good one. "I think you need a rest, and pity poor Aaron. He's been out there all morning with no breakfast and practically snowed in."

Clint moved to stand in front of her. He touched her cheek. "Aaron's fine." He bent and brushed his lips across hers in a sweet kiss. "So am I, Annabelle. This has been a *memorable* morning."

She leaned against his powerful body and had to fight the need to drag him back to bed. "For me, too."

"You fix breakfast and I'll shovel my way out to Aaron and bring him in to eat."

"Oh, dear." She just knew Aaron would know how they'd spent the morning.

Clint placed a quick, parting kiss on her lips. "Aaron is a gentleman." Clint put on his heavy jacket and jammed his hat on his head. "Besides, any man would envy me my morning."

Annabelle threw a cup at him. He ducked, grinned and raced out the door.

She dressed quickly, then broke eggs into a bowl for pancakes. Cold weather like this, men needed good food that stuck to their bellies. She glanced out the window at Clint shoveling his way to the barn.

Annabelle hummed as she measured flour into the bowl. They had a new life together, she thought. The pain and fear behind them now, they deserved to be happy. Clint would put his guns away and she would make a home for him. With this remarkable husband of hers, she felt safe for the first time in her life.

Chapter Ten

"I don't understand!" she cried.

"Sure you do, honey. Let's go over it again." Clint wrote the figures on the slate. "Here, try again." He gave her an encouraging smile and handed her the chalk.

"I don't understand. If two times two is four and two plus two is four... well, it's all the same."

Her lower lip stuck out in the sweetest little pout. It was all he could do to keep from nibbling on it. He shuddered as a wave of pure need swept through his body.

Hell, he had to concentrate on her lessons. Outside a storm raged. He couldn't leave the cabin and he couldn't keep her in bed day and night. Although the idea did have a certain appeal.

"Now look here, Annabelle, you're not even trying." He got up and brought a jar of white beans to the table. He had to find the means to help her. He made three groups of beans with three beans in each pile. He pointed to the piles. "Now how many do I have?"

"Beans or bunches?"

"Either one." He suppressed his smile.

She looked at the beans and moved her lips. He knew how badly she wanted to understand. He'd never seen a woman so eager to learn.

She raised her eyes and they held the sparkle they always did when she'd figured out something. "I think I see." She pointed at the beans.

"Three plus three is six, but three plus three plus three is nine. So, three times three . . . multiplying gives me a shortcut to the nine."

He grabbed her off the apple box, pulled her onto his lap and nuzzled her neck. "That's right. Now all you have to do is memorize those tables I wrote out for you."

"Good grief, that will be a chore. Besides, with you kissing my neck I can't think much about figuring what numbers do." She tipped her head to give him an easier time of it.

Clint rose with her in his arms and flopped down onto the bed. "I suppose if I have to pick out the most important of the two, I'll kiss your neck."

Annabelle shifted in his arms and looked into his eyes. She ran her fingers through the heavy waves of his hair and smoothed his mustache. Her look turned serious.

"What's on your mind, honey?" Clint asked.

"I have to tell you, these past few weeks have been the happiest of my life." She laid her head on his chest and let out a contented sigh.

"Me, too." He hugged her and realized the truth of his statement. With her he experienced a softness in his life he'd never known before; never suspected existed. Only memories of his childhood came even close to the happiness he felt with her. "Back when I was a kid. It was a good time then. But this is the best."

She sighed again. "You're a lucky man. I don't believe I could ever say I was a child."

He tipped up her chin and saw the sad expression in her eyes. "You mean living with the Bodines?"

She nodded. "They took a great pleasure in making my life miserable."

"What do you mean?" She had never spoken much about her childhood and he suddenly needed to know.

"I don't want to talk about it. I just want to talk about now. How happy I am, how safe I feel in your arms."

His heart expanded with his love for her. "Talk to me, honey. It's important for us to know each other."

"I guess so. It's just that it was so..."

"Awful?"

She released a long, trembling sigh. "Awful was the good days."

"Were the Bodines that bad?"

"They were poor white trash and considered me even lower." Annabelle's mind turned back to her earliest memories of work and beatings and the words began to pour out. She felt as if she were purging her soul.

"My momma died when I was born. They took her in when our home burnt down and all the slaves left. I suppose they hoped some relative of mine would eventually come along and pay them for my care." She rolled onto her back and stared at the ceiling. "But nobody ever did. After the war, there just wasn't any of my family left." She reached out and took Clint's hand and pressed it to her cheek.

"They had nine children, all boys. Mean bullies, liars and thieves, all of them. I swear their main purpose in life was to cause me misery." A sob broke from her lips. "They thought it a fine joke that the daughter of the plantation owner was being raised by croppers."

Clint gathered her into his arms. "Go on, honey."

She told him of her life in the shadow of her family's burnt-out plantation. How the Bodines laughed at her comedown in life. Of the drudgery of her existence.

Throughout her story, Clint's solid presence comforted and soothed her. Finally she told him of the Bodines' last assault on her. How LaMar took her away with golden promises. Clint held her tight and whispered soft words and stroked her back. She had never felt so close to another person. She had never felt so much love—even if he hadn't said the words—or felt so safe.

After breakfast on Christmas Eve, Annabelle began her preparation of the feast she planned for that afternoon.

She rubbed the venison roast with mustard seed and wild garlic. The last big pumpkin was brought up from the cool space below the floor and cut into pieces, then put to cooking for the pies. She made a salad of apples, walnuts and raisins. The smell of sugar cookies filled the air and carrots and potatoes rested in pots, ready for the stove.

Covered with flour, she was rolling out piecrust when Clint and Aaron hauled in a small tree they had cut near the edge of the clearing.

"Where do you want this, honey?"

She stood with a hand over her heart. "I've never had a Christmas tree." She dabbed her eyes with her apron and pointed to her wonderful new window. "Over there."

Aaron secured the tree to the stand he'd made. "There, missus. It looks just fine." His pleased grin spread over his face.

Clint handed her a package wrapped in an old flour sack and tied with twine. "Here, sweetheart. This will finish things up, just like town folks."

She sat down and carefully unwrapped the package. She gasped in delight. Ornaments. At least twelve. All made of wood and gaily painted.

"Oh, they are beautiful."

Clint knelt beside her. "Aaron made them. See this one?" He held up a wooden figure. "A toy soldier. I just described one I'd had as a kid and Aaron made it right off. I never saw anything like it." The small soldier hung from Clint's finger by a thin piece of twine.

Annabelle held up a Saint Nicholas, a church, brightly colored circles and an overfed bear. She looked at these two wonderful men who had come into her life and knew a peace she'd never felt before. Her luck had changed. "I thank you from the very center of my heart for this lovely tree and these beautiful ornaments. This must be the best Christmas ever."

Aaron grinned, then dug inside his jacket. "Here, missus. For the top of the tree."

In his huge hand rested a delicately carved and painted angel.

Clint and Aaron wore silly, pleased smiles. They looked like two small boys who had made a wonderful surprise. They had. Tears rolled down her cheeks and she covered her face with her hands and sobbed.

Clint pulled her into his arms. "Hell, Annabelle. We wanted to make you happy." The puzzled expression on his face matched the one on Aaron's.

"You—you . . . did . . . have."

"Why you cryin', missus?"

"Be-because I . . . am so ha-happy."

Clint held her away and wiped her tears with the apron. "Shoot, honey. You don't sound happy."

She struggled out of his arms and punched his chest. "Don't you tell me if I'm happy or not. Don't you think I know?" She flung her arms around him and hugged him tight.

This woman is a wonder, he thought. Like lightning, she goes from surprise to tears to anger to love. What a delightful bit of femininity. He lowered his head and kissed her flour-dusted hair. He loved the lively feel of it beneath his lips.

"Annabelle, you want to sort this out for us two stupid men?"

She pushed away from him and wiped her eyes on her apron again. She sniffed and then bestowed a glorious smile on them. "I've never in my life been part of a Christmas celebration. I've never had a tree or people around me who cared about me." She walked over to Aaron and held out her hands to him. "I thank you Aaron Parker for your kindness. The ornaments are truly beautiful."

Aaron ducked his head and smiled his wide, wonderful smile. "The only Christmas I've ever seen was through a window or two. So you see this is kind of my first one, too, missus."

Clint reached out and brought her down to sit on his lap. "My last Christmas was when I was nineteen. So you see, honey, this is important for all of us."

Suddenly she jumped up. "And a fine Christmas it will be. You men bring me some extra flour and sugar from the barn. I don't have any gifts for you, but I'll fix you the finest Christmas Eve dinner you ever had, and tomorrow—"

"Big storm moving in tomorrow, missus."

"You just worry about bringing me wood for the stove and I'll keep it cooking."

She hustled the dishes into a basin and poured hot water over them. She wiped the table clean and brought down her pie pans from the cupboards. It came to her as she worked that she had never been in a household where so much smiling went on.

The men stood and watched her dash around. She stopped with her hands on her hips. "Well, go on. Standing around doesn't get things done." She shooed them toward the door. "And potatoes. I need more potatoes."

In the barn, Clint took a large package from its hiding place behind the flour barrel. Armed with Martha Cummins's list of feminine needs, Aaron had returned from his last trip to town loaded down with presents for Annabelle. Clint prayed she would accept his gifts with the love he felt in the giving. If she even recognized his feelings as love.

"Mister Clint?"

He turned and looked over at his hired hand, who was fast becoming a good friend. "Yeah, Aaron?"

"I need to tell you...uh...how much all this means to me." He made an encompassing gesture.

"This isn't much of a place to stay, Aaron." Clint glanced around the barn and marveled at the homey section Aaron had built in one corner.

"It's all I need," Aaron said. "'Till I gets me a woman." He rubbed his chin in thought. "I'd like to find me what you've found with the missus." He looked over at his cot. "'Cept maybe I'll have to make me a wider cot." His grin revealed his thoughts well enough to Clint.

He nodded in agreement. "When we get the house built, you and that woman you're going to find can have the cabin until you can build a better place."

"That's mighty generous of you, Mister Clint." Aaron's voice cracked with emotion.

"A man needs his own place, Aaron. I never thought I'd have a home again. I don't think Annabelle has any idea how much I wanted a life like this one." He felt a shimmer of fear roll down his spine. "I pray every day now, Aaron, that nothing or no one will take it away from me." He forced the thought from his mind and smiled. "However, I do recall dreaming of a soft, docile little woman who would agree sweetly with me and tend to my every need."

Aaron laughed loudly. "Well, Mister Clint, some-where your dream took a different road."

Clint gazed through the dimness of the barn and his smile widened. "A road for the better, Aaron. With that rambunctious female in the cabin I got fire and surprises. She does keep a man on his toes." He slowly shook his head in wonder at his luck.

He remembered last Christmas Eve, standing out-side a church in Dodge City. He listened to carols be-ing sung and watched the families leaving at the end of the service. His gut had hurt so bad with wanting. Wanting the home those people went to. Wanting the children racing through the snow, eager for the morning to come. He longed to be with his own family in Philadelphia.

Now, with Annabelle, he had a chance for it all. His home. His family. His wife. He felt his throat tighten and he sent up another prayer asking protection for the life being created here on this small ranch at the foot of the Sierra.

Clint awoke to the mingling smells of freshly baked bread, apple pies and coffee. His stomach growled and he marveled that he could be hungry after last night's feast.

He figured a man could want for nothing more in his life. He ran his hand over the place where Annabelle should be and smiled. Well, perhaps one thing more.

He rolled over and watched her. Desire for her pooled heavily in his groin and he wondered how he could stop her determined activity and coax her back into bed.

She was a sight. She had flour on her freckled face and down the bodice of that damned blue dress. Her hair escaped the faded ribbon that was meant to hold it out of the way. He did love her hair. It seemed to announce to the world that under it was a woman of difference, a woman who knew her own mind, and woe unto the person who wanted to change it.

He watched her graceful movements from table to stove to sink and his need for her grew to insistent proportions. "Annabelle?" he said softly. "Come here."

She moved to the bed. "Clint, I need you to get up. I need more—"

"Me." He ran his hands under her skirt and found her bare bottom. "We're going to have to get you some drawers, honey."

She swatted at his hands and tried to move away. "Never mind about my lack of underpinnings. Just get your lazy carcass out of that bed. I need more wood for the stove."

He forced her closer to the bed. "What you need, my love, is me inside you." He moved his hands between her soft thighs and discovered her familiar, welcoming dampness.

Her eyes closed as she savored his words. *My love.* She licked her lips as she anticipated his kiss. She knew she would always make time for this. Still, she had so much to do. "Clint, I have two more pies...oh, Lordy." His intimate caresses drove all thoughts of pies and cooking right out of her head.

"Annabelle," Clint whispered against the sweet shell of her ear, and brought her down beside him.

"Mmm."

"Come on, honey. You've a starving man here." He stroked her cheek.

"Mmm." She pushed his hands away from her face and over her breasts.

"Big day ahead of us, you know. It's Christmas morning."

With a lurch, Annabelle sat up and looked down at her grinning husband. "Damn you, Clint Strand." She ran her knuckles over her eyes, trying to fight off the drowsy sensual haze he brought her to. "I've hundreds of things to do this morning and you dragged me back into bed.''

''Seems to me you crawled in willingly.''

She leaned over him, her nose close to his. ''If I was made of snow and ice, I'd melt willingly into your bed and you know it.'' She got up, then turned back to him. ''And you take advantage of that fact.''

''I am not a stupid man, Annabelle,'' he said, his shoulders shaking with laughter. ''Of course I do. I'm ready for you all the time, honey.''

She glanced down at the tented covers over his hips and couldn't prevent a smile forming on her lips. ''You'd best be careful. You might be mistaken for a Christmas tree in need of decoration. Watch out or you'll find it tied with red ribbons and one of Aaron's fancy wooden ornaments.''

''You've got the only ornament I'll ever wear.'' He positively leered at her.

''Get out of that bed,'' she said, stamping her foot on the floor, ''before I dump cold water on your... Christmas tree.''

Clint leapt from the bed, pulled her into his arms and gave her a hearty kiss. ''Merry Christmas, sweetheart.''

She gazed into his wonderful blue eyes and knew all the love she felt must shine through to him. She caressed his stubbled cheek and rose up on tiptoe to give him a soft kiss. ''You are all the Christmas I need, Clint Strand.''

He held her close against his chest and they stood quietly in each other's arms.

Clint cleared his throat and stepped back. ''This is an important day, honey, and I'm still a hungry man, but I'll settle for pancakes." He moved away and pulled on his clothes. "I'll go get Aaron. He must think we'll never get out of bed."

She punched him and he laughed as he left the cabin.

Aaron set down his third cup of coffee and patted his full belly. "Missus, you are one fine cook. I don't believe I ever had a better breakfast."

Annabelle smiled her thanks and started to clear up the table.

Clint took the dishes from her and set them by the dry sink. He marched her over to the bed, ignoring the puzzled look on her face. "Get in there and keep your eyes closed." He pulled the curtains together behind her.

"Clint?" What was that man up to? she wondered.

"Just hush up and don't peek."

She squeezed her eyes shut and put her hands to her breast. He must have brought her a present. Goodness, she'd never had a present in her whole life. She felt the strong quickness of her heart as it beat with anticipation.

She heard the men leave the cabin. They must have hidden her present in the barn. It seemed forever before they returned. She could hear the rustle of paper and their whispering. The temptation to part the curtains just a little was so strong Annabelle felt perspiration form on her forehead.

"All right, honey. Come on out."

Now that she had permission, she couldn't leave the cozy safety of the bed. Suddenly, the curtains were jerked open and Clint stood before her with a boyish grin on his handsome face.

"Well, what're you waiting for?" He pulled her to her feet and stepped aside so she could see the table.

It was piled with packages wrapped in bright calico. She thought there must be ten or twelve.

"Sit down, missus," Aaron said. "These are all for you." His grin was as foolish as Clint's.

Tears threatened and she looked helplessly at both men. "But I..." She cleared her throat. "I don't have—"

Clint gave her a quick hug and sat her down at the table. "Open them, Annabelle. It's Christmas and the lady of the house has presents from her men." He and Aaron pulled up the apple boxes and sat down. Clint handed her a flat, square package. "Start with this one." He looked as eager as a young child.

She couldn't speak and only nodded at him. She slowly removed the wrapping and found a beautiful sketch of a table and chairs. A puzzled look on her face, she said, "It's a lovely drawing, but—"

Aaron interrupted. "It's from me, missus. I'm goin' to build that for you."

"But, Aaron," she said, stunned at his gift, "it's so much and must be very difficult to do."

"No, ma'am. Mister Clint is goin' to get me a lathe. I can do most anything with one of those." He nodded his head in firm agreement with himself.

She smoothed the sketch on her lap and the lump in her throat grew to alarming size. She looked up into the eyes of the smiling man. "Thank you, Aaron. It will be the most wonderful table and chairs in the valley."

He beamed with delight.

"Here, Annabelle, open this one." Clint handed her a large, soft package.

She swallowed the lump in her throat, tore open the gift and found lengths of bright cotton. Enough for four dresses. There was a bright green, nearly the color of her eyes. A lemon yellow, a patterned violet and a deep, rusty color.

She buried her face in the new-smelling material and desperately tried not to cry all over it.

Clint pulled her hands away from her face, a worried look on his. "Honey?"

She shook her head to let him know she was all right. It took a minute to find words. "I'm fine. It's just . . . just so much."

Clint let out his breath. "Hell, for a moment I thought you hated the colors. I just never want to see you in blue again."

Happiness filled her and she laughed and kissed him. "I promise. No more blue."

Clint kept her moving through the packages. There was material for new crisp sheets for their bed. A big copper kettle for soups and stews. Sweet-smelling soap from London! Yards of ribbon to put on her new dresses and in her hair. A wonderful lotion for her hands.

Finally the tears fell. Never in her life had she been so happy or felt so appreciated. These men gave her a feeling of importance she'd never known was possible.

Clint pulled her onto his lap and rocked her back and forth. "I take it, Mrs. Strand, these are tears of happiness?"

She nodded and sniffed against his strong chest.

"Well, hold still. I've got two more presents for you, honey."

She lifted her head and gazed at him through teary eyes. "Oh, Clint. You've already given me so much."

He held her close. "Not nearly enough, Annabelle. The day you marched into that saloon you gave me the greatest gift I've ever had. A chance for the life I'd dreamed of. All this—" He made a gesture toward the presents. "All this is just a way of saying thank-you." He nodded at Aaron, who reached under the table and brought out two small packages.

Clint gave her the biggest one. She opened it and gasped at what she found. A book! A slim volume with bright lettering on the cover. "But I can't—"

"You will, sweetheart. That's a reader. I'm going to teach you to read."

She held the book tight to her chest and closed her eyes in sheer wonder. To know how to read; it was the greatest gift of all. More tears found their way from beneath her tightly closed lids.

"Don't collapse on me yet, honey. There's one more present." Clint placed a small, square box in her hands.

It was wrapped in a piece of red velvet and tied with a narrow gold ribbon. Where on earth, she wondered, had he found such lovely fabric? It would go into her tin box along with the green. She carefully took off the wrapping and opened the little box. Inside lay a shiny gold wedding band. He took it from its white velvet nest and placed it on a stunned Annabelle's finger.

"With this ring I thee wed." He looked fierce and determined, as if he expected her to argue. "Forever, Annabelle."

She felt she might explode with joy. How could something as crazy and outrageous as their marriage turn out to be so glorious? she wondered.

"Well, hell, Annabelle. Say something."

She ran her hands over his wonderful, handsome face. "This is the most precious moment of my life." She leaned forward and placed a tender kiss against his warm lips.

He tugged her close. "And I promise you, nothing will ever change it. Merry Christmas, Annabelle."

She burrowed against his strong, warm, safe body and sighed in contentment. "Merry Christmas, Clint."

She loved him.

Deep in the very pulse of her body, strong feelings of love had settled in and found a welcome home. The love she'd needed to give all her life flowed in her blood and seeped out through her skin.

She loved him.

Clint to love her. He hadn't said the words, but his every action spelled love to her. They still wrangled and teased and even fought sometimes. Who wouldn't, holed up in one room for the long winter? But he took care of her in hundreds of loving ways.

She wrapped herself in the coat Martha had brought to her in the bad days after the baby died. She pulled a woolen cap over her curls then stepped out onto the porch to watch Clint and Aaron lay down boards over the mud from the house to the barn. Last night's snow had been light, the last gasp of winter. She could feel spring in the light breeze caressing her face.

Water dripped from the melting icicles hanging from the roof, leaving deep holes in the shaded ice. Snow-laden pine branches gave up their burdens with great swooshes and the heavy white stuff plopped to the ground. Her peach trees stood out stark and bare against the icy mountain backdrop. But she knew that inside their branches, spring juices would soon flow.

A time of rebirth and flowering. Annabelle knew that feeling. She had it all the time now. Love is the spring in my life, she thought as she saw Clint and Aaron laugh at some shared joke and pat each other on the back.

The two men had become fast friends over the past months. On the good weather days they worked on improving Aaron's quarters in the barn or on the chicken coop. One stormy day, they'd built two more shelves for her in the cabin.

In February the men repaired the bed. She could feel herself blush with the memory of how that poor bed had finally given up. Clint had teased her about their "winter recreation activities" and told her he hated for spring to come, as he'd have too much to do to stay in bed trying to keep her satisfied. She'd punched him.

Her wonderful memories of the deep winter were interrupted by Clint's call. She ran to the barn, eager to be with him every minute she could.

"Come on in here, Annabelle. See what Aaron's made now."

The men sat on either side of an empty, upside-down barrel. On top sat a narrow board with holes in it.

"Can you believe it?" Clint asked. "A cribbage board."

She glanced at Aaron, who had a pleased expression on his face. "Well, it is a very nice board. You did a fine job, Aaron." She felt nervous about this. Clint acted as though she should know what the board was for. "I suppose I'd be excited if I knew what it did."

"It doesn't do anything." The disgusted look on his face told her what he thought of her statement.

"What good is a board with holes in it?"

"Hell, Annabelle, it's a game. Sit down, we'll show you."

She sat, but it didn't look like much of a game to her.

Clint opened a deck of cards. "Now, the ace can be high or low. Next is the king—"

"I know, after that comes the queen," she said.

Clint reached over and rumpled her hair. "Right. Pay attention, this gets tricky." He explained the point system and the cards they would use.

"Why don't you play with all the cards?" It seemed to her a game couldn't last very long with so few cards.

"That's just the way it's done. See these little pegs? This is how we keep score."

"Of what?" She felt sure this game was beyond her.

"Of the points! Are you paying attention?" Impatience edged its way into his voice.

"Yes! Just show me how to play the damned game!"

Clint blew his breath through clenched teeth. "Each of us gets five cards. We decide which ones to keep and which to get rid of. We bid on our hands, then have to make the points we bid. We lay down our melds and that starts our points. When we take the bid that tells us how many points we have to make—"

Annabelle shot off her seat and started for the barn door.

"Annabelle! Where are you going?" Clint hollered.

"In the house. Where the queen belongs."

He stomped over and pulled her back to her seat. "Sit down. This is a good game for two people and I want you to learn it."

She rolled her eyes heavenward and prayed for strength.

"Don't look like that. You're going to love this. Now, where were we? Okay. This is how you count your points." He began laying cards on the table and switched them around so fast she couldn't keep track.

"Fifteen-two. Fifteen-three. Fifteen-four and two is six. See how easy it is?"

She just stared at him and wondered if he'd gone crazy. Or maybe she had, to sit here and listen to this. She stood up. "I'm going in the house."

"Annabelle, you're not trying."

"Trying what! Not one word you've said makes sense to me. Just because you know the rules you think they'll soak in through my skin. Fifteen this, fifteen that. I don't know what you're talking about and I don't want to." She plopped down on her box.

Clint pulled her onto his lap. "I'm sorry, honey. I really like cribbage. I thought it would be great for us to play together. I just got overexcited."

She rested her head on his shoulder and sighed. "All right. I'll try, but go slow and explain each part to me."

"I will, promise. Now sit across from me and we'll start over."

Annabelle looked around the barn. "Where's Aaron?"

"He snuck out when we started fighting."

She felt indignant at his words. "We don't fight."

Clint grinned. "Then how come we do all that making up?"

She blushed to her toes when she thought of how they made up. "I guess we do have a tiff now and then."

He shuffled the cards and dealt them out. "I used to play this game with my father and grandfather. My mother wanted me to learn whist, but cribbage was my game."

Carefully, she set her cards down on the barrel. When he'd told her of the train robbery, he'd also told her about his family. In the back of her mind she'd worried about how they would take to her. "Your folks? They must be pretty fancy people."

Wrapped up in the cards in his hands, Clint missed the cautious tone of her voice. "Fancy? I suppose so."

"Their friends must be from the best families."

"Uh-huh."

"I suppose you'll want to see them again sometime?"

Her voice had dropped to a mere whisper and finally caught his attention. She sat with her hands folded in her lap and gazed off into the dim recesses of the barn. His mind whipped back over her questions and he cursed himself for not listening.

He leaned over the barrel and took her hand. He guided her around and onto his lap. "Why are you worried about my folks?" He knew why but needed her to talk about it.

She snuggled close and spoke to his neck. "When you go home, I can wait here for you. I won't mind, I promise."

He forced her trembling chin up and saw the sparkle of tears in her eyes. "Now why would I go back there without you?"

"I'm not exactly what your family would consider a proper person. I'd be as out of place as a turnip in a strawberry patch."

"Listen to me, Annabelle Strand. You are my wife and my family would welcome you and take you into their hearts."

"Are you sure? Seems to me that rich—"

"They are rich, but not cruel and overtaken by their position." How could he make her see how special she was? Give her the confidence she needed? "You're a lot like my ma."

Annabelle pulled back and stared at him. "You are trying to make me feel better, Clint Strand."

"Maybe, but it's true. My mother is a gentle woman, but she is strong and fights for her place and opinions. She is loving and is not a nose-in-the-air society type."

Settling back in his arms, Annabelle reached up and stroked his mustache. "Just the same, I'm not the kind of person they would have expected you to marry."

"Honey, they gave up expecting anything of me years ago. You're the only one with the right to expect anything from me now." He squeezed her tight. "Another thing, Mrs. Strand. This is my home, not the one back in Philadelphia."

Her smile made his heart race and he lowered his lips to hers.

When the kiss ended, Annabelle said, "I promise before we go to see your folks, I'll stop swearing."

Clint laughed so hard he nearly toppled them both to the ground. He nuzzled her neck and wished it was night so he could take her to bed. But he really did want her to learn to play cribbage. "I think the road will be in good enough shape to go to town soon," he said to get his mind off the wonderful smell of her neck. She had bathed in the soap he'd given her at Christmas.

Annabelle rushed to her feet, all interest in the confusing card game gone. "How wonderful. I can see Martha. Maybe fresh vegetables have come from Sacramento. I'd dearly love to have a tomato." She stopped suddenly. "Do you really think the town...the people will..."

"Everyone will treat you fine, honey. Don't you worry about that. Now sit down and let me teach you this card game."

The firmness of his tone assured her that he would never let anything happen to her. She sat primly, hands folded in her lap, while he explained the impossible game.

Chapter Eleven

Spring! Annabelle sat by the stream and drew in the sweet smell of the new season. The Sierra were still heavily capped with snow, but in the meadow all was fresh and new. Like her life with Clint, spring promised the future.

She cherished the long winter days and nights. She and Clint learned to live together. He was such an easy man to be with. His patience in teaching her to read, his unfailing good humor—his lovemaking. He taught her loving was a joyous experience, a glorious one.

She picked up one of the buckets and dipped it into the cold, clear water. When she set it down and reached for the other, she saw Clint striding toward her. She shaded her eyes from the bright sunlight and smiled.

She loved watching him. His loose-hipped walk made her mouth water. And his blue eyes; well, she just lost her heart when he watched her, his gaze all hot and needy. She unconsciously licked her lips and wiped her hand on her skirt. She felt her readiness for him swell between her legs and blushed.

"Annabelle, honey, if you don't stop looking at me like I was your next meal, I just may have to lay you

down on this nice green grass and make love to you."
He stood with one hip cocked and his hands in the back
pockets of his denim trousers.

"Get that pleased look off your face, Clint Strand.
The good Lord didn't put you on this earth just to satisfy the female population." She turned her back to
him and brought her disorderly feelings under control. She leaned down for the other bucket.

Clint grabbed her by the waist and whirled her
around. He kissed her until she felt dizzy. He was a
man for kissing. Seemed to Annabelle kissing was one
of his favorite things—hers too, now.

"Maybe," he said when he had her weak-kneed. "I
figure he put me here just for your satisfaction." He
kissed her nose. "And I'll tell you, Mrs. Strand, keeping you satisfied is a full-time occupation. I don't believe I have time for doing much else."

She stared into his eyes and felt her love for him fill
every nook and cranny of her body. She wrapped her
arms around his waist and leaned against him. She
could stand here with him all day in the warm sun.

Clint tipped up her face. "You're very quiet."

She nodded her agreement, then laid her head back
against his chest.

"You all right, Annabelle?"

She nodded again and sighed contentedly.

He wrapped her in his arms and rubbed her back. "I
told you I'd haul the water."

"I know. I just wanted to be outside."

"It's been a long winter."

The rhythmic movement of his hands and the welcome heat of the sun lulled her into a near doze. "A
wonderful winter."

"It was that." He nuzzled her neck and set her away from him. "I'll carry the buckets back." He hefted both of them and motioned her to come with him. "Aaron and I are going into town. I thought you might want to tag along."

"Town?" Delight filled her. She felt ready to face whatever came her way now. Secure in Clint's care of her, she drew new strength from him and their special life together.

"Yep. I decided we owed the population of Pleasant Valley proof we made it through the winter without killing each other."

She punched him in the arm. "I don't care what they think."

"Yes you do, honey. You want to be accepted by them just as I did."

Annabelle stopped. "Did? What do you mean, did?"

Clint set down the buckets. "Just that. Did. They do accept me now. Have since before, uh, winter."

"I don't understand. What happened to make a gunfighter—you—acceptable to the town?"

"The money, Annabelle. Money you've never asked about. Money goes a long way toward making a person acceptable, even welcome."

She'd avoided the topic of his money like the plague. She'd been so afraid. "I thought maybe you'd—"

"Stolen it?" Clint interrupted.

"Well, yes! You've killed people. Is it so strange I'd think you might have stolen from them?" She hated herself for the words and dearly wished she could recall them, but that's just what she'd thought.

Clint grabbed her hard by the arms and shook her. Fury etched sparks in his eyes and hardened the line of his mouth. "I've never killed wantonly or drawn first in my life. I've never stolen from any man, woman or *child*. What the hell kind of a man do you take me for?" He trembled with anger.

She broke his grip and flung herself against him. She wrapped her arms around his waist and held on. "A wonderful man. A man who's given me everything." She tilted her head back, rose on her toes and kissed his tense lips until they softened.

"I'm so sorry," she said. "I'm hateful and selfish and I felt guilty. I didn't know anything about you. I've never once really asked about the money, just made stupid guesses about it. Please forgive me, Clint?"

His arms tightened about her. "Ask me now, Annabelle."

She leaned against him. "Where did you get the money?"

"From my grandmother."

Pulling back from him, eyes wide, she asked, "Grandmother?"

He sighed heavily. "I did have one and she left me and my sister each a trust fund when she died. It's been in the bank for eight years. I never had a reason to draw on it before. I had it in my mind maybe someday I'd head for Mexico or even Canada to escape the life I led. But I kept putting off the decision. I didn't really want to live outside the States. This is my country, honey. I didn't want to leave it. Then we got married and I saw this ranch and what we could have here."

Once again he began stroking her back. "Don't you realize yet, honey, how much all this means to me?"

Annabelle nodded against his strong chest. "As much as to me, I suspect." She felt his face move against her hair in agreement. "Do you forgive me?"

"I'll always forgive you, Annabelle."

"You act like I'll be needing your forgiveness a lot."

"You are an impulsive woman." He grinned down at her.

She pushed him away, flipped her skirt and marched off toward the cabin. "Let's head for town," she hollered over her shoulder.

When Clint and Annabelle pulled up in the wagon in front of the general store, she experienced a moment of uneasiness. This was her first trip into Pleasant Valley since their marriage. In spite of Clint's assurance, she felt some doubt about her welcome. When Jed Cummins crossed the street from the livery with a warm smile for her, most of her uncertainty fled. She still had the women to face.

"Look what spring brought into town," Jed said. He moved to the side of the wagon and assisted Annabelle down. He looked carefully at her and nodded. "You're looking fine, Annabelle."

She smiled and smoothed out her new green dress. "That's only 'cause I am." She grabbed his hand and squeezed it. "Thank you." She didn't want to talk about the baby, but she needed him to know she appreciated his kindnesses.

Jed flushed. "Just being neighborly."

Good manners prevented Annabelle from commenting on the months in her life without neighborly overtures from him or anyone in Pleasant Valley.

Clint came around the wagon and held his hand out to Jed. "Good to see you, Jed. I've got a list that'll empty old Fillmore's shelves."

"That'll take some doing. He got five loads in from Sacramento this month and more coming." Jed turned to Annabelle. "Martha saw your wagon coming in and ran over to the tea shop to wait for you. She does love that place."

Annabelle grinned and looked inquiringly at Clint. She wanted to pursue her friendship with Martha.

"Go one, honey," he said. "I can manage fine. You can come on later and pick out any feminine needs you have."

She dug in her reticule and gave him the list he had helped her with. "I'll be back in a bit."

Jed took the list and scanned it quickly. "I'll help Clint. It'll be ready for you."

Rough wood walls painted pale pink and windows draped in flower-sprigged cotton attested to the fact that the tearoom catered to women.

The owner of the shop, Charlotte Janeway, pointed to a small table in the far corner where Martha waved. "Come on in, Mrs. Strand. Martha's busting with spring fever and town news."

Annabelle smiled at Martha and sat down. "Since you're the only person in here, did you think I wouldn't find you?"

"I'm just so glad to see you," Martha said. She motioned to Charlotte to bring their tea. "Besides, I wanted to be the first to invite you to the picnic."

"Picnic?"

"Every spring. Three Sundays from now, right after morning service." Charlotte brought the tea and

Martha spooned sugar into hers with a liberal hand.
"The town council decides on a project and we raise
means, in labor or money, at the picnic." She took a sip
of her tea. "This year the men will build new desks for
the school. The money raised will buy the lumber and
the fittings."

"I—I don't know, Martha. I—"

"Of course you'll come!"

"I'm not sure the people will—"

"They will!"

Annabelle sat back and smiled at Martha. "You
don't even know what I'm trying to say."

"Yes I do. You think you won't be welcome." She
pushed Annabelle's cup nearer to her. "Drink your
tea."

"What makes you so sure I'll be welcome. And
Clint? How about him?" She wasn't sure she could
face the townspeople again. And certainly not in a large
group. She felt her anxious heartbeat. What if people
turned up their noses at her and Clint? How could he
be so sure everyone had forgotten his past? Did his
money make that much difference? Never having had
much, Annabelle felt her judgment in this unsure.

Martha filled her cup again and, after adding heaping spoonfuls of sugar, stirred it with a determined
motion. "Listen here, Annabelle Strand. You're some
kind of wondrous character in this town. The women
think you're courageous and adventurous. Something
most of them never had a chance to be. And the men?
Why, they say Clint stole something from you and you
just made him give it back. Makes perfect sense to
them." She chuckled. "Although most of them are

glad it's Clint and not them that have to deal with you. You are feisty, Annabelle."

Annabelle knew her jaw had to be hanging down to her lace collar. Life just seemed to throw one surprise after another at her these past few months. First a hard-bitten gunfighter turned into a gentle, caring man. Now mean, uncaring people in Pleasant Valley accepted her impulsive, dangerous act as something else entirely—and praised her for it.

Martha reached out and patted her hand. "Don't fret over it, child. Drink your tea."

Annabelle looked at the nearly empty sugar bowl and began to laugh. "You've cleaned out that sugar and most likely gained five pounds."

Martha's hearty laugh rang through the tea shop. She patted an ample hip with one hand. "My Jed, he likes a full-figured woman. Makes it easy to find me in the bed."

Annabelle and Martha came into the store to find Mr. Fillmore waiting on Judaline Jennings.

Regardless of how diligently the woman had tended her, Annabelle still felt wary of Judaline. Some part of her still waited anxiously for Judaline and her banker husband to come with the sheriff and throw her off the ranch, and now she wondered why they hadn't. It must be the banker, maybe even the sheriff, who didn't want to face down Clint.

Judaline turned and saw the two women. She looked Annabelle over carefully. "So, you made it through the winter?"

"Good afternoon to you, too, Judaline," Annabelle said. Lord, what a difficult woman.

"Humph! It's going to rain."

Martha stepped up to the counter to check Annabelle's boxes against her list. "Judaline, you are quicker to find a dark cloud than you are a dollar."

Judaline's eyes narrowed and she glared at Martha. "I know how many dollars you and Jed owe the bank."

"And every one of them will be paid on time, as they always are, so quit rubbing your hands together," Martha retorted.

Annabelle felt she had to intervene. After all, Judaline and her husband hadn't foreclosed on her property when she had been unable to make the payments. "Now, Martha—"

Judaline's gaze snapped to Annabelle. "Just because that gunfighter you married paid your mortgage, don't think that makes us friends." She fairly gloated. "I can't imagine that prosperous Philadelphia family of his will welcome the likes of you. Money buys a lot of things, but not station. You'll find that out."

"Paid?" A stunning surprise overcame Annabelle. Why hadn't he told her? He'd spent lots of money fixing up the ranch, but it never entered her mind he would pay off her debt. His family? He had assured her they would accept her. Maybe Judaline was right.

The banker's wife smirked at Annabelle's confused expression. "Didn't tell you, did he? Keeping little secrets from you, is he? A man like that isn't to be trusted."

Annabelle assessed the pleasure Judaline got from her announcement and she had the greatest desire to knock the wind out of the hateful woman's sails.

"Judaline, I think more than anyone in this town you need a friend. I'm making that offer to you now." She held out her hand and prayed Judaline would take it.

Expressions of wonder, anger and confusion raced over Judaline's face. She riveted her gaze to Annabelle's and shook her head slowly. Suddenly, she whirled around and raced from the shop.

"Well," said Martha, "I've never seen that one at a loss for words before." She chuckled. "That was a sight. I do believe I saw those fierce eyes of hers tear up. You have made a fearsome enemy, Annabelle, or neutered an old one."

Annabelle had no time for wondering about Judaline. She turned to Mr. Fillmore. "Where's Clint?"

"He said he had to go to the bank and the lumberyard." He looked at the grandfather clock against the wall. "I'd say the lumberyard by now." He glanced at Martha. "Jed went with him."

Annabelle left Martha behind without another word. The bank was right across the street. She would go there first. She flung open the door.

Hervey Jennings glanced up from his conversation with another man. He smiled and walked toward her with his hand held out in greeting. "Mrs. Strand! I'll bet you're looking for that husband of yours?"

Annabelle couldn't find the spit to make a single word to answer the banker's friendly greeting.

"He left just a few minutes ago for the lumberyard." Jennings gave her a warm smile. "He has great plans for that place of yours."

"Mr. Jennings, Judaline told me Clint paid off my mortgage. Is that true?" She felt stupid and embarrassed. This man knew more about her life than she did.

Jennings looked uneasy. "Well, yes, he did, Mrs. Strand. Back last . . . I'm sorry my wife broke the news to you. It's not her place to do so."

Annabelle studied the banker and decided he was sincere. "Why does she hate me so?"

Taking her arm, he led her out onto the boardwalk. He seemed so distraught Annabelle felt terrible about asking him the question.

"I'm not one to discuss my family, Mrs. Strand, but I feel you are owed some explanation." He sighed and gazed off into the distance. "Judaline comes from a background not, uh, unlike yours. Her mother . . . well, she . . . let's just say there are similarities. Also, we lost four children shortly after each was born. We were not lucky in giving healthy life to our children."

Tears sparkled in his eyes and Annabelle felt totally at a loss as to what to do. She placed her hand on his arm. "Mr. Jennings, please don't say any more. I offered my friendship to Judaline. I hope someday she can accept it. I will not withdraw my offer."

"You are an understanding woman, Mrs. Strand." He patted her hand.

"Only recently, Mr. Jennings. Only lately have I had the time or someone to teach me."

She shook Jennings's outstretched hand, then fled to find Clint.

She found him at the lumberyard in a huddle with Simon Wilson and Jed. Ignoring the presence of others, she accosted Clint. "I would like to speak privately with you, please."

Clint turned and knew immediately that Annabelle bubbled with emotion. He knew her so well by now. She was hurt. What the hell had happened to her? Had one of those old biddies snubbed her?

"What's wrong, honey?"

"I need to talk to you."

Hell, was she mad at him? He grabbed her by the arm and dragged her to a dim corner of the yard. "What's going on, Annabelle?"

"You owe me some explanations, Clint."

He sighed and knew he was in for it. He pulled her down to sit on the lid of a nail keg. "All right, what's got you all stirred up now?"

"You paid off the mortgage on the ranch."

He eased off his hat and wiped his brow with his forearm. She must have gone to the bank looking for him and Jennings had shot off his mouth. "You've been to the bank." He jammed his hat back on his head.

"I suppose everyone in this town knew about it but me?"

"Didn't it once occur to you that the sheriff hadn't been around to toss you out on the road?"

"Yes. No." That was a bald-faced lie. "Well, yes. Not really." He tipped his head and she could tell he didn't believe a word she said. "Well, blast it, I didn't think much about it. Well, not too much. I...I had other things on my mind." She had lost the baby, then herself in grief. Then all her thoughts were taken up with Clint and her growing feelings toward him. "I guess I thought they were all afraid of you."

"Annabelle. Look at me."

She glanced up into his eyes.

"I paid off the ranch the day you . . . lost the baby. That's when I did it. And the sheriff is not afraid of me. I settled things with him the same day I went to the bank. We understand each other."

"Why didn't you tell me?" She felt terribly hurt he'd kept this from her. She also understood the ranch no longer belonged to just her. Before, even with their marriage, she could still pretend it was all hers. Now he'd bought and paid for it. So it was more his now.

Clint knelt in front of her. "Honey, you weren't ready to hear about it or you'd have asked some questions." He tipped her chin up. "You tend to ignore things you don't want to talk about. The ranch is still in your name, Annabelle. You just have to ask me to leave."

She knew he meant it. He didn't lie to her. It was her own fault if she didn't know things; she didn't ask anything when she felt uncertain of the outcome. She also knew, above all things, she didn't want him to leave.

"You want me to go?"

She shook her head.

"Why?"

She shrugged.

"Come on, why?"

She jumped up and stomped toward the street. She turned back to look at him still on his knees in the sawdust. "We're doing fine together, aren't we?"

"Yes."

Even in the dim light she could see the sparkle in his eyes. "Then why are you talking about leaving?"

He stood and brushed off his trousers, then strode right up to her. "I wanted you to know you always have a choice where we are concerned."

She didn't fully understand this man. No matter how cranky she got, he treated her with patience and humor. She appreciated the patience, but the humor riled her at times. Each day her love for him grew stronger.

She reached up and stroked his mustache. "I...thank you for paying off the ranch. I..." She couldn't say what she really wanted to say. She dropped her hand to her side and closed it into a fist.

He ran a hand through her wild hair, dislodging her bonnet. There was something else disturbing her, he knew it. "What, honey?"

"Judaline said your family is...they won't like me."

"That woman is just being spiteful, honey. I know my family better than she does. They will love you."

And I love you, Clint Strand. "I have to make sure Mr. Fillmore has everything in the wagon." She ran from the lumberyard, fear beating a cowardly rhythm in her heart. She'd almost told him she loved him. Crazy, that's what she was. Plumb crazy. If ever a man needed an excuse to leave, an unwanted love was it.

Clint watched her go, then smiled. She was getting close to admitting her feelings for him; he saw it in her eyes. He chuckled. They both were so damn cautious, he thought as he followed her out. Soon he'd bring this foolishness to a stop and declare himself. He just hoped to hell he read her right. With Annabelle, he never knew for sure.

The grove beside the church filled with families and food. Colorful booths were decorated with gay ribbons and brightly painted signs advertised mouth-watering treats for sale. The laughter of children competing in one-legged races and hoop-rolling contests filled the spring air. For the first time since her arrival in Pleasant Valley, Annabelle felt a part of the town.

She propped her chin on her hands and leaned her elbows on the counter of the booth, breathing in the sweet scent of berry pies, new green grass and the pungent smell of beef cooking over a wood fire.

The men had gone over to the far field for the turkey shoot. Clint had only been gone for about thirty minutes and she missed him.

"You're daydreaming, girl." Martha slapped a small boy's grimy hand away from a fruit pie.

"Mmm. I'm just being happy."

"You're just being pregnant."

Shocked, Annabelle quickly straightened. "How did you know that?"

Martha waved her arm in a broad gesture. "Somewhere out there I have seven children. I know pregnant." She looked at Annabelle through narrowed eyes. "You told that man of yours yet?"

"No. I thought I'd wait a bit, you know, until I'm sure." Truthfully, she felt scared to death to tell him. He just might ride out in the middle of the night. She didn't have the slightest idea how he'd feel about it. She wanted him to be as happy about it as she.

"Well, I'm sure. You have the look. Better tell him."

"Why? He doesn't tell me everything." It still rankled that he hadn't told her about paying off the mortgage. She knew she was being unreasonable, but she couldn't help it. She wanted to share everything, good or bad, with him.

Martha laughed and patted Annabelle on the arm. "Land sakes, child. That's just men. They don't think women need to know everything that's going on." Her laugh grew even heartier. "Poor souls. They still haven't figured out we usually find out anyway. Most times even guess before they do."

Annabelle sighed. "Not me. Half the time he's in the middle of something before I even notice he's been doing it."

"It'll come. You've had a bad time. Now you're just falling in love. Keeps a body off her senses."

"I'm not in love," Annabelle lied. She was so far gone she feared falling off the edge of the world. She would if he left her now.

"Who're you trying to fool? Yourself? You watch every move that man makes. He can't take a step without that heart of yours taking it with him. Love shines right out of your eyes. I swear I can feel your heartbeat and see your mouth water. Don't tell me you aren't in love. It fairly sparkles all over you."

Panic shot through Annabelle and she searched the crowd, looking for him. "Do you think he knows it?" She prayed he didn't.

"He is not stupid."

Annabelle wrung her hands and chewed on her bottom lip. Surely he would have said something. Since he hadn't, did that mean he didn't want to acknowledge it? Didn't want her to be in love with him?

Martha took her by the shoulders. "Stop worrying yourself into a tizzy. The man dotes on you, can't you tell?"

"He does?"

Martha heaved a mighty sigh and looked disgusted. "Annabelle, use that head of yours. Think! Would he have done all he has if he didn't care about you?"

"He cares about making a home, starting a new life. I just came with the ranch."

"I give up!" Martha said, opening her arms in surrender. "Play dumb. Keep your mind closed against the truth." She suddenly smiled. "That's a pretty elaborate house he and Aaron are designing for a man that doesn't care about the woman who'll live in it."

Annabelle froze. "What house?" she asked, her words slow and deliberate.

"Oh, lands! I suppose he's planning on surprising you and I've put my big foot right in it." Martha looked chagrined.

Annabelle ducked under the counter. "I'll kill that man," she muttered, and took off in the direction she'd seen Clint go.

"Friend, I think you might be in some trouble," Jed said as he watched Annabelle march toward them.

Clint turned and saw Annabelle storming his way under a full head of steam. "You may be right, Jed. She sure looks in a fury." His mind raced trying to figure out what had her going now. He carefully hid a smile. He loved it when she fairly bubbled over with anger. Making up with his wife was something he looked forward to with pleasure. It more than compensated for the arguments.

"Clint Strand," she said, coming to a stop in front of him, hands on her hips, "are you planning to build yourself a house?"

He couldn't stop the smile. She looked so furious. He didn't mind a bit. She brought that same fire, same intensity to their lovemaking. He was a lucky man, he figured, to be given all that passion. "I'm planning on building *us* a house." So much for his surprise.

"I can't believe this. Are you forever going to be doing things behind my back? Don't you think I have a right to say how I want a house built?"

"I guess I figured you wouldn't argue about how much lumber and how many nails. That's about as far as I've gotten."

Guilt rushed through her as she thought of her own secrets, her love for him, her pregnancy. She had no right to be angry with him, take her frustrations out on him. He wanted to surprise her, that's all. She acted from fear and hated it. Would she ever trust completely his promise to stay? If she just felt sure of his love . . .

"I'm sorry, honey. I wanted to surprise you. I didn't think about the special things you might want in your house. I'm sorry. I'll show you the plans when we get home."

She slumped, her anger suddenly gone. "No, I'm sorry for being so—" She stopped abruptly when she saw a big, fierce-looking man come up behind Clint.

"Beating up on women now, Strand."

Clint whirled and in the same motion shoved Annabelle behind him.

"No, I don't beat up women. Only men who don't mind their business." Clint didn't know this man, but he recognized the unspoken challenge and felt the old sickness rise inside his gut and choke him with despair. It had all been too good to be real and now his past had found him again. God, if only Annabelle was home and not here to witness this. He didn't feel a moment's uncertainty as to the outcome. One way or another.

"Clint?" She stepped beside him and her voice sounded fragile and fearful in his ears.

"Annabelle, get out of the way." He didn't take his eyes off the other man as he tried to release his arm from her grip.

"What's happening? I don't understand." She plucked at his shirtsleeve to get his attention.

"Jed!" Clint called out to his friend. He grabbed Annabelle's fingers and uncurled them from his gun arm. "Get her out of here, right now!"

Jed pulled Annabelle away. "I've got her, don't worry."

"Clint!" she cried to him.

"Move, Annabelle. Get the hell away from here, now."

He backed away some distance from the man and settled his hands on his gun belt. "What's on your mind?"

The man mirrored Clint's actions and cocked a heavy dark eyebrow. "Just ridin' through. Stopped at the saloon and heard you were in town. Thought I'd see if all the stories about you are true."

"They are."

The stranger shrugged and hitched up his gun belt. "Some things a man's got to find out for himself."

Clint nodded his understanding. In the background, he heard Annabelle struggling and arguing with Jed and Martha. He had to clear all thoughts of her from his mind. He needed every bit of concentration he could muster. He pulled the dark cloak of his experience around him and took cautious comfort as the knowledge of the old life fired his blood; the sounds around him faded. Only he and the stranger existed now.

The man he faced had murder in his eyes, like so many before. For a final second Clint opened his mind and heard Annabelle one last time. Her voice, in the background, pleading with him; it might be the last time he heard her. It surely would be if he lost his concentration. He shut down all thoughts of her and the life they had together, all thoughts of what he had to lose now; more than just his life.

The sound of her voice drifted from his mind, replaced by a montage of faces. Faces of all those desperate men striving to create themselves in the folktales of others. Men with the fear of death in their hearts and denial of death in their eyes.

Clint drew in a deep breath and released it slowly. He felt the cold, sure hands of control steady his nerves, quiet his stomach. This part of his life he knew as well as the lines in the palms of his hands. His heart beat at an even pace now and his eyes saw every movement the man made, no matter how subtle.

Clint was ready.

The surface of his skin sensed the waves of anxiety coming from the man. His need to prove himself against Clint radiated across the distance between them and Clint knew before the draw he would walk away whole this time, in body anyway.

The stranger's draw, Annabelle's scream and Clint's shot merged in his mind and fused in his heart. Without going to the fallen body, he knew he had killed the man.

Clint drew in a deep breath of fresh spring air. He raised his face to the warm sun and felt the joy, the urgency of life race through his mind, his body and his soul.

Alive!

Once again he'd come through alive. Once more fate dealt the cards in his favor.

Clint turned to where Annabelle stood, held fast in Jed's grip. Horror, written with a heavy hand, stared at him from her eyes. Her gaze flashed away and locked on the dead body. She looked bewildered, as if she couldn't believe what she saw.

Weariness washed over Clint, replacing the brief moment of exultation that being alive brought him. What now? What would she do? Her usual unpredictability had been a constant fascination to him. Now it worried his mind and tugged at his heart. He couldn't begin to guess what the next few moments would bring.

He started toward her, anxious to touch her, to make physical contact with her. All at once he was surrounded by men from the town.

"Hell of a shot, Clint."

Someone patted him on the back.

"By God, I wouldn't have believed it. You let that shooter draw first!"

Clint angled his head, trying to find Annabelle in the crowd of people converging on him.

"I'll bet we never see the likes of that again in Pleasant Valley," said a man behind Clint.

He had to get to her. Had to explain, needed to touch her fresh, clean skin. To run his shaking hands through her wonderful red hair.

"Boy, you sure showed that fella."

Clint wanted to shout at them to get away, to leave him alone. To let him get to Annabelle. Suddenly he saw her. Wrapped in Jed's arms, she hid her face against his chest, drew from him the comfort Clint wanted to give her. Comfort he doubted he had the right to give her now.

He saw the sheriff coming toward him and wondered if, for the first time in his life, he was going to be arrested.

Sheriff Jensen nodded at Clint. "You know this fella?"

"No. But I know his kind."

"He was in the saloon, braggin' on what a fine shot he was. One of the loggers let it slip you were here and were the best shot around." He shook his head. "Like lightning to dry prairie grass, this—" he motioned to the dead man "—this had to happen."

"You taking me in?"

"Hell no. I just hope this is the last damn fool to come into town with famous on his mind."

Clint looked at Annabelle; she still stared at the dead gunfighter. "I had no choice."

Sheriff Jensen put his hand on Clint's arm. "I know that." He looked around at Annabelle. "You better get her out of here. We'll take care of... him." His grip tightened. "Don't let that loudmouth in the saloon worry you. This town can keep its mouth shut. I'll see to that."

"I appreciate your help and concern," Clint said.

"Where'd you last see this Docker fella?"

"Tucson."

"I'll send a wire. See if he's still there."

This man had the authority to order Clint to leave town. A warm feeling of belonging filled his chest. His words stuck in his throat and he could only nod his thanks. He left the sheriff and shouldered his way through the crowd of men, making his way to Annabelle, still wrapped in the shelter of Jed's arms.

Clint held out his hand to her.

She looked at it as if she expected it to be covered in blood. Unconsciously, Clint wiped it on his trousers and held his hand out to her once again. If asked later, he would have said his heart stopped beating while he stood there reaching out to her.

With shaking fingers, she stopped the trembling of her mouth. Part of her wanted desperately to take his hand, to touch him, to prove to herself he still lived. The other part? It wanted to run from this man. This stranger who stood before her with his hand out, a hard look in his eyes and a firm white line around his mouth.

Who is he? her mind cried out. *He looks so closed up, so frozen. Where is the beguiling grin that takes my heart each time he flashes it at me? Is there no warmth behind the frozen blue of his eyes? When he touches me now, will I still trust him not to hurt me?*

Her fear overcame all other feelings. Her fear of Clint, this man she loved. She needed some time away from him to sort out the disorder of her thoughts, her feelings. "I—I think I'll go home with, uh, Martha and Jed."

Martha fairly hissed at her. "Don't be a fool, Annabelle Strand. Take your man's hand and go with him. He needs you, so stop this foolishness."

Annabelle glanced around at the crowd of men who'd been treating Clint like a hero. They waited to see what she would do. *She* didn't know what she would do! She realized Clint's hand still reached for her. It shook! He was afraid! Afraid she wouldn't stand by him.

Her heart, acting bravely on its own, reached out, and she followed hesitantly with her hand, unsure she did the right thing until she saw the grateful expression in his eyes.

Clint took off his hat and with his forearm wiped the sweat rolling down his face. What the hell could he say to her? She didn't understand this at all. His experience reassured him that he couldn't have afforded to just wound the gunman, but Clint felt a bitter relief; he was alive but he had done murder in front of Annabelle.

Chapter Twelve

They rode down Mosquito Road toward the cabin on Jed's borrowed wagon, their horses tied behind by their reins. Clint was reminded of their first ride together, after their shotgun wedding in the saloon. After another shooting.

Somehow this time seemed even worse. Now he and Annabelle had established a new life together; they had plans. Now his resurfaced past jeopardized everything. No, be honest, he told himself. *He* endangered their life together. Just his presence put her in danger. His decision to eliminate the stranger—the way he'd done all the others—made their future even more uncertain.

By killing the challenger, Clint drove his hopes for a new, peaceful life with Annabelle farther from his grasp. He could have tried to talk the gunfighter out of it, attempted to persuade him that killing wasn't the answer.

Deep inside he heard the cynical but truthful laughter. He would be dead now if he had tried that fool stunt. In his old life, hesitation meant suicide. You shot or got shot. Dead.

The memory of the moments after the shooting came roaring into his mind.

Another dead body at his feet. Annabelle's eyes widened in shock. All color drained from her face, leaving her freckles in bold relief against her pale skin. Her head moving back and forth in denial of what had happened. She had backed away from him as if she'd expected him to physically hurt her. He had felt waves of apprehension coming from her, and he nearly staggered under the knowledge that she feared him.

He glanced at her. She sat with her chin nearly resting on her chest, her shoulders slumped; she looked so defeated. He had never seen her like this. Annabelle always met life head-on. No mincing of words, no holding back her feelings. She might give in to tears for a minute or two, but before he knew it she was up fighting for what she wanted.

Now she seemed beaten down, crushed by life. He despised himself for being the cause of her sadness and silent condemnation. He thought of all the times he would have paid a healthy sum to silence her sharp tongue. Right now he'd pay all he owned if she would go into one of her tirades. Anything to break the dismal quiet of their ride.

She slowly straightened her back and turned toward him. He knew she had come to a decision by the determined look in her eyes. He felt her gaze move over him as if it were a touch. She searched his face as if she'd never seen him before, as if he were a stranger.

He felt tiny cracks open in his heart.

She is going to tell me to leave.

"I'll tell you one thing for certain, Clint Strand. *That* is the last time *that* is going to happen. When we get home, I expect you to throw out those guns. I never want to see one in your hands again.'' She gave a firm nod of her head, emphasizing her words.

In his mind, Clint experienced relief and rage all at the same moment. Relief she hadn't told him to go and rage that she felt she could dictate something as important as this.

"For God's sake, Annabelle. I can't do that. My guns are the only thing that stand between you and a bullet.''

She leaned toward him and poked him in the chest with a finger. "And what stands between you and a bullet? The good Lord you just called upon? If you don't carry guns, no one will shoot at you.''

That she couldn't see the absurdity of her statement astonished him. He pulled the wagon to a stop in front of their home and jumped down. He stomped around to her side and jerked her off the seat. He dragged her into the house and plopped her down in the new chair Aaron had built.

"For a pretty smart woman, you can be damn dumb sometimes—''

"Don't you throw my lack of book learn—''

"Shut up, Annabelle. This has nothing to do with books! This has to do with common sense, me—and fifteen years of watching my back. Without guns I am a dead man! Maybe not today, or tomorrow, but that day always exists. Without my guns I am committing suicide. Can you understand that?''

He paced in front of her, filled with frustration, and wished he had a drink of whiskey.

She slammed her hand on the table. "It was guns that got you into trouble in the first place. If you hadn't had the guns you wouldn't have got mixed up with those robbers and that woman.''

"For God's sake, Annabelle, you are the limit. The last I heard, you thought I was a hero for saving that woman's life.''

"Well, you were, but somebody else would have done it.''

"Not very damn likely.'' He sat down at the table and took her hand. "Try to understand, at least a little bit, what my life has been. Since that day of the train robbery, I've been good at only one thing, staying alive. I've been able to do that because of my guns.''

She pulled her hands away. "You have to understand me too, Clint. I've lost everyone I've ever cared about and some, like my mother, I never even knew.'' She reached out and touched his face. "I don't want to lose you.''

She watched as the hardness of his eyes and mouth were momentarily softened by her words, only to be replaced by a look of grim determination.

"What do you want me to do when some gunslinger faces me down? Duck? Say, 'Oh, please, mister, don't shoot. My wife made me put away my guns.''' He rose from his seat and marched to the door. "That'll guarantee to make you a rich widow for sure, Annabelle. Maybe that's what you really want.'' The door slammed behind him.

Stunned, she sat with her face in her hands, tears streaming between her fingers. How could he think that? She dropped her hands to her lap and searched out her feelings as dispassionately as she could.

Do I want him to leave now that I've seen this side of him?

Right after the gunfight, she might have said yes, when the horror of it was still with her. Almost immediately she threw off that thought. She would not give in to her usual need to do something *right now* to change the direction her . . . their lives had taken.

She had felt so afraid. Afraid of the man who sat beside her in the wagon, disquiet in his eyes. Fear of losing all they had begun together invaded her thoughts.

Ever fearful of being left alone again, Annabelle felt even more terrified of what this killing might bring to them—yet another gunman to challenge Clint.

What did he want of her? Absolution? Understanding? If she couldn't give either, would he leave her? Did he expect this—this kind of thing to frequent their lives forever? Could she raise a child, knowing a killer might come to the mountains and devastate their lives again?

She rose and went out onto the porch. Weariness enfolded her. She felt depleted of all energy. The soothing sounds of the stream beckoned her and she had the strongest need to lie in the new spring grass and close out the world and all its problems. To find herself again.

She went down the steps and around the wagon. Clint was unhitching the team. Suddenly, anger overtook her again and she challenged him.

"What happens ten years from now—if you're still alive—when your eyes aren't as sharp and your hand's not so steady? What then? Do I just stand aside and watch you die?"

A stillness came over him. Amazed, she saw the hard, cold mask of the gunfighter return. The steel-nerved man she'd witnessed for the first time at the picnic surfaced. A man alone, apart. A man she didn't know.

"You'll do whatever has to be done, Annabelle. Just as I do." With a grim set to his jaw and his shoulders straight, he turned his back to her. Leading the horses, he walked into the dim interior of the barn.

Aaron looked up from sanding a fine piece of mahogany. "Home early, Mister Clint?"

He unharnessed the horses and began rubbing them down. "I might be leaving here soon."

"Seems a mite strange decision for a happy man." Aaron put down the wood and walked over to help Clint with the horses.

"I may not have any choice. I was challenged today, at the picnic."

Aaron nodded. "Reckon it was always a possibility. Looks like you made it out whole."

"Yep. This time." Clint backed the horse into the stall and hung the oat bag under his nose.

"The fella dead?"

"Mmm-hmm."

"The missus? She not takin' it well, I guess."

"She wants me to put away my guns."

Aaron finished with the horse and put him in the stall to feed. He sat down on a low stack of lumber and gazed at the floor between his boots. After a few moments, he glanced up. "Don't know, Mister Clint. Don't seem like a smart move to me."

"It's not and I can't." Clint scooted over a case of tinned goods and sat opposite Aaron. "She's afraid.

Hell, I can understand that. I'm afraid, afraid something will happen to her.''

"Man'd be pretty dumb to come around this place lookin' for trouble, what with the both of us here."

"That's true. Docker sure wouldn't. He likes to ambush or backshoot." Clint shook his head. "I don't know, Aaron. Maybe Annabelle and I just need some time apart, you know. To think about what we want from each other."

"Seems to me that can change all the time." Aaron grinned. "With women, it can change from day to day."

Clint smiled. "It sure can with Annabelle." His thoughts turned serious once again. "The sheriff'll be out here soon. He's checking with Tucson to see if Docker's still around there. If he is, you and me may take a trip to Sacramento to pick up that horseflesh we've been talking about."

"I'd surely like to get back to cowboyin', Mister Clint. My best times are breakin' horses."

"Yeah. I've spent a good deal of time working on someone else's ranch, moving someone else's cattle. Those were the good times. When I could let down my guard and just enjoy the feel of a horse between my legs and a good card game in a bunkhouse. But it never lasted long enough. Eventually someone would recognize me. I'd have to move on."

"Your bunkhouse days are gone. You're the boss man."

"Not yet, Aaron. Not until Annabelle can accept me as a partner here. After today, I'm not sure of anything." He stared off into the gloom of the barn. "D'you think you could ramrod this place, Aaron? It isn't much now, but with horses and a few cattle, a bunkhouse for men, it could be a good spot to settle down.''

Aaron rose and dipped water from a barrel and filled the coffeepot. He tossed in a handful of ground coffee, set the pot on the stovetop and turned to Clint. ''You'd trust me with the runnin' of the stock and men?''

''I would.''

''I'd be mighty proud to accept, Mister Clint.''

Clint got to his feet and held his hand out to Aaron. They shook hands and Clint left the barn. Even if he had to leave for good, his worries lessened now he knew Aaron would run things for Annabelle.

Annabelle hung out the wash on the new sturdy lines Aaron had strung for her. She looked toward the rise, where Clint sat beneath a tall mountain oak.

Five days since the picnic and not many more than five words had passed between them. She badgered, nagged and pushed at him, but he wouldn't talk to her. Finally, he began sending messages to her by way of Aaron.

She hated it. Aaron hated it. She suspected Clint hated it.

He wanted her to give in completely. Of course, she wanted the same from him. Like two gunfighters waiting for the other to draw first. She almost smiled at the thought, but smiling was a hard thing to come by these days.

The nights were little better. They entered their bed and lay like corpses. Yet during the night one would reach for the other and their lovemaking became furious and desperate, as if they were storing memories for the hard times to come.

Aaron came from the barn to stand before her, shuffling his feet in the dust.

"For heaven's sake, Aaron, stop acting like a ten-year-old caught stealing cookies."

He straightened his big body and took off his hat. "Missus, I surely dislike this, totin' words 'tween you and Mister Clint. I despise it, for a fact."

She pinned a pillowcase to the line and put her hands on her hips. "Do you suppose I like it? That man is as stubborn as a billy goat. What's he want now?" She bent over to pull a sheet out of the basket.

Aaron grinned. "Mister Clint says he's stayin' up on the rise to stake out the house. Says he might be late for dinner."

"You tell him that he'll be lucky if he gets any dinner at all."

"I don't know, missus. Mister Clint surely likes your cookin'." He chuckled and put his hat back on. "He won't like it, but I'll tell him, missus."

Not another minute, she told herself. She wouldn't put up with it another minute. "Never mind, Aaron. I'll tell him myself. I'm putting an end to this foolishness right now." She heard Aaron's relieved sigh.

She dropped the wet sheet into the basket and strode up the rise. She would somehow force him to talk with her, to end this terrible emptiness between them.

Clint watched her storm up the rise. He knew this morning they couldn't go on like this, both of them wanting something the other couldn't give. He would go to Sacramento. The sheriff had come out yesterday with the news that Docker had left for Mexico. It was safe to go for the horses. Even safe enough to take Aaron with him.

If he left, Annabelle could settle in her own mind whether she wanted him to stay for good. He felt it only fair to give her the time she needed without the pressure of his presence.

Coming to a stop in front of him, she put her fists on her hips and stamped her foot. "I've had enough of this silence, Clint Strand. You will talk to me, now!"

Slowly, he got to his feet and hooked his thumbs in his belt. "I'm leaving in the morning, Annabelle."

"No!" The cry burst from her lips before she could stop it.

He unhooked his thumbs and cradled her face in his hands. "I think we need some time away from each other. I'm taking Aaron. We'll go to Sacramento and look over the stock. Herv told me there's some fine horseflesh to be had there."

"Are... are you coming back?" Her throat closed so tight she barely got out her words.

"Yes. I want to be here with you, honey. But I think we both have to think about what we want and how we're going to manage getting it." He pulled her into his arms and held her tight. "We'll work it out somehow, whatever's best."

She hated the sad look in his eyes, as if he didn't really believe his own words. She should tell him about the baby. It might make him happy, then he'd stay. He wouldn't leave her if he knew she carried his child. She pushed away and searched his beloved face.

"I'm... I'm..."

"You're what, sweetheart?"

She couldn't do it. If he needed to be away from her, she couldn't hold him that way. "I'm sure you're right. When you come back we'll sit down and, as you say, work it out."

He smiled and brought her close again. "Good girl."

That evening, with a heavy heart, Annabelle put supper on the table. *He'll be gone in the morning.* She didn't want to be alone again. Perhaps he would let her go with them. There was no reason for her to stay here.

He said they needed time apart. Annabelle resisted this idea with every beat of her heart. He might get used to being away from her. He might get shot. He might even decide life in Philadelphia is better, easier, safer. He might leave her in Aaron's care and just go home to his wealthy family back East. She couldn't let this happen.

She could hear Clint and Aaron washing up outside. She stepped to the open door and watched them dry their faces and hands. She would just say it.

"I want to come with you."

Clint hung the towel on the hook over the washbasin. He ran his fingers through his sandy hair, then looked up at her. "No, Annabelle. Aaron and I will be traveling fast. It's fifty hard miles on horseback to Placerville, then a hot, dirty ride on the train to Sacramento."

She knew he was right, but her fear of being left filled her heart and drove reason from her mind. "I don't care. I want to go."

"Next time, honey." He came up the steps and took her in his arms.

"Will there be a next time?" Her words were muffled against his chest. "What if you get challenged in Sacramento?"

Clint took her chin in his hand and forced her to look at him. "My hand is steady and my eyes sharp. I promise. There will be a next time."

"What about Docker?" she pressed.

"Honey, you heard the sheriff. Docker's on his way to Mexico. That's a long way from here."

She sagged against him with relief. He hadn't ever lied to her. "All right, I'll stay here."

"That was never in doubt."

She punched him in the ribs.

Clint laughed for the first time in days. The sound of its richness made her smile back at him. Maybe they would be fine. He rubbed his ribs and wondered how many little bruises she'd leave on him over the next thirty or so years. He'd just have to make her kiss them away.

"I'm starving, wife."

"I'll say one thing, Clint Strand. Whether you even got a meal today *was* in doubt." She glanced over at the tall dark man grinning at them. "Right, Aaron?"

"I got to tell you, Mister Clint, food was a dubious thing around here today. I'm surely glad you decided to talk to the missus. Otherwise we'd be eatin' oats with the mule."

Clint laughed and drew Annabelle inside to the table. "A man's just got to be aware of a woman's limits, Aaron. One side of the line, the vittles are just fine. Go over the line and you'll sport a hollow belly for sure."

Annabelle sliced roasted chicken onto Clint's plate. "Better watch your mouth or you'll be sporting an empty bed."

Clint grabbed her hand and placed a sizzling kiss in her palm. "Now, why would you deny yourself all that pleasure, woman?"

Aaron laughed right out loud. Clint pulled her into his lap and Annabelle hid her heated face against his warm, muscled chest.

This is our last night together, she thought as she lay next to Clint. No, not our last. He *will* be back. He promised.

"How long will you be gone?" Her voice sounded sad even to her.

"A month. Maybe longer."

She swallowed hard to keep the tears away. She hadn't dreamed it would be that long.

Clint reached over and pulled her close. He knew she worried he wouldn't return. Hell, he didn't want to leave, but he believed they needed time to search out their feelings and needs. He couldn't do that around Annabelle. She was such a lively presence in his life; she took up too much of his thoughts. Besides, he needed to stock the ranch and he couldn't do it in Pleasant Valley. He had to go to Sacramento. If he returned without being challenged, maybe he could consider her plea to give up his guns.

He squeezed her to reassure her. "Before you know it we'll be home. The time will go by fast, honey."

She burrowed even closer. "For you, maybe. Not for me. You and Aaron will be traveling, buying horses, drinking in the saloons. All those things men do."

Suddenly, she rose up on an elbow and he swore he could feel her fierce gaze in the dark.

"Don't you dare take up with any of those women in the saloons." He heard the anger in her voice over something that hadn't even happened and, as far as he was concerned, wouldn't happen.

He rolled over and trapped her beneath his body. "You listen to me, sweetheart. I'm going to buy horses, not women. You are the only one I want in my bed. What we have here is more than I ever dreamed I'd have with a woman, let alone my wife. Hell, Annabelle, I never even thought to have a wife."

"You're not sorry, then—that I forced you to marry me?"

"You didn't force me. I could have taken that gun from you whenever I wanted." He felt her go still as the night outside their window. He knew she wrestled with his statement and waited for her furious outburst.

She relaxed against him, slipped her arms around his neck and pulled him down to meet her lips. "Make love to me, Clint. I don't want to think about anything but this night. Make me forget about Docker, the danger, about your leaving. About everything. Just make love to me until it fills my body and my mind."

His arms closed around her and held her to him as if he could draw her in through the very pores of his skin. As if by pressing her closer than ever he would merge them into one being.

He absorbed the feel of her naked body against him. Their skin seemed to blend and cover them both under a blanket of desire so strong, so essential, Clint knew he would never forget this night as long as he lived.

He found every secret she owned. He reveled in her textures. The brisk feel of hair, the silky-smooth inner part of her. The dark, feminine well that promised him endless delights. He wanted to burn the feel of her, the scent of her, into his brain.

When he at last plunged into her, Annabelle thought she might faint from the sheer joy of possessing him in her body. She wanted to cleave to him so strongly this mating would remain with her for all the days of his absence.

He rose above her, all power, all desire, all male. She sensed the small tremblings begin and cried out silently to him, *I love you.*

While Clint readied his bedroll, Annabelle made bundles of food for their journey. There weren't many places for them to get food or supplies between Pleasant Valley and Sacramento. Placerville, the first town of any size, was a good fifty miles away.

A knock on the door signaled Aaron had the horses ready. Clint shouldered his bedroll and Annabelle followed him out the door with the food packages.

Aaron relieved her of her burden and fitted the bundles onto the horses. "Looks like we'll be eatin' fine on the road, missus."

She tried to give him a smile but knew she didn't do too well. "It's a long trip. Can't have my men going hungry."

Clint finished tying on his belongings and turned to her. "I'll send a wire to Jed at the livery when I reach the train station in Placerville and again in Sacramento. He can have one of the boys ride over with it."

She wrapped her arms around his waist and hugged him tight. She searched his eyes, memorizing the bright blue and the deep lines radiating from them. "You look tired."

He smiled down at her. "Considering you kept me awake most of the night, woman, what do you expect?"

She felt a blush heat her skin and she nuzzled against his chest. "I just wanted to be sure you felt content before you left."

"I'm content all right. Content and exhausted. Be lucky if I don't fall off my horse before we leave town."

She gave him a mock frown. "I swear, men complain if things are too good or too bad. No pleasing you."

"I'm pleased, Annabelle. Pleased right out of my drawers."

How would she stand it when he had gone? His wicked sense of humor. His laughter and teasing. "I'll miss you, Clint. I hoped after last night you—"

"Might have changed my mind?"

She nodded and knew her hope shone out of her eyes.

"Have you?"

She shook her head. She still hated his guns and wanted them gone from their life.

"Then there isn't much to say. I can't agree to what you want, Annabelle. All my experience tells me it's wrong."

He gave her a quick hug and leapt into the saddle. "I'll stop at the bank. Herv will be ready to help you with money if you run out. Just go ask for it, it's yours. Get anything you need at the general store. I'll settle up when I get back." He pulled on the reins to calm the frisky horse. "There'll be men out to start on the house. Jed and Martha will keep in touch. You'll be fine."

She wanted to scream, I won't be fine without you. But she didn't. She nodded her agreement. "Be careful."

Clint kicked his horse and rode down the road.

Aaron took the reins and walked his horse over to where Annabelle stood.

"I'll watch his back, missus."

Annabelle held up her hand. He enfolded it in his large one. "I thank you, Aaron."

She watched them until they disappeared in the early morning light.

Chapter Thirteen

Annabelle's gaze followed Martha around her kitchen as she bustled about putting pans of freshly risen bread dough into the oven and shooed noisy children from the room.

Martha reached for the coffeepot and poured two cups. She sat across from Annabelle and heaved a grateful-sounding sigh. "Feels good to be off my feet. Well, how long's he been gone?"

"Better than three weeks." Annabelle, her chin cupped in one hand, idly scraped dough from the breadboard with a fingernail.

"Land sakes, you sound like he's been gone forever."

"He might be."

Martha spooned four teaspoons of sugar into her cup and took a sip of her coffee. "Do you really think he won't be back?"

Annabelle shrugged.

"You are a goose. That man's not going to run out on you. He loves you."

Again, Annabelle shrugged.

"What makes you so uncertain of Clint?"

Annabelle chewed on the yeasty-tasting dough. "We had a fight."

"*A* fight? I have to tell you, child, Jed and I fight all the time. He may appear soft-spoken, but he can get his dander up mighty high." She refilled her cup and spooned her usual heaping teaspoons of sugar into the coffee. "Do you see me living alone? No sir. Fighting . . . arguments are part of living together."

"Maybe. I told Clint to throw away his guns, that I never wanted to see them again."

Martha slammed her cup on the table, splashing the dark liquid onto the oak surface. "Appears to me you want that man dead instead of in your bed." She laughed. "I made a rhyme."

Annabelle rose from her chair, nearly tipping it over. "This is *not* funny. That's what *will* happen to him if he accepts every challenge that comes his way. He'll be dead!"

She grabbed a rag from the sink board and wiped up the spilled coffee. "It's not funny. He was furious when I asked . . . demanded he give up his guns. That's when he decided to leave." She moved back to the sink and pumped water over the rag. "Must be nice to have a pump."

"You'll have one in that house that's going up. Clint said he knew that was one of your great desires." Martha took the cover off a cake plate and sliced through a sweet-smelling loaf. "Here, sit down and have some date bread. Made it early this morning."

"That's another thing." Annabelle took a bite and chewed furiously. "There's men up on the rise every morning working on that house and the bunkhouse. When I ask about it, they just smile and say, 'Your husband arranged for it, Mrs. Strand.'" She took another big bite. "Just like he does everything."

"Seems to me, Annabelle, you are mighty hard to please. You've got a strong man who'll take care of you and your child. A good man who fairly dotes on doing things for you, and all you do is complain. I have to tell you, I don't understand it for a minute."

"I know." Annabelle sighed. "He's been so good to me, Martha. He treats me like I was special."

"Maybe you are to him."

"I just want to be part of the plans he makes for us. He didn't tell me about the pump."

"Maybe he likes to surprise you. Jed did the same thing. Stashed me off in Sacramento while he had this place built. I was furious with him. But he knew me and my needs well. I wouldn't change one board of my home." She looked around her kitchen, a pleased expression on her face.

Annabelle had to smile at her contented friend. She rose, took her shawl off the back of her chair and wrapped the soft wool around her shoulders. "Time for me to go. I've got animals to feed and water."

Martha walked Annabelle outside and watched her unhitch her horse. "How long are you going to be able to ride?"

"As long as I need to, I guess." She shoved her foot in the stirrup and heaved herself onto the placid animal. "Clint said that to me the other day. That I'd have to do whatever I need to be done. He was right and I'm feeling fine. A lot better than the last time." It suddenly dawned on her that she could talk about the loss of her child without the sting of bitter tears.

Martha moved to the side of the animal and patted Annabelle on the knee. "You ride slow and easy. And stop worrying about your man and those guns. Jed says Clint's the finest shot there is. He will live to be a crotchety old man. As long as he's around you'll be safe."

"That's what I've been trying to tell you. As long as he's around."

"That's not what I meant, and you know it."

"But it's what I've been saying all along, Martha. I need him around to feel safe, but now if he's wearing his guns, I don't feel safe at all. When I asked him to take them off for good, he left me. Now I should feel safe and I don't."

She kicked her horse and moved down the road. Without turning, she waved goodbye to her friend.

When she neared the cabin she noticed the workmen had left the site of the new house. She felt so tired. She might have to give up riding soon, she thought. The movement of the horse made her feel queasy. She shouldn't have eaten so much of Martha's baking. It didn't rest easy on her stomach.

She slid down from the horse and wrapped the reins around the porch railing. She would lie down for a short while before she fed the animals. There was plenty of time before dark for chores.

Dust clung to her skirt and she brushed it off before going inside. No use dragging in more to sweep out. She put her hand on the doorknob. The door crashed open and a bone-crushing grip yanked her inside, nearly pulling her arm from its socket.

"What—"

"Shut up and sit down," a whiskey-cured voice demanded.

She was slammed down onto an apple box. Her hair fell around her face and she frantically brushed it back to see the man who stood before her.

Dear God, he is huge, she thought. He loomed over her, his very size a threat. Much bigger than Aaron and rough-looking, he smelled of sour sweat and liquor.

"Who...who are you?" She hated the quaver in her voice, but he terrified her.

"Where is he?" His voice rasped down her spine and bumps rose on her skin.

"Wh-who?" *I know who this man is.* The realization hit her like a blow to the gut. The murderous look in his eyes, the vicious slant of his mouth, his fetid breath. He embodied every image she had ever had of the man who wanted to kill Clint. *Bull Docker!*

He grabbed the front of her dress and pulled her to her feet, bringing her even closer to him. "Don't play dumb with me, sweetheart. Where is he?"

Annabelle shook her head. "I don't know who...who you mean." Her heart throbbed in her throat, and when she tried to swallow, she nearly choked.

He pushed her away a little and glared into her eyes. His mouth tightened even more and his eyes seemed to flash hatred at her. "It don't pay to act stupid with me, little girl. I want that son-of-a-bitch who shot my brother."

She felt shock roll through her body as his free hand drew back. *He's going to hit me!* The blow snapped her head and the metallic taste of blood flowed over her tongue.

"He's gone!"

Still holding her by the front of her dress, he shook her hard. "Where is he?"

"S-s-stop. Please stop shaking me." She felt sure she would throw up, humiliating herself when she needed to be strong before this man, needed to convince him Clint was gone forever.

He slammed her back on the box and leaned over her, his foul, hot breath flowing over her skin. She gagged, then gagged again.

He moved away quickly. "You sick?"

She nodded and rushed for the sink. She pulled a pan from its hook, bent over and lost everything in her stomach.

The man watched her. Silent. Menacing.

She poured water from the crock over a cloth and wiped her face. Her hands shook so hard she feared she would drop the cloth.

"You through pukin'?"

"Y-yes. I think so."

"Sit down." His words weren't tenderly spoken, they were a demand.

"I have to lie down." She felt the weakness spread through her body, a warning to take to her bed.

He grinned and she noticed a tooth gone from the front of his mouth. She shivered and felt chilled to the bone.

"I could lie down, too." His grin widened and took on a lecherous look.

"No! I'll be fine." Dear Lord, help me, she prayed. She grabbed the damp cloth and wiped her face again.

"Now, I'm going to ask you one more time. Where is Clint Strand?"

All at once fury raced through her. This man wanted to kill Clint. She felt the blood return to her face and steel return to her backbone. "I told you. He's gone. Left me for good."

He slapped her again. She fell off the box to the floor. *Dear God, he'll kill me if I can't convince him Clint's gone and not coming back.*

She wiped the blood from her mouth with the hem of her skirt. "I swear to you, he's not coming back."

He reached down and wrenched her to her feet. He loomed over her, a living threat. "Now, tell me. Why would he leave a pretty little girl like you?"

"I'm pregnant."

His gaze widened for a second, then narrowed. "Not good old Clint. His *honor* wouldn't let him." He made honor sound like a dirty word. "Oh no, he'd stick by you."

Her mind raced frantically to find the argument that would send this terrible man away. "I . . . I insisted he give up his guns."

With both hands he held her away from him and stared at her as if she were crazy, something strange and unknown. "You *what?*"

She watched the incredulous look on his face and knew she'd found the answer. She eased herself from his loosened grip and moved back a little. "I told him to give up his guns or give up me." She shrugged. "He gave up me."

Laughter boomed through the cabin. "Maybe there's hope for him yet." He pulled out a box and sat down heavily. "Little girl, you played the wrong card. A man like Clint, a man like me. Guns keep us alive."

He's not like you! The realization screamed through her. Clint and this animal were nothing alike. Clint would never hit her or threaten her. A niggling of understanding grew in her mind of what would happen to Clint, to her and their baby, if Clint put away his guns.

"Are...are you Bull Docker?" She had to know for sure, to warn Clint somehow.

The huge man flashed his gap-toothed grin. "Told you about me, did he?"

She lifted a shoulder. "He mentioned you."

He quickly reached out and grabbed her arm. "Did he tell you I would kill him—and why?"

She tried to free her arm, but he held on tight. "Yes! He told me. Your brother tried to backshoot him."

He slapped her once more. "That's a lie!"

Annabelle reeled against the table and grabbed the edge to keep from falling. She knew his words were the lie. Clint would never shoot without a good reason. She understood this now. Now, when it might be too late.

He released her. "I'll kill him. Believe it. When we meet again, one of us will die. And I don't intend it be me."

She wiped her lip with the back of her hand. "Well, you won't meet him here. He's gone to Canada."

He drew his thick black brows together and raised his fist to hit her again.

Annabelle jumped from her seat and moved out of range. "I swear it!" It felt as if her blood would explode in her head. Pain pounded in her skull and she felt dizzy with fear. He might still kill her if he got angry enough or didn't believe her. "He's been gone over three weeks. He won't be back!"

He watched her, his eyes merely slits in his face. She could almost hear his thoughts weighing her words for truth. Please, God, let him believe me, she prayed again. I've got to convince him, got to get him out of here.

"Fix me some food."

"What?" His sudden demand left her confused.

"Are you deaf as well as stupid? I'm hungry. Give me some of what's in that pot on the stove. Make it fast."

Annabelle quickly took a plate from the cupboard, filled it with savory stew and set it in front of Docker.

He waited, just looking at her.

She realized she hadn't given him anything to eat with. She placed a knife and fork beside his plate and backed away from the table.

"Sit over there." He pointed with the fork to the box across from him.

She sat. It wouldn't do to anger him further.

He shoved the stew into his mouth as if he hadn't eaten in days. "Better than that slop they give you at the hotel."

"They let you stay at the hotel?" She couldn't believe any hotel keeper would let such a man bed down in his establishment.

Docker's confident grin spread over his stubbled face. "Little girl, I stay wherever I want. I might even decide to stay here, with you. That bed looks damn good to me."

Horror and loathing galvanized Annabelle and she shot to her feet. She grabbed the bread knife off the sink. "I'll kill you if you touch me, then I'll kill myself."

Docker roared with laughter. "Sit down and shut up. I'd take a good whore anytime before I'd take you. Hell, a man wants a willing woman in his bed and a whore's always willing."

He shoved his empty plate away and got to his feet. His assessing gaze traveled over her.

She felt the bile rise in her throat and tightened her grip on the knife.

Docker wiped a grubby hand over his mouth.

Annabelle moved back a step and brought the knife up between them.

Docker's smile wrote terror in her heart.

"Yeah," he said. "A good whore every time. She knows what to expect and what to give. She's worth every dime."

Suddenly the knife weighed fifty pounds and her hand dropped to her side.

He moved so swiftly she didn't see the blow coming. Her head hit the edge of an apple box as she fell, spraying stars behind her eyelids. Sprawled on her back with his legs straddling her waist, she instinctively knew it was spurned masculine pride that had knocked her off her feet.

He stepped back and snatched her up with him. "I'm going but I'm not leaving you in here to put a bullet in my back." He dragged her through the door and around the back of the cabin.

"I don't have a gun." She struggled to free herself from his bruising hold.

"So you say." He pulled her along to where his horse was tied to the clothesline pole.

"I don't!"

"Little girl, I'm still alive 'cause I don't believe many people."

He untied his horse and started to mount.

From the barn came Velvet's pleading bellow to be milked.

Docker came to a dead stop and stood still as a rattler waiting to strike.

Velvet sounded again.

Docker tightened his grasp on Annabelle's wrist and started for the barn, dragging her along.

"What are you doing?" she asked, puzzled by his direction. She thought for sure he finally was leaving.

"Who's in the barn?"

"No one! My God, that's only my cow."

Docker didn't stop, just kept moving toward the barn. "We'll see."

He cautiously opened the barn door and stepped to one side, taking Annabelle with him.

"You're crazy. Honestly, it's only my cow."

He turned his head and glared at her. "Shut up."

"Fine, make a fool of yourself over a dumb cow." She cursed her fool tongue for its imprudent words.

Docker jerked her close and his breath turned her stomach sour. "If I was a fool, I'd have been dead years ago, little girl."

Suddenly he released her, kicked the door open and went through firing.

Annabelle screamed.

Velvet bellowed.

Docker quit shooting. The silence rose thick and heavy around them.

Velvet bellowed again.

Docker fired.

Velvet fell to the straw-covered dirt floor, her legs kicking and blood bursting from her heart.

Annabelle stood with both hands covering her mouth and tears streaming down her face. Velvet! Docker had shot Velvet, her precious cow.

Docker grabbed her shoulder and whirled her around. "Tell Strand when you see him, he'll be as dead as that cow."

He shoved his gun back into its holster and left Annabelle standing in the dim light of the barn. One thought screamed through her mind.

Dear Lord, he didn't believe me.

At dusk, the sheriff found Annabelle in the barn, holding Velvet's head in her lap.

"Mrs. Strand? Annabelle? What the hell happened here?"

She raised her tear-streaked face. "He shot my cow."

Sheriff Jensen knelt beside her. "Who?"

"Docker. Bull Docker."

"Damn. I was hoping against all the good sense I have that he hadn't found you."

"You saw him? Why didn't you stop him? Why did you let him come out here?"

"I've been over to Marysville to a trial. I just got back. Folks in the town said a gunfighter was in the saloon looking for Clint. I'm not sure how he found out about you. Nobody's admitting they told him. I'm going to ask some mighty strong questions when I get back to town."

Annabelle stroked Velvet's head. "He shot my cow. For no good reason, he just shot my cow."

"I imagine he had reason enough. To scare you, to make a point."

"He succeeded. I'm more than scared."

The sheriff eased Velvet's head from Annabelle's lap and gently brought her to her feet. "Come on, my dear. You can't stay here alone. I'll hitch up the wagon and take you over to Martha's. You can stay there until Clint gets back from Sacramento."

"I'll ride my horse, she's still saddled." She felt somehow separated from her body. She knew she moved at Sheriff Jensen's side, but couldn't feel the ground beneath her feet, the early chill of the spring air—anything. "Clint may not come back, you know."

"When he gets my wire, he'll come back."

Annabelle stopped and gripped his arm. Her heartbeat sped up and fear chased the blood through her veins. "He can't! Docker will kill him."

Jensen patted her hand. "Now, you rest easy. We aren't going to let that happen. Things will be just fine."

"Why do men always say that to women?"

The sheriff didn't answer her, he just tugged at her arm.

Annabelle went with him, but she didn't think for one minute things would be fine.

"Aaron Parker here will be my foreman. Any of you have trouble taking orders from him?" Clint looked at the four men he'd hired to work the horses and cattle. "If you do, now's the time to ride out. He's the boss, that's final."

One of the older men stepped forward. He looked trail-worn and weather-beaten. "I always figured a man should be judged by the horse he rode and how he treated that horse. I saw him riding it out with that rangy, mean-minded bronc today. He's no pasture man. All I need to know."

"Mr. Strand," said another man. "We, the men and I, talked it over. We'd be pleased to ride with you. Aaron here, we figger him to be a square shooter, got a fine hand with his animal. Good enough for us."

Clint smiled as the other two cowhands nodded in agreement. "It'll be hard work. We're building from scratch."

"Ain't nobody drowned in their own sweat as I know of."

All of them laughed and Clint felt the thrill of a new beginning rush through his belly. These were good men; they respected Aaron's knowledge and skill. "Fine, we'll see you in the morning." He shook hands with the newly hired men and they left for the saloon to have a final drink before the trip to Pleasant Valley.

Clint rested his forearm on the corral railing and looked over the fifteen horses he'd purchased over the past few days. He'd bought more than he planned, but six of the mares carried foals. A bargain at half the price.

"What do you think, Aaron?"

"I'm thinking we sure need that new barn, Mister Clint. Some of those mares'll have to be inside soon."

Clint smiled, brimming with pleasure. "That's true enough." He slapped Aaron on his broad back. "Well, friend, we are in the horse business in a big way."

"You still plannin' on buying some cattle?"

"Yep. I'll start looking the stock over tomorrow. We'll have them shipped by rail to Placerville, then drive them to the ranch."

"Good thing you hired on those men today. You and me, we'd have some time takin' this bunch back alone." He waved at the horses. "Just hope the bunkhouse is done. Got a feelin' those men won't like sleepin' in a spring rain."

"They're used to weather." Clint pointed to a huge black horse trotting possessively around the mares. "That fellow there is going to be a handful, even with four of us trying to manage him."

A beautiful smile spread over Aaron's face. "He and I are goin' to have an understandin'."

Clint laughed at the eagerness with which Aaron looked forward to gentling the stallion. "He may break a few of your bones first."

"Mebbe."

"I still can't see why you weren't satisfied with that sorrel. He was saddle-broke at least. This one here, hell he isn't even green-broke."

"Yessir, that's it exactly." Aaron's eyes gleamed with excitement.

Clint slapped Aaron on the back again and turned to leave. The hotel manager's son ran toward them, hollering. "Mr. Strand! Mr. Strand! I got a wire for you."

Clint fished a coin out of his pocket and gave it to the boy. "Thanks, son."

The boy looked at the coin and smiled widely. "Thank *you*, Mr. Strand." He turned and ran back in the direction of the hotel.

Clint and Aaron began a slow walk following the boy as Clint tore open the wire. He came to a sudden stop and felt the blood leave his face.

"I've got to go back, now."

"What's happened, Mister Clint?"

He took off his battered Stetson and wiped his forehead with his sleeve. "Docker's been to the ranch. He hurt Annabelle." He shoved the wire at Aaron.

"Uh, you know I can't read it, Mister Clint."

"Sorry, Aaron, I'm not thinking too clearly." He strode toward the hotel and motioned Aaron to follow him. "We've got to hire a couple of more men to help you with the horses. I have to send the sheriff a wire and let him know I'm on my way."

When they reached the hotel, Clint started up the steps. Aaron stopped. "I can't go in there. I'll wait out here."

Fury flooded Clint's brain. He grabbed Aaron by the arm and pulled him along. "We fought a damn war so you can go in that hotel. I don't have time for any of that stupidity."

When they reached the desk Clint saw the startled look in the clerk's eyes. "I don't want to hear one word out of your mouth about my friend here, you understand?"

The nervous clerk nodded. "Yes sir, Mr. Strand."

"Fine. I need to send a wire."

The clerk pushed a form over to Clint and flicked his gaze over Aaron. Clint frowned and the man moved away a few steps and tried to smile.

Clint quickly wrote his message and gave it to the clerk. "I want this sent *immediately*. I'm checking out right now." He turned to Aaron. "Come up with me while I pack and line up what I need you to do."

The clerk cleared his throat.

Clint whirled on the man. "It's bad enough a fine man like Aaron Parker has to sleep in the livery, but if you make one move to stop him coming to my room, I'll beat the living hell out of you."

The clerk ran out of the hotel, Clint's wire gripped in his white-knuckled fist.

"Come, Aaron."

Clint stood in the livery stable and tied his bedroll onto the back of his saddle. The cowboys and Aaron listened as Clint outlined what he wanted done.

"Leave tomorrow. Take your time." He bent over and tightened the cinch under the animal's belly. "I don't want those horses injured because you think you have to hurry. I'll take care of the trouble at home."

"I understand, Mister Clint," said Aaron. "Make it easy on the horses."

Clint turned to the other men. "Any of you fellas have problems leaving tomorrow? Any second thoughts about my foreman?" Clint noted the surprise on Aaron's face, but after the scene in the hotel he wanted to make sure of these men. "If any of you have reservations, leave now. Better now than have troubles later on."

The men stood silent. None left.

Clint gave a short nod and leapt into the saddle. "I'll see you all soon."

As he rode away, he prayed he'd be alive to see them again.

* * *

The ride back to Pleasant Valley was the longest of Clint's life. Every mile seemed like two. Every hour seemed three. He felt sure by the time he arrived Docker would have wreaked final havoc in his world and ended all his dreams of a good life with Annabelle.

Guilt rode the saddle with him. He'd left her to face Docker alone. He should have been there to care for her, to protect her. Instead, he'd been miles away playing the big rancher, deceiving himself that he'd finally beat the deadly game. What a fool.

When the road to Jed's place loomed ahead, Clint felt a bone-weary relief invade his body. Was Annabelle all right? How badly had Docker hurt her? Was Docker still around? That didn't seem likely. If he was, he would have ambushed Clint somewhere on the trail.

He rode the trail home with a tingling sensation between his shoulder blades. What the hell was Docker waiting for? To bring Clint down in front of the people in town? To humiliate him as he finally ended Clint's life?

He brought his exhausted horse to a stop in front of Jed's house. He slid from the saddle and patted the heaving animal's sweat-stained neck. "Thanks, old boy. You did fine."

Suddenly, the door opened and Annabelle ran out and flung herself into his arms. "Thank God, you're here." She hugged him so hard he could barely breathe. She looked up at him, then frowned. "What the devil are you doing here, Clint Strand? That Docker person is looking to kill you."

"You are as contrary as ever, my sweet. Let me look at you." Clint ran his fingers into her hair and held her head still. He saw her swollen, scabbed lip, the dark bruises on her face.

"I will kill him, Annabelle. For every bruise, for every mark on you, I will put a bullet in him. I promise you." He felt full of a hatred as deep and wide as the Mississippi—swirling and roiling, trying to overrun the banks of his control.

She shoved herself away from him. "Are you crazy? Do you think that's what I want? I want you alive and warm beside me. I want us to have children to watch us grow old. You go after him and all I'll have is another body to bury."

She crushed herself against him and moaned with her desperate need for him.

Jed and Martha stood on the porch and watched the two of them hang on to each other. Martha moved down the steps. "Will you come in and have a bite, Clint."

Annabelle looked at her friend. "No, thank you, Martha. We need to go home."

Clint would have sold his soul right that minute for a "bite." But he could see Annabelle's need to go home.

"I thank you, Martha. For the offer and for taking care of my wife. I think she's right. We need to go home."

He sensed Annabelle had a lot to say and didn't want to say it in front of their friends. Clint felt sure he had the battle of his life ahead of him.

Chapter Fourteen

Clint slid once more off his weary horse and lifted Annabelle down from hers.

"I'll take care of the horses and be in soon." Clint needed a little time to prepare himself for the argument to come. Annabelle's tense silence on the ride home warned him of her mood.

"Fine." She climbed the steps without looking back. "I'll fix you some supper."

"Fine. I'll feed Velvet."

Annabelle whirled on him and he was astonished to see tears flow from her eyes. "Docker shot Velvet! She's dead!"

His anger refueled at the cruelty Annabelle had had to witness. "That son-of-a-bitch! I don't care what you say, I'm going to kill him."

She felt her tears dry up like a pond in a drought. "I've had all the talk of killing I can stand." She turned and continued up the steps. "Wash up before you come in for supper."

Clint watched Annabelle move her food around her plate, little of it going into her mouth. His hunger drove him to eat every bite of the delicious chicken pie. His last meal had been eaten in haste hours ago.

He put down his fork and cleared his throat. They had to talk this out.

"Annabelle, we've—"

"Clint, I think—"

"Go on, honey. Tell me what's on your mind."

He saw her hand tremble as she raised her coffee cup and took a small sip. Her skin, normally so full of color, looked pale and drawn, the bruises in stark relief against its whiteness. He reached out and put a hand over hers, which was drawn into a tight fist on the table. "Go on, sweetheart."

She took a shuddering breath. "We have to leave here."

If she had told him she was dying, he wouldn't have been more astonished. He tried to hide his surprise. "Why?"

Her brows rose in a questioning arch. "Why? Because of Docker, that's why."

"Docker's not driving us from our home."

Her shoulders slumped and her voice softened. "He will kill you, Clint. He's unfeeling and vicious."

Clint felt his anger rising. "Hell, Annabelle. Don't you have any confidence in me? That I can keep myself alive, keep us alive?" The expression on her face made his heart feel so sad.

"I don't think you can make that kind of a promise. He isn't the kind of man you can count on coming at you face-to-face."

How could he make her understand how it was with him and Docker? "Honey, listen to me. I have this...crazy kind of feeling whenever Docker's around. I know, don't ask me how, but I know. I—''

She rose before him, angrier than he'd ever seen her. ''That's horse hockey, Clint Strand. I want to leave here. I want *us* to leave here. We can go to Canada or back where your folks are. Anyplace!''

He stood and took her trembling body in his arms. ''Shh, shh, sweetheart. Don't get so riled up. Let me take care of this.''

Annabelle thought she might explode with rage at his typical male response. What is the matter with him? she thought. Can't he see we might die? She pushed away from him. ''Stop treating me like a child! I could be dead now. I'm alive, but not because of any manly action on your part with your precious guns.''

She saw the color drain from his face but couldn't stop. ''I was alone when that man came here! You can't be here all the time.'' She felt out of control now. ''He can kill either one of us anytime he wants. He'll shoot you in the back. Unlike you, he has no honor! *We have to get out of here!*''

Clint ran a hand over his face and tried to tamp down his fury with her and his disappointment that she didn't trust him or his skill and experience. That she would taunt him with his inability to protect her every minute. Yet a small part of his heart beat stronger because she recognized his honor.

He pulled her back into his arms, seeking to comfort her—himself—by holding her. ''I don't mean to make light of what you're saying. I do understand how you feel, but he will follow us, Annabelle. Unless I kill him, he will find us. His hatred of me is so complete, nothing but a bullet will stop him.''

He felt trembling movements roll through her body. It took him a second to realize she was gagging. He released her quickly and she raced to the sink and threw up in a basin.

Stunned, he poured water over a cloth and held it to her forehead. He braced her against his body while again and again she gave in to the waves of nausea that racked her.

Finally she slumped, and he caught her up in his arms and took her to their bed. He ripped back the quilt and laid her down gently.

He went to the sink and poured more cool water on the cloth, then returned to the bed. He wiped her face and mouth. "Honey, I'm sorry. I guess I didn't realize how upset this has made you."

Her eyes flew open. "Upset?"

"Well, sure. To make you upset enough to—"

"You are truly a fool, Clint Strand." She turned away from him and faced the wall.

Confusion settled over his brain. What the hell did she mean? A fool? He was only trying to make her understand— He grabbed her shoulder and rolled her over.

"What's the matter with you, Annabelle?"

She looked at him as if he were stupid.

"Why . . . why are you so sick?"

She raised one dark red brow.

Clint felt his heart stop for a second, then kick up its beat so fast he thought he might pass out. Slowly, he stretched out on the bed beside her. He wrapped her solidly in his arms and kissed her forehead. She snuggled against him, tucking her head under his chin.

"Honey?"

"Yes, Clint?"

"Are . . . are you . . . a baby?"

"Yes, Clint."

He felt tears sting his eyes. For years this was what he had wanted. His own woman. His own place. His own child. Now he understood why she wanted to leave. To protect her child. He had no choice. He had to give her this chance to have her child. Their child.

"It will take me a couple of days to get things settled, before we can leave."

She arched away from him, searching his face. "Do you mean it?"

"Yes." He brought her back, close. "You will be giving up everything here you love."

He felt her shake her head against his chest. "I'll be taking everything I love with me."

His heart felt warm and full. At last she felt confident enough to tell him of her feelings for him. "Do you love me, Annabelle?"

"Oh, yes."

"I love you, too, sweetheart." He felt humbled that she cared enough for him to leave her ranch. The home she needed so desperately. The home that spelled roots, permanence, to her.

Pushing aside all thoughts of Bull Docker and the danger he represented, Annabelle let waves of happiness roll through her. Never in her life had she felt a moment of such pure bliss. He loved her. "Are you happy about the baby?" She had to know.

"I figure a man couldn't get much happier."

"You mean it?"

"Annabelle, I don't say things I don't mean. You and the baby are all that's important to me. We'll take the train back to my folks and stay there until the baby's born. Then we'll see."

All at once desire so basic, so elemental, for her filled his body. He needed to be inside her, to mate with her. "I want to make love with you, sweetheart. Will it hurt you? Is it all right?"

She wrapped her arms around his neck and nuzzled him. "Yes, Clint, please."

Early the next morning the sheriff came riding up to the house. Clint stepped out on the porch. "Come on in, Will, and have a cup of coffee. We just finished breakfast."

"I'll do that, thanks." Will Jensen tied his horse and brushed the dust from his hat.

When the men came through the door, Annabelle turned from the stove with the pot in her hand. "Good morning, Sheriff. Sit down and join us."

"Thanks, Annabelle. I could use that coffee. There's a nip in the air this morning."

Clint settled himself at the table and took a sip from his cup. "You have something special on your mind, Will? It's a little early for a social call."

"I just wanted you to know I got a wire that Docker's been spotted in Placerville."

Annabelle experienced a rush of relief. They would have time to leave town before Docker returned.

Clint reached over and placed his hand on hers. "We'll have to be careful. I'd hate to meet him on the trail." He paused briefly and took a swallow from his cup. "He'll be back. Annabelle told him I went north. Placerville's south and west." He paused then continued. "Will, we're leaving town for a while."

The sheriff looked surprised. Annabelle felt sure he'd expected Clint to stay in Pleasant Valley for a showdown with Docker. Men!

Clint frowned and she instantly knew that leaving would brand him a coward in the eyes of some people. The sheriff for one. She hated forcing him this way, but she couldn't live with the threat of Docker hanging over their lives. She didn't believe for a minute Docker would follow them to Philadelphia.

Clint cleared his throat and shifted uneasily in his chair. "I've got to get Annabelle away from here. She's expecting."

The sheriff nodded his understanding.

"I'm...we're going into town today to make arrangements with Herv for the property. Aaron will move in here and run things for us while we're gone. He's coming with horses and the men to work them. The bunkhouse is ready and Aaron knows what to do."

Surprised, Annabelle squeezed his hand. "When did you make all these plans?"

"Last night, after—"

"After supper?" Her face warmed when she realized he hadn't slept after their lovemaking. He must have made all these plans then.

Clint grinned knowingly at her. "Right. After supper." He turned back to the sheriff. "I'm giving Jed my power of attorney. Herv can help Aaron with the finances. Sam at the lumberyard can make sure the house gets finished. I want this place looked after while we're gone. I only wish I'd had time to buy cattle before this broke."

Uncaring that the sheriff witnessed what he did, Clint pulled Annabelle onto his lap. "I want to come back here someday, honey. This is where we belong. Somehow, someday, we'll manage it.''

She rested her head on his shoulder. "Thank you, Clint."

The sheriff got to his feet. "Let me know how to get in touch with you. I'll try to keep tabs on Docker for you."

"I appreciate that, Will."

"You riding out soon?"

"Yes. We'll catch the train in Placerville to Sacramento, then on to Philadelphia. I'll leave word on how to reach me."

"Fine. I'll see you then before you go."

Clint lifted Annabelle off his lap and rose to shake the sheriff's hand. "I want to thank you again, for watching over my wife."

Will smiled and cuffed Clint on the arm. "All part of the job, son. You and the missus take care."

Annabelle buckled the last strap on one of the new valises. All four were packed. Everything was done.

Yesterday they delivered the last of their food to Jed and Martha, along with the power of attorney.

They said tearful goodbyes and promised to write. Lord, she hated to leave, but it had to be.

Clint opened the door and stamped the dust off his boots before coming in. "The animals are fed and watered. Jed will check them tomorrow and Aaron should be here any day now. I wish I could see him before we left, but there's no help for that. You ready in here?"

"Yes." She moved to him and wrapped her arms around his waist. "I know you hate this. It means everything to me that you're doing this for me."

He held her close. "For us, honey. Stop worrying about me. I'm fine with this move. It makes good sense and you and the baby will be safe. That's all that matters now."

Through the open door, Annabelle saw a rider coming fast up the road. "Someone's coming." She felt a chill creep up her spine and raise the soft hairs on her neck. Deep in her heart she knew they had waited too long. Trouble rode that horse.

Clint released her and stepped out on the porch. "Hell, honey. That looks like . . . *Judaline?*"

Annabelle moved beside him and he put an arm around her. She hung on to his waist and the front of his shirt for dear life. That woman! She never brought anything but bad news.

Judaline jumped off the heaving animal and ran to the foot of the steps. Her normally pristine dress was covered with dust and her usually tightly wound hair hung in damp hanks around her face.

She reached out a pleading hand to Clint. "You've got to come." Her voice trembled with fear. "That man—Docker—has killed the sheriff." She gasped a deep breath. "Herv is wounded and Docker has him hostage in the saloon. The doctor can't get inside to help Herv."

Annabelle stepped forward, fury racing in her blood. "Get out of here, Judaline. Get out of here!"

Clint pulled her back against him and held her tight. "Is anyone else in the saloon?"

Judaline shook her head. "I don't think so. I don't know for sure. Everyone's too afraid to go in. You've got to come."

"No!" Annabelle cried. "We're leaving town. Get out of here. Find someone else."

"Hush, honey. I've got to go. There isn't anyone else."

She whirled to face him. "You promised!"

"I can't walk away from this. I'm the reason he's here. It's me he wants."

Annabelle watched the guise of the gunman settle over him. The muscles around his eyes tensed and his body became rigid. She watched her laughing, tender husband disappear and the stranger, the gunfighter, take his place. She knew she had lost.

He walked into the cabin. In a moment he came out, strapping on his guns. He bent over to tie the leather thongs around his thighs.

Annabelle, driven by a force too powerful for her to understand, moved down the stairs to stand in front of Judaline.

"Damn you. *Damn you.* You've given me nothing but heartache and trouble." Every part of her body shook with rage.

Judaline drew herself up and looked Annabelle right in the eyes. "I don't want my husband to die."

Annabelle's laugh rang out, filled with bitterness. "But you're willing to get my husband killed to save yours?"

"Yes!"

Judaline looked appalled at her own answer, but Annabelle knew at least this woman was honest. How she hated her at this moment.

Annabelle hauled back her right hand and slapped Judaline so hard she nearly fell to the ground. Judaline rubbed her cheek and gave Annabelle a look that she could swear was almost like respect.

Clint grabbed her arm. "For God's sake, Annabelle."

Judaline touched Clint on the shoulder. "No. I understand. I'd do the same myself. Perhaps worse."

Annabelle didn't want this woman's understanding. "Get out of here, Judaline." She turned slowly and looked at Clint. A coldness descended over her and in her shattered heart she told him goodbye. "Go with her if you have to. But don't come back here."

His eyes narrowed into mere slits and she saw the muscles work in his jaw and knew he was furious with her. She couldn't help herself. She couldn't bear to see him lying dead in the dust. She could not live through this again.

He stepped off the porch and walked to the barn. When he returned with his saddled horse, he stopped in front of her. "Are you sure? Is this the way you want it?"

The words begging him to stay were trapped behind the lump in her throat, fighting to be free. She merely nodded.

Clint mounted his horse. "Let's go, Judaline."

Annabelle turned away from them and wearily climbed the steps, went inside her home and closed the door.

She washed and dried the dishes and put them away in the fine cupboards Aaron had made. Lord, what would Aaron think when he came home? Would he stay and help her or go with Clint? If Clint lived. She ruthlessly pushed the thought of his death from her mind.

She jerked the sheets off the bed to change them. The muslin held the fragrance of his body. She pressed the sheet to her face and inhaled the musk of him, the scent of their last lovemaking.

She closed her eyes and saw him once again, wounded and unconscious in this bed. Strong and masculine, fighting for his life; the hours passing as she cared for him and fought for him, prayed over him, beseeched him to live. She shook the image from her mind. She hadn't gone through such an ordeal to see him throw his life away in this senseless manner.

He was being reckless with the life they had both fought for. Suddenly the image of Clint digging a hole next to her child's grave flashed into her brain. She remembered his anger at her willingness to slip and stay in some dreamworld where pain and disillusionment couldn't happen. Telling her to climb into that dark hole had shocked her into fury and back into the real world.

Annabelle sat down at the table and faced the truth. At every turn, no matter how outrageous her behavior, he had never given up on her. He teased, he reasoned, he fought back. When she tried to get him to leave, he refused—at first out of a sense of obligation, later a need to find the same roots for a home that she sought. He taught her numbers, how to write, to read.

He was as stubborn as she, just as full of fight for what he believed in. Most important of all, he never would have walked out on her when she needed him— even if she told him to go.

The love in her heart for him swelled and its pounding reached her brain. What the devil was she doing? How could she have let him go off—perhaps to die—alone? Without her. What kind of selfish love would allow her to turn her back on him now, when he needed her trust more than ever?

Would he believe she really loved him at all? My God! She had to go to him. She ran frantically to the barn for her horse. How long had he been gone? Would she be in time? She quickly saddled the mare, leapt on her back and raced down the road.

Annabelle reined in her horse at the entrance to the livery. She slid down and called out, "Jed?"

Martha came out of Jed's small office, tears streaming down her face. "It's about damned time, Annabelle Strand."

Jed came up behind his wife. "Now, Martha," he scolded.

"'Now, Martha,' nothing. Where have you been, child?'

"Home, feeling sorry for myself. Where is he?"

Jed walked to her side and took her hand. "Standing in the middle of the street with Docker. They're looking to kill each other."

"Then I'm not too late." She nearly slumped to the floor with relief.

"Late?" Jed asked. "Too late for what?"

"To stop this, of course."

"Annabelle, you're as likely to stop a raging river at full flood. One of those men will die this day. It's out of your hands."

"No it's—"

Shots rang through the air and Annabelle swayed with fear. Jed grabbed her.

"Let me go!" She flew out of his arms and ran down the street driven by a need so strong she didn't even see Docker. All she could see was Clint down in the dirt. Blood streamed down one side of his face. She came to a dead stop.

"Clint!" Her scream echoed through the silence.

She had to get to him, to help him, to stop the life-blood flowing from his body. She started forward but a strong hand grabbed and jerked her to a stop.

Furiously she fought whoever held her. "Let me go! Dammit, I have to go to him."

"Stop it, you little she-devil. You're not going anywhere."

Annabelle froze, then looked over her shoulder. Docker! He held her in a steellike grip. She snapped her head around to look at Clint. He had raised himself up on one elbow. His other hand still held his gun.

"You heard her, Docker. Let her go and we'll finish this—man to man."

"Clint! No! Stay down, you're hurt." Was he crazy? Docker would kill him if he got up.

"It's finished, Strand. One more bullet and you're done for."

"Always the coward, right, Bull? Just like your brother. Back-shooters the both of you. Shooting men when they're down."

Docker's grip on her tightened so she feared she might not be able to take her next breath. What could she do to stop this horror?

"Shut up, Strand. I've got your woman now. I can just as easy shoot her."

"Yep," Clint said, easing up a little off the ground. "Back-shooter and a woman-shooter. A real brave man, aren't you? Hiding behind a woman's skirts."

Close to her face, Annabelle heard Docker growl his fury. She had to figure out a way to help Clint. If she could distract Docker... If she just wasn't so afraid. If she did the wrong thing, Clint would be killed. She would be killed. Dear God, help me, she silently prayed.

She called on her anger and her faith and glared at Clint. "Well, are you satisfied now? You're damn near dead and this slimy bastard has me. Seems like your fancy plans didn't work too well."

He scooted up a little more and balanced his body with one hand. The last thing he'd expected was to see Annabelle flying down the street, heedless of the danger, coming to his rescue. What the devil had changed her mind?

He wiped the blood out of his eyes to see her better, to try to see the change, the reason for her unexpected appearance. Her fear shimmered around her. Yet fury—at him or Docker?—sparked in her green eyes. His Annabelle was radiating complex emotions all at the same moment.

He felt so tired, so weak. His vision wavered and he called on every bit of strength he had to keep from easing back in the dust and closing his eyes—giving up. In spite of his efforts his eyelids began to close and he felt himself slipping down.

"Clint!" Her scream reached some deep place in his brain, some ember of life still able to fight.

He pulled himself upright. He stretched out his legs and clutched his weapon in his gun hand. God, it felt so heavy. A part of him wanted to laugh; suppose it was too heavy to lift? Suppose he was too weak to pull the trigger? That last ember of life taunted him: *then Annabelle will die.*

Clint straightened his shoulders, wiped away the blood once more and called on pure guts and his love for Annabelle. Everything in the world he wanted and loved struggled for him within the arms of a killer. And it was his fault. He'd brought this danger to her and now he needed her aid to get them out of this.

There was no choice for Clint. He had to clear his mind of the danger to Annabelle. Had to call on that cold, clear-thinking part of him again to save this brave woman he loved. He had to gather his rage for Docker and use it to save her.

"Why did you come, Annabelle? To see me get killed? To see the end of this?"

Clint's fury reached her in white-hot waves. She felt Docker's hold loosen just a little. *Good!* She swallowed her rising fear. She had to find the words to enrage Clint even more. To make him want to live long enough to get rid of Docker, then shake her teeth out of her head for getting herself into this danger.

"I've been told what a fine shot you are, Clint Strand. I expected to see this foul-breathed goat in the dust, not the man I love." Docker's grip tightened again. Damn, she'd have to stop insulting him.

She taunted Clint again. "You don't look like such a fine shot, lying there in the dirt."

Clint struggled to his knees and shook his head to clear his mind. He wiped his wound with his shirt-sleeve. By God, she knew exactly what she was doing and she challenged him as no other person had. A flash of a past conversation ignited that remaining ember to a flame. Would she remember?

She felt his intense gaze bore into her brain. She expected hatred but found only an intensity she struggled to understand. He wanted something from her. What? Oh Lord, what? What? Desperately, she tried to marshal her thoughts. What did he want her to do? She nearly cried from the effort to understand. Docker held her so tight around her stomach she thought she might throw up.

Clint spread his knees a little and wiped his hand on his trouser leg. His expression was hard and his eyes so fierce . . . they sent her a message! *Get ready, Annabelle!*

"What do you want me to do, Annabelle? *Duck?*"

Like two rivers flowing together to make one, their thoughts merged and she understood. She paused only a second, then flashed Clint a smile and collapsed, boneless, in Docker's arms.

Thrown off balance, he swore viciously and tried to pull her to her feet, but she kept her body limp, dead weight.

Clint fired.

Annabelle screamed.

Docker fell dead, on top of Annabelle.

Clint threw down his gun and staggered to her side.

She looked up at him and twisted her body. "Well, don't just stand there. Get this filthy man off me."

Clint rolled Docker off, lifted her to her feet and brushed the dust off her face. "Are you all right?"

He still looked like that gunfighter who'd left her at home. "Yes. I'm fine." She took the edge of her skirt and wiped the drying blood from his face. "You need the doctor."

"I'm fine. It's not serious, a scratch."

"It looks serious. You've lost a lot of blood."

His smile only tipped one side of his mouth, barely moved his mustache. "Still arguing with me, Annabelle?" He stepped back from her, then turned to pick up his gun from the ground. "Take care of yourself, and . . . the baby."

She couldn't have felt more stunned if he'd melted into his boots right there in front of her. Didn't he hear her a minute ago say that she still loved him? "You're leaving!"

"Yep. I'll rest at the hotel tonight and make that Placerville train tomorrow." He turned to leave. "I'll be in the saloon. Tell Jed I need to see him. I'll leave my whereabouts with Herv so you can let me know about the...kid. Don't worry about money, there's plenty in the bank." He walked slowly over to the saloon, climbed the steps and went inside.

Money! Money? She felt so hot with fury she wouldn't have been surprised if her hair caught on fire. She whirled and headed for the livery. *We'll see, Clint Strand. We'll just see about that!* Money!

Clint called out to the bartender. "Whiskey."

The man came over, poured the shot and handed Clint a clean bar rag. He smiled his thanks and the bartender smiled back. "Drink's on the house, Mr. Strand. It's a pleasure to serve you."

"I appreciate it." Clint wiped the blood from the slight wound in his forehead.

The man went to serve another customer and Clint downed the shot. Surprised at its smoothness, he realized the bartender had given him some special stock. Well, he'd leave town with fine whiskey in his belly anyway.

A pat on the back caused him to turn. Jed stood beside him. "Buy you one for the road, friend?"

"Hell yes, Jed. Then I'll buy you one, then you buy and—"

"Your money's no good in here today." Jed waved the bartender forward. "Put the bottle on the bar."

The barman nodded and set a tall slender bottle in front of them. A bottle with a label!

Jed laughed. "Very special treatment. I haven't seen a label for a long time."

The man behind the bar smiled. "I figure I owe Mr. Strand an apology." He shrugged. "Seems the best way to give it."

Clint held out his hand to the man. "Accepted."

The barkeep took Clint's hand. "Appreciate it."

Jed poured the drinks. "So. You're really leaving."

"That's what Annabelle wants."

"What do you want?"

A bitter laugh broke through Clint's stiff lips. "Annabelle."

"Stay and fight for her."

"No. She's right. I'm a danger to her and the baby. Better I hightail it out of here. Head for Canada or somewhere. Maybe Mexico."

"You speak Mexican?"

"I can learn."

"Guess so." Jed downed his drink and poured another. "Sheriff's dead, you know. You could run for his office. I expect gunfighters would steer clear of Pleasant Valley if you were the law."

"Maybe. Maybe not. Might bring even more trouble."

"No. I figure with a badge on your shirtfront, they'd avoid you like typhoid."

"What time is it?" Clint asked.

Jed took his timepiece out of his watch pocket. "Just after ten. Seems like it should be later with all that's happened this morning. What'd you need to know the time for?"

"I don't know. I thought—"

"Maybe enough of it had passed that Annabelle might cool down and come for you?"

"Wishful thinking, I guess. Annabelle doesn't cool down very fast."

"You're acting the fool."

"Maybe."

"Go after her."

"Nope. I've caused her enough grief."

The room stilled abruptly and Clint felt the short hair on the back of his neck rise. Bile rose in his throat. Not so soon! He'd prayed to get out of town before another trigger-happy gunfighter challenged him.

He tensed and resettled his guns on his hips.

Jed eased slowly out of the way.

With careful movements, Clint turned to face—*Annabelle!*

She marched through the crowd of curious men, leading Mrs. Fillmore, who carried a rolling pin; Felicity Whitehall, who sported a long yellow ruler; and Hepsaba Mills, who carried a Bible. Clint thought it might be the same one Reverend Mills had used at a certain marriage ceremony.

Martha followed directly behind Annabelle and wore a satisfied smile. Judaline brought up the rear. A strange position for her, Clint thought. She usually led the Tuesday Club in their endeavors. This looked like Annabelle's show.

Belly first, she came to a stop in front of Clint. "Here he is, ladies. A coward, running away from his wife and child."

"Careful, Annabelle," Clint said.

"Humph!" Judaline said, obviously not giving up her leadership role completely.

"Humph!" the Tuesday Club echoed.

Clint took off his hat. "Ma'am?" he asked through a barely suppressed grin.

"Don't you 'ma'am' me, you ... deserter!"

"You know why I'm going, Annabelle."

"All I know is I love you, and if you don't get on your horse—"

"Now, honey, I—"

"And ride home and—"

"Use that wild red head of—"

"And get in our bed—"

"Bed!" the Tuesday Club gasped.

"Bed, Annabelle?" Clint could hardly stop his laughter.

"You've got till the count of ten before I shoot you right where you stand." She fumbled in the folds of her skirt and brought up a six-shooter—it looked suspiciously like Docker's—and shoved it into Clint's ribs.

"Now, sweetheart—"

"One."

"Let's talk this—"

"Two."

"Over, and—"

"Three." She poked him even harder.

"Hell!"

Laughter rang out in the saloon.

"Four."

Clint, with great deliberation, put on his hat. Then, with a sleight of hand that left Annabelle with her mouth open in surprise, he took the gun from her.

He whirled the chambers and threw her a condemning glance. After carefully emptying the bullets onto the bar, he shoved the gun in his belt. "Don't want to take a chance on ruining old do—"

"Clint!" Annabelle's face turned as red as her hair.

He leaned over and swept her into his arms. "Nothing to say, sweetheart?"

She shook her head and buried her face in his neck.

He grinned down at her. "I like that part about being in your bed."

She nodded her head vigorously.

"Bed!" gasped all but two of the Tuesday Club.

Martha grabbed Jed and pulled him toward the swinging doors. "Sounds like a good idea to me."

Judaline walked over to Herv and held out her hand. Herv looked shocked, then smiled and took her hand with his good arm, the other being in a sling. They followed Jed and Martha out of the saloon.

When Clint reached the entrance, one of the customers called out, "Told you you'd have your hands full with that one, Strand."

Clint looked down at the bundle of fire in his arms and grinned wickedly. She was a challenge all right.

Not to his life, but to his heart—and she'd won the draw. "Don't you worry, I've got *her* figured out." He placed a hot, wet kiss on her willing lips, shouldered his way through the doors and never looked back.

* * * * *

Harlequin® Historical

WARRIOR SERIES

The WARRIOR SERIES from author
Margaret Moore

It began with A WARRIOR'S HEART (HH #118, March 1992)—the
unforgettable story of Emryss Delanyea, a wounded Welsh
nobleman who returns from the crusades with all thoughts of
love put aside forever . . . until he meets the Lady Roanna.

Now, in A WARRIOR'S QUEST (HH #175, June 1993), healer
Fritha Kendrick teaches mercenary Urien Fitzroy to live by his
heart rather than his sword.

And, coming in early 1994, look for A WARRIOR'S PRIDE, the
third title of this medieval trilogy.

If you'd like to order A WARRIOR'S HEART, A WARRIOR'S QUEST or CHINA BLOSSOM
(HH #149, November 1992), the prequel to A WARRIOR'S QUEST, please send your name,
address, zip or postal code, along with a check or money order for $3.99 plus 75¢ postage
and handling ($1.00 in Canada), for each book ordered, payable to HARLEQUIN READER
SERVICE, to:

In the U.S.
3010 Walden Avenue
P.O. Box 1325
Buffalo, NY 14269-1325

In Canada
P.O. Box 609
Fort Erie, Ontario
L2A 5X3

WAR1

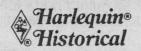

TEXAS

TEXAS HEART—A young woman is forced to journey west in search of her missing father.

TEXAS HEALER—A doctor returns home to rediscover a ghost from his past, the daughter of a Comanche chief.

And now, TEXAS HERO—A gunfighter teaches the local schoolteacher that not every fight can be won with a gun. (HH #180, available in July.)

Follow the lives of Jessie Conway and her brothers in this series from popular Harlequin Historical author Ruth Langan.

THREE UNFORGETTABLE HEROINES
THREE AWARD-WINNING AUTHORS

MAVERICK HEARTS

A unique collection of historical short stories that capture the spirit of America's last frontier.

HEATHER GRAHAM POZZESSERE—over 10 million copies of her books in print worldwide
Lonesome Rider—The story of an Eastern widow and the renegade half-breed who becomes her protector.

PATRICIA POTTER—an author whose books are consistently Waldenbooks bestsellers
Against the Wind—Two people, battered by heartache, prove that love can heal all.

JOAN JOHNSTON—award-winning Western historical author with 17 books to her credit
One Simple Wish—A woman with a past discovers that dreams really do come true.

Join us for an exciting journey West with
UNTAMED
Available in July, wherever Harlequin books are sold.